DANGER;

OR, WOUNDED IN THE HOUSE OF A FRIEND.

T. S. ARTHUR

1st WORLD
LIBRARY
Literary Society

Danger; or Wounded in the House of a Friend

T. S. Arthur

© 1st World Library, 2007
PO Box 2211
Fairfield, IA 52556
www.1stworldlibrary.com
First Edition

LCCN: 2007920699

Softcover ISBN: 978-1-4218-4010-9
Hardcover ISBN: 978-1-4218-3910-3
eBook ISBN: 978-1-4218-4110-6

Purchase *"Danger; or Wounded in the House of a Friend"*
as a traditional bound book at:
www.1stWorldLibrary.com/purchase.asp?ISBN=978-1-4218-4010-9

1st World Library is a literary, educational organization dedicated to:

- Creating a free internet library of downloadable ebooks

  - Hosting writing competitions and offering book publishing scholarships.

Interested in more 1st World Library books?
contact: literacy@1stworldlibrary.com
Check us out at: www.1stworldlibrary.com

1ˢᵗ World Library Literary Society

Giving Back to the World

"If you want to work on the core problem, it's early school literacy."

- James Barksdale, former CEO of Netscape

"No skill is more crucial to the future of a child, or to a democratic and prosperous society, than literacy."

- Los Angeles Times

Literacy... means far more than learning how to read and write... The aim is to transmit... knowledge and promote social participation."

- UNESCO

"Literacy is not a luxury, it is a right and a responsibility. If our world is to meet the challenges of the twenty-first century we must harness the energy and creativity of all our citizens."

- President Bill Clinton

"Parents should be encouraged to read to their children, and teachers should be equipped with all available techniques for teaching literacy, so the varying needs and capacities of individual kids can be taken into account."

- Hugh Mackay

PREFACE

ALL efforts at eradicating evil must, to be successful, begin as near the beginning as possible. It is easier to destroy a weed when but an inch above the ground than after it has attained a rank growth and set its hundred rootlets in the soil. Better if the evil seed were not sown at all; better if the ground received only good seed into its fertile bosom. How much richer and sweeter the harvest!

Bars and drinking-saloons are, in reality, not so much the causes as the effects of intemperance. The chief causes lie back of these, and are to be found in our homes. Bars and drinking-saloons minister to, stimulate and increase the appetite already formed, and give accelerated speed to those whose feet have begun to move along the road to ruin.

In "THREE YEARS IN A MAN-TRAP" the author of this volume uncovered the terrible evils of the liquor traffic; in this, he goes deeper, and unveils the more hidden sources of that widespread ruin which is cursing our land. From the public licensed saloon, where liquor is sold to men—not to boys, except in violation of law—he turns to the private home saloon, where it is given away in unstinted measure to guests of both sexes and of all ages, and seeks to show in a series of swiftly-moving panoramic scenes the dreadful consequences that flow therefrom.

This book is meant by the author to be a startling cry of "DANGER!" Different from "THE MAN-TRAP," as dealing with another aspect of the temperance question, its pictures are wholly unlike those presented in that book, but none the less vivid or intense. It is given as an argument against what is called the temperate use of liquor, and as an exhibition of the fearful disasters that flow from our social drinking customs. In making this argument and exhibition the author has given his best effort to the work.

T. S. Arthur

CHAPTER I

SNOW had been falling for more than three hours, the large flakes dropping silently through the still air until the earth was covered with an even carpet many inches in depth.

It was past midnight. The air, which had been so still, was growing restless and beginning to whirl the snow into eddies and drive it about in an angry kind of way, whistling around sharp corners and rattling every loose sign and shutter upon which it could lay its invisible hands.

In front of an elegant residence stood half a dozen carriages. The glare of light from hall and windows and the sound of music and dancing told of a festival within. The door opened, and a group of young girls, wrapped in shawls and water-proofs, came out and ran, merrily laughing, across the snow-covered pavement, and crowding into one of the carriages, were driven off at a rapid speed. Following them came a young man on whose lip and cheeks the downy beard had scarcely thrown a shadow. The strong light of the vestibule lamp fell upon a handsome face, but it wore an unnatural flush.

There was an unsteadiness about his movements as he descended the marble steps, and he grasped the iron railing like one in danger of falling. A waiter who had followed him to the door stood looking at him with a half-pitying, half-amused expression on his face as he went off, staggering through the blinding drift.

The storm was one of the fiercest of the season, and the air since midnight had become intensely cold. The snow fell no longer in soft and filmy flakes, but in small hard pellets that cut like sand and sifted in through every crack and crevice against which the wild winds drove it.

The young man—boy, we might better say, for, he was only nineteen—moved off in the very teeth of this storm, the small granules of ice smiting him in the face and taking his breath. The wind set itself against him with wide obstructing arms, and he reeled, staggered and plunged forward or from side to side, in a sort of blind desperation.

"Ugh!" he ejaculated, catching his breath and standing still as a fierce blast struck him. Then, shaking himself like one trying to cast aside an impediment, he moved forward with quicker steps, and kept onward, for a distance of two or three blocks. Here, in crossing a street, his foot struck against some obstruction which the snow had concealed, and he fell with his face downward. It took some time for him to struggle to his feet again, and then he seemed to be in a state of complete bewilderment, for he started along one street, going for a short distance, and then crossing back and going in an opposite direction. He was in no condition to get right after once going wrong. With every few steps he would stop and look up and down the street and at the houses on each side vainly trying to make out his locality.

"Police!" he cried two or three times; but the faint, alarmed call reached no ear of nightly guardian. Then, with a shiver as the storm swept down upon him more angrily, he started forward again, going he knew not whither.

The cold benumbed him; the snow choked and blinded him; fear and anxiety, so far as he was capable of feeling them, bewildered and oppressed him. A helmless ship in storm and darkness was in no more pitiable condition than this poor lad.

On, on he went, falling sometimes, but struggling to his feet

T. S. Arthur

again and blindly moving forward. All at once he came out from the narrow rows of houses and stood on the edge of what seemed a great white field that stretched away level as a floor. Onward a few paces, and then—Alas for the waiting mother at home! She did not hear the cry of terror that cut the stormy air and lost itself in the louder shriek of the tempest as her son went over the treacherous line of snow and dropped, with a quick plunge, into the river, sinking instantly out of sight, for the tide was up and the ice broken and drifting close to the water's edge.

CHAPTER II

"COME, Fanny," said Mr. Wilmer Voss, speaking to his wife, "you must get to bed. It is past twelve o'clock, and you cannot bear this loss of rest and sleep. It may throw you all back again."

The woman addressed was sitting in a large easychair with a shawl drawn closely about her person. She had the pale, shrunken face and large, bright eyes of a confirmed invalid. Once very beautiful, she yet retained a sweetness of expression which gave a tenderness and charm to every wasted feature. You saw at a glance the cultured woman and the patient sufferer.

As her husband spoke a fierce blast of wind drove the fine sand-like snow against the windows, and then went shrieking and roaring away over housetops, gables and chimneys.

"Oh what a dreadful night!" said the lady, leaning forward in her chair and listening to the wild wail of the storm, while a look of anxiety, mingled with dread, swept across her face. "If Archie were only at home!"

"Don't trouble yourself about Archie. He'll be here soon. You are not yourself to-night, Fanny."

"Perhaps not; but I can't help it. I feel such an awful weight here;" and Mrs. Voss drew her hands against her bosom.

T. S. Arthur

"All nervous," said her husband. "Come! You must go to bed."

"It will be of no use, Wilmer," returned the lady. "I will be worse in bed than sitting up. You don't know what a strange feeling has come over me. Oh, Archie, if you were only at home! Hark! What was that?"

The pale face grew paler as Mrs. Voss bent forward in a listening attitude.

"Only the wind," answered her husband, betraying some impatience. "A thousand strange sounds are on the air in a night like this. You must compose yourself, Fanny, or the worst consequences may follow."

"It's impossible, husband. I cannot rest until I have my son safe and sound at home again. Dear, dear boy!"

Mr. Voss urged no further. The shadow of fear which had come down upon his wife began to creep over his heart and fill it with a vague concern. And now a thought flashed into his mind that he would not have uttered for the world; but from that moment peace fled, and anxiety for his son grew into alarm as the time wore on and the boy did not come home.

"Oh, my husband," cried Mrs. Voss, starting from her chair, and clasping her hands as she threw them upward, "I cannot bear this much longer. Hark! That was his voice! *'Mother!'* *'Mother!'* Don't you hear it?"

Her face was white as the snow without, her eyes wild and eager, her lips apart, her head bent forward.

A shuddering chill crept along the nerves of Mr. Voss.

"Go, go quickly! Run! He may have fallen at the door!"

Ere the last sentence was finished Mr. Voss was halfway down stairs. A blinding dash of snow came swirling into his face as he opened the street door. It was some moments before he could see with any distinctness. No human form was visible, and the lamp just in front of his house shone down upon a trackless bed of snow many inches in depth. No, Archie was not there. The cry had come to the mother's inward ear in the moment when her boy went plunging down into the engulfing river and heart and thought turned in his mortal agony to the one nearest and dearest in all the earth.

When Mr. Voss came back into the house after his fruitless errand, he found his wife standing in the hall, only a few feet back from the vestibule, her face whiter, if that were possible, and her eyes wilder than before. Catching her in his arms, he ran with her up stairs, but before he had reached their chamber her light form lay nerveless and unconscious against his breast.

Doctor Hillhouse, the old family physician, called up in the middle of that stormy night, hesitated to obey the summons, and sent his assistant with word that he would be round early in the morning if needed. Doctor Angier, the assistant, was a young physician of fine ability and great promise. Handsome in person, agreeable in manner and thoroughly in love with his profession, he was rapidly coming into favor with many of the old doctor's patients, the larger portion of whom belonged to wealthy and fashionable circles. Himself a member of one of the older families, and connected, both on his father's and mother's side, with eminent personages as well in his native city as in the State, Doctor Angier was naturally drawn into social life, which, spite of his increasing professional duties, he found time to enjoy.

It was past two o'clock when Doctor Angier made his appearance, his garments white with snow and his dark beard crusted with tiny icicles. He found Mrs. Voss lying in swoon so deep that, but for the faintest perceptible heart-beat, he would have thought her dead. Watching the young physician closely as he stood by the bedside of his wife, Mr. Voss was quick to perceive something unusual in his manner. The professional poise and coolness for which he was noted were

T. S. Arthur

gone, and he showed a degree of excitement and uncertainty that alarmed the anxious husband. What was its meaning? Did it indicate apprehension for the condition of his patient, or— something else? A closer look into the young physician's face sent a flash of suspicion through the mind of Mr. Voss, which was more than confirmed a moment afterward as the stale odor of wine floated to his nostrils.

"Were you at Mr. Birtwell's to-night?" There was a thrill of anxious suspense in the tones of Mr. Voss as he grasped the physician's arm and looked keenly at him.

"I was," replied Doctor Angier.

"Did you see my son there?"

"Yes, sir."

"At what time did you leave?"

"Less than an hour ago. I had not retired when your summons came."

"Was Archie there when you left?"

"No, I think not."

"Are you sure about it?"

"Yes, very sure. I remember now, quite distinctly, seeing him come down from the dressing-room with his hat in his hand and go through the hall toward the street door."

"How long ago was that?"

"About an hour and a half; perhaps longer."

A groan that could not be repressed broke from the father's lips.

"Isn't he at home?" asked the young physician, turning round quickly from the bed and betraying a sudden concern.

"No; and I am exceedingly anxious about him." The eyes of Mr. Voss were fixed intently on Doctor Angler, and he was reading every varying expression of his countenance.

"Doctor," he said, laying his hand on the physician's arm and speaking huskily, "I want you to answer me truly. Had he taken much wine?"

It was some moments before Doctor Angier replied:

"On such occasions most people take wine freely. It flows like water, you know. I don't think your son indulged more than any one else; indeed, not half so much as some young men I saw there."

Mr. Voss felt that there was evasion in the answer.

"Archie is young, and not used to wine. A single glass would be more to him than half a dozen to older men who drink habitually. Did you see him take wine often?"

"He was in the supper-room for a considerable time. When I left it, I saw him in the midst of a group of young men and girls, all with glasses of champagne in their hands."

"How long was this before you saw him go away?"

"Half an hour, perhaps," replied the doctor.

"Did he go out alone?"

"I believe so."

Mr. Voss questioned no further, and Doctor Angler, who now understood better the meaning of his patient's condition, set himself to the work of restoring her to consciousness. He did

T. S. Arthur

not find the task easy. It was many hours before the almost stilled pulses began beating again with a perceptible stroke, and the quiet chest to give signs of normal respiration. Happily for the poor mother, thought and feeling were yet bound.

Long before this the police had been aroused and every effort made to discover a trace of the young man after he left the house of Mr. Birtwell, but without effect. The snow had continued falling until after five o'clock, when the storm ceased and the sky cleared, the wind blowing from the north and the temperature falling to within a few degrees of zero.

A faint hope lingered with Mr. Voss—the hope that Archie had gone home with some friend. But as the morning wore on and he did not make his appearance this hope began to fade away, and died before many hours. Nearly every male guest at Mrs. Birtwell's party was seen and questioned during the day, but not one of them had seen Archie after he left the house. A waiter who was questioned said that he remembered seeing him:

"I watched him go down the steps and go off alone, and the wind seemed as if it would blow him away. He wasn't just himself, sir, I'm afraid."

If a knife had cut down into the father's quivering flesh, the pain would have been as nothing to that inflicted by this last sentence. It only confirmed his worst fears.

The afternoon papers contained a notice of the fact that a young gentleman who had gone away from a fashionable party at a late hour on the night before had not been heard of by his friends, who were anxious and distressed about him. Foul play was hinted at, as the young man wore a valuable diamond pin and had a costly gold watch in his pocket. On the morning afterward advertisements appeared offering a large reward for any information that would lead to the discovery of the young man, living or dead. They were accompanied by minute descriptions of his person and dress. But there came no response. Days and weeks passed; and though the advertisements were repeated and newspapers called public attention to the matter, not a single clue was found.

A young man, with the kisses of his mother sweet on his pure lips, had left her for an evening's social enjoyment at the house of one of her closest and dearest friends, and she never looked upon his face again. He had entered the house of that friend with a clear head and steady nerves, and he had gone out at midnight bewildered with the wine that had been poured without stint to her hundred guests, young and old. How it had fared with him the reader knows too well.

T. S. Arthur

CHAPTER III

"HEAVENS and earth! Why doesn't some one go to the door?" exclaimed Mr. Spencer Birtwell, rousing himself from a heavy sleep as the bell was rung for the third time, and now with four or five vigorous and rapid jerks, each of which caused the handle of the bell to strike with the noise of a hammer.

The gray dawn was just breaking.

"There it is again! Good heavens! What does it mean?" and Mr. Birtwell, now fairly awake, started up in bed and sat listening. Scarcely a moment intervened before the bell was pulled again, and this time continuously for a dozen times. Springing from the bed, Mr. Birtwell threw open a window, and looking out, saw two policemen at the door.

"What's wanted?" he called down to them.

"Was there a young man here last night named Voss?" inquired one of the men.

"What about him?" asked Mr. Birtwell.

"He hasn't been home, and his friends are alarmed. Do you know where he is?"

"Wait, returned Mr. Birtwell; and shutting down the window, he dressed himself hurriedly.

"What is it?" asked his wife, who had been awakened from a heavy slumber by the noise at the window.

"Archie Voss didn't get home last night."

"What?" and Mrs. Birtwell started out of bed.

"There are two policemen at the door."

"Policemen!"

"Yes; making a grand row for nothing, as if young men never stayed away from home. I must go down and see them. Go back into bed again, Margaret. You'll take your death o' cold. There's nothing to be alarmed about. He'll come up all right."

But Mrs. Birtwell did not return to her bed. With warm wrapper thrown about her person, she stood at the head of the stairway while her husband went down to admit the policemen. All that could be learned from them was that Archie Voss had not come home from the party, and that his friends were greatly alarmed about him. Mr. Birtwell had no information to give. The young man had been at his house, and had gone away some time during the night, but precisely at what hour he could not tell.

"You noticed him through the evening?" said one of the policemen.

"Oh yes, certainly. We know Archie very well. He's always been intimate at our house."

"Did he take wine freely?"

An indignant denial leaped to Mr. Birtwell's tongue, but the words died unspoken, for the image of Archie, with flushed face and eyes too bright for sober health, holding in his hand a glass of sparkling champagne, came vividly before him.

T. S. Arthur

"Not more freely than other young men," he replied. "Why do you ask?"

"There are two theories of his absence," said the policeman. "One is that he has been set upon in the street, robbed and murdered, and the other that, stupefied and bewildered by drink, he lost himself in the storm, and lies somewhere frozen to death and hidden under the snow."

A cry of pain broke from the lips of Mrs. Birtwell, and she came hurrying down stairs. Too well did she remember the condition of Archie when she last saw him—Archie, the only son of her oldest and dearest friend, the friend she had known and loved since girlhood. He was not fit to go out alone in that cold and stormy night; and a guilty sense of responsibility smote upon her heart and set aside all excuses.

"What about his mother?" she asked, anxiously. "How is she bearing this dreadful suspense?"

"I can't just say, ma'am," was answered, "but I think they've had the doctor with her all night—that is, all the last part of the night. She's lying in a faint, I believe."

"Oh, it will kill her! Poor Frances! Poor Frances!" wailed out Mrs. Birtwell, wringing her hands and beginning to cry bitterly.

"The police have been on the lookout for the last two or three hours, but can't find any trace of him," said the officer.

"Oh, he'll turn up all right," broke in Mr. Birtwell, with a confident tone. "It's only a scare. Gone home with some young friend, as like as not. Young fellows in their teens don't get lost in the snow, particularly in the streets of a great city, and footpads generally know their game before bringing it down. I'm sorry for poor Mrs. Voss; she isn't strong enough to bear such a shock. But it will all come right; I don't feel a bit concerned."

But for all that he did feel deeply concerned. The policemen went away, and Mr. and Mrs. Birtwell sat down by an open grate in which the fire still burned.

"Don't let it distress you so, Margaret," said the former, trying to comfort his wife. "There's nothing to fear for Archie. Nobody ever heard of a man getting lost in a city snow-storm. If he'd been out on a prairie, the case would have been different, but in the streets of the city! The thing's preposterous, Margaret."

"Oh, if he'd only gone away as he came, I wouldn't feel so awfully about it," returned Mrs. Birtwell. "That's what cuts me to the heart. To think that he came to my house sober and went away—"

She caught back from her tongue the word she would have spoken, and shivered.

"Nothing of the kind, Margaret, nothing of the kind," said her husband, quickly. "A little gay—that was all. Just what is seen at parties every night. Archie hasn't much head, and a single glass of champagne is enough to set it buzzing. But it's soon over. The effervescence goes off in a little while, and the head comes clear again."

Mrs. Birtwell did not reply. Her eyes were cast down and her face deeply distressed.

"If anything has happened to Archie," she said, after a long silence, "I shall never have a moment's peace as long as I live."

"Nonsense, Margaret! Suppose something has happened to him? We are not responsible. It's his own fault if he took away more wine than he was able to carry." Mr. Birtwell spoke with slight irritation.

"If he hadn't found the wine here, he could not have carried it away," replied his wife.

T. S. Arthur

"How wildly you talk, Margaret!" exclaimed Mr. Birtwell, with increased irritation.

"We won't discuss the matter," said his wife. "It would be useless, agreement being, I fear, out of the question; but it is very certain that we cannot escape responsibility in this or anything else we may do, and so long as these words of Holy Writ stand, *'Woe unto him that giveth his neighbor drink, that putteth the bottle to him and maketh him drunken'*, we may well have serious doubts in regard to the right and wrong of these fashionable entertainments, at which wine and spirits are made free to all of both sexes, young and old."

Mr. Birtwell started to his feet and walked the floor with considerable excitement.

"If *we* had a son just coming to manhood—and I sometimes thank God that we have not—would you feel wholly at ease about him, wholly satisfied that he was in no danger in the houses of your friends? May not a young man as readily acquire a taste for liquors in a gentleman's dining-room as in a drinking-saloon—nay, more readily, if in the former the wine is free and bright eyes and laughing lips press him with invitations?"

Mrs. Birtwell's voice had gained a steadiness and force that made it very impressive. Her husband continued to walk the floor but with slower steps.

"I saw things last night that troubled me," she went on. "There is no disguising the fact that most of the young men who come to these large parties spend a great deal too much time in the supper-room, and drink a great deal more than is good for them. Archie Voss was not the only one who did this last evening. I watched another young man very closely, and am sorry to say that he left our house in a condition in which no mother waiting at home could receive her son without sorrow and shame."

"Who was that?" asked Mr. Birtwell, turning quickly upon his wife. He had detected more than a common concern in her voice.

"Ellis," she replied. Her manner was very grave.

"You must be mistaken about that," said Mr. Birtwell, evidently disturbed at this communication.

"I wish to Heaven that I were! But the fact was too apparent. Blanche saw it, and tried to get him out of the supper-room. He acted in the silliest kind of a way, and mortified her dreadfully, poor child!"

"Such things will happen sometimes," said Mr. Birtwell. "Young men like Ellis don't always know how much they can bear." His voice was in a lower key and a little husky.

"It happens too often with Ellis," replied his wife, "and I'm beginning to feel greatly troubled about it."

"Has it happened before?"

"Yes; at Mrs. Gleason's, only last week. He was loud and boisterous in the supper-room—so much so that I heard a lady speak of his conduct as disgraceful."

"That will never do," exclaimed Mr. Birtwell, betraying much excitement. "He will have to change all this or give up Blanche. I don't care what his family is if he isn't all right himself."

"It is easier to get into trouble than out of it," was replied. "Things have gone too far between them."

"I don't believe it. Blanche will never throw herself away on a man of bad habits."

"No; I do not think she will. But there may be, in her view, a

T. S. Arthur

very great distance between an occasional glass of wine too much at an evening party and confirmed bad habits. We must not hope to make her see with our eyes, nor to take our judgment of a case in which her heart is concerned. Love is full of excuses and full of faith. If Ellis Whitford should, unhappily, be overcome by this accursed appetite for drink which is destroying so many of our most promising young men, there is trouble ahead for her and for us."

"Something must be done about it. We cannot let this thing go on," said Mr. Birtwell, in a kind of helpless passion. "A drunkard is a beast. Our Blanche tied to a beast! Ugh! Ellis must be talked to. I shall see him myself. If he gets offended, I cannot help it. There's too much at stake—too much, too much!"

"Talking never does much in these cases," returned Mrs. Birtwell, gloomily. "Ellis would be hurt and offended."

"So far so good. He'd be on guard at the next party."

"Perhaps so. But what hope is there for a young man in any danger of acquiring a love of liquor as things now are in our best society? He cannot always be on guard. Wine is poured for him everywhere. He may go unharmed in his daily walks through the city though thousands of drinking-saloons crowd its busy streets. They may hold out their enticements for him in vain. But he is too weak to refuse the tempting glass when a fair hostess offers it, or when, in the midst of a gay company wine is in every hand and at every lip. One glass taken, and caution and restraint are too often forgotten. He drinks with this one and that one, until his clear head is gone and appetite, like a watchful spider, throws another cord of its fatal web around him."

"I don't see what we are to do about it," said Mr. Birtwell. "If men can't control themselves—" He did not finish the sentence.

"We can at least refrain from putting temptation in their way," answered his wife.

"How?"

"We can refuse to turn our houses into drinking-saloons," replied Mrs. Birtwell, voice and manner becoming excited and intense.

"Margaret, Margaret, you are losing yourself," said the astonished husband.

"No; I speak the words of truth and soberness," she answered, her face rising in color and her eyes brightening. "What great difference is there between a drinking-saloon, where liquor is sold, and a gentleman's dining-room, where it is given away? The harm is great in both—greatest, I fear, in the latter, where the weak and unguarded are allured and their tastes corrupted. There is a ban on the drinking-saloon. Society warns young men not to enter its tempting doors. It is called the way of death and hell. What makes it accursed and our home saloon harmless? It is all wrong, Mr. Birtwell—all wrong, wrong, wrong! and to-day we are tasting some of the fruit, the bitterness of which, I fear, will be in our mouths so long as we both shall live."

Mrs. Birtwell broke down, and sinking back in her chair, covered her face with her hands.

"I must go to Frances," she said, rising after a few moments.

"Not now, Margaret," interposed her husband. "Wait for a while. Archie is neither murdered nor frozen to death; you may take my word for that. Wait until the morning advances, and he has time to put in an appearance, as they say. Henry can go round after breakfast and make inquiry about him. If he is still absent, then you might call and see Mrs. Voss. At present the snow lies inches deep and unbroken on the street, and you cannot possibly go out."

T. S. Arthur

Mrs. Birtwell sat down again, her countenance more distressed.

"Oh, if it hadn't happened in our house!" she said. "If this awful thing didn't lie at our door!"

"Good Heavens, Margaret! why will you take on so? Any one hearing you talk might think us guilty of murder, or some other dreadful crime. Even if the worst fears are realized, no blame can lie with us. Parties are given every night, and young men, and old men too, go home from them with lighter heads than when they came. No one is compelled to drink more than is good for him. If he takes too much, the sin lies at his own door."

"If you talked for ever, Mr. Birtwell," was answered nothing you might say could possibly change my feelings or sentiments. I know we are responsible both to God and to society for the stumbling-blocks we set in the way of others. For a long time, as you know, I have felt this in regard to our social wine-drinking customs; and if I could have had my way, there would have been one large party of the season at which neither man nor woman could taste wine."

"I know," replied Mr. Birtwell. "But I didn't choose to make myself a laughing-stock. If we are in society, we must do as society does. Individuals are not responsible for social usages. They take things as they find them, going with the current, and leaving society to settle for itself its code of laws and customs. If we don't like these laws and customs, we are free to drift out of the current. But to set ourselves against them is a weakness and a folly."

Mr. Birtwell's voice and manner grew more confident as he spoke. He felt that he had closed the argument.

"If society," answered his wife, "gets wrong, how is it to get right?"

Mr. Birtwell was silent.

"Is it not made up of individuals?"

"Of course."

"And is not each of the individuals responsible, in his degree, for the conduct of society?"

"In a certain sense, yes."

"Society, as a whole, cannot determine a question of right and wrong. Only individuals can do this. Certain of these, more independent than the rest, pass now and then from the beaten track of custom, and the great mass follow them. Because they do this or that, it is right or in good taste and becomes fashionable. The many are always led by the few. It is through the personal influence of the leaders in social life that society is now cursed by its drinking customs. Personal influence alone can change these customs, and therefore every individual becomes responsible, because he might if he would set his face against them, and any one brave enough to do this would find many weaker ones quick to come to his side and help him to form a better social sentiment and a better custom."

"All very nicely said," replied Mr. Birtwell, "but I'd like to see the man brave enough to give a large fashionable party and exclude wine."

"So would I. Though every lip but mine kept silence, there would be one to do him honor."

"You would be alone, I fear," said the husband.

"When a man does a right and brave thing, all true men honor him in their hearts. All may not be brave enough to stand by his side, but a noble few will imitate the good example. Give the leader in any cause, right or wrong, and you will always find adherents of the cause. No, my husband, I would not be alone in doing that man honor. His praise would be on many lips and many hearts would bless him. I only wish you were

T. S. Arthur

that man! Spencer, if you will consent to take this lead, I will walk among our guests the queenliest woman, in heart at least, to be found in any drawing-room this season. I shall not be without my maids-of-honor, you may be sure, and they will come from the best families known in our city. Come! say yes, and I will be prouder of my husband than if he were the victorious general of a great army."

"No, thank you, my dear," replied Mr. Birtwell, not in the least moved by his wife's enthusiasm. "I am not a social reformer, nor in the least inclined that way. As I find things I take them. It is no fault of mine that some people have no control of their appetites and passions. Men will abuse almost anything to their own hurt. I saw as many of our guests over-eat last night as over-drink, and there will be quite as many headaches to-day from excess of terrapin and oysters as from excess of wine. It's no use, Margaret. Intemperance is not to be cured in this way. Men who have a taste for wine will get it, if not in one place then in another; if not in a gentleman's dining-room, then in a drinking-saloon, or somewhere else."

The glow faded from Mrs. Birtwell's face and the light went out of her eyes. Her voice was husky and choking as she replied:

"One fact does not invalidate another. Because men who have acquired a taste for wine will have it whether we provide it for them or not, it is no reason why we should set it before the young whose appetites are yet unvitiated and lure them to excesses. It does not make a free indulgence in wine and brandy any the more excusable because men overeat themselves."

"But," broke in Mr. Birtwell, with the manner of one who gave an unanswerable reason, "if we exclude wine that men may not hurt themselves by over-indulgence, why not exclude the oysters and terrapin? If we set up for reformers and philanthropists, why not cover the whole ground?"

"Oysters and terrapin," replied Mrs. Birtwell, in a voice out of which she could hardly keep the contempt she felt for her husband's weak rejoinder, "don't confuse the head, dethrone the reason, brutalize, debase and ruin men in soul and body as do wine and brandy. The difference lies there, and all men see and feel it, make what excuses they will for self-indulgence and deference to custom. The curse of drink is too widely felt. There is scarcely a family in the land on which its blight does not lie. The best, the noblest, the purest, the bravest, have fallen. It is breaking hopes and hearts and fortunes every day. The warning cross that marks the grave of some poor victim hurts your eyes at every turn of life. We are left without excuse."

Mrs. Birtwell rose as she finished speaking, and returned to her chamber.

T. S. Arthur

CHAPTER IV

"MR. VOSS," said the waiter as he opened the door of the breakfast-room.

Mr. and Mrs. Birtwell left the table hurriedly and went to the parlor. Their visitor was standing in the middle of the floor as they entered.

"Oh, Mr. Voss, have you heard anything of Archie?" exclaimed Mrs. Birtwell.

"Nothing yet," he replied.

"Dreadful, dreadful! What can it mean?"

"Don't be alarmed about it," said Mr. Birtwell, trying to speak in an assuring voice. "He must have gone home with a friend. It will be all right, I am confident."

"I trust so," replied Mr. Voss. "But I cannot help feeling very anxious. He has never been away all night before. Something is wrong. Do you know precisely at what time he left here?"

"I do not," replied Mr. Birtwell. "We had a large company, and I did not note particularly the coming or going of any one."

"Doctor Angier thinks it was soon after twelve o'clock. He saw him come out of the dressing-room and go down stairs about that time."

"How is Frances?" asked Mrs. Birtwell. "It must be a dreadful shock to her in her weak state."

"Yes, it is dreadful, and I feel very anxious about her. If anything has happened to Archie, it will kill her."

Tears fell over Mrs. Birtwell's face and she wrung her hands in distress.

"She is calmer than she was," said Mr. Voss. "The first alarm and suspense broke her right down, and she was insensible for some hours. But she is bearing it better now—much better than I had hoped for."

"I will go to see her at once. Oh, if I knew how to comfort her!"

To this Mr. Voss made no response, but Mrs. Birtwell, who was looking into his, face, saw an expression that she did not understand.

"She will see me, of course?"

"I do not know. Perhaps you'd better not go round yet. It might disturb her too much, and the doctor says she must be kept as quiet as possible."

Something in the manner of Mr. Voss sent a chill to the heart of Mrs. Birtwell. She felt an evasion in his reply. Then a suspicion of the truth flashed upon her mind, overwhelming her with a flood of bitterness in which shame, self-reproach, sorrow and distress were mingled. It was from her hand, so to speak, that the son of her friend had taken the wine which had bewildered his senses, and from her house that he had gone forth with unsteady step and confused brain to face a storm the heaviest and wildest that had been known for years. If he were dead, would not the stain of his blood be on her garments?

T. S. Arthur

No marvel that Mr. Voss had said, "Not yet; it might disturb her too much." Disturb the friend with whose heart her own had beaten in closest sympathy and tenderest love for years—the friend who had flown to her in the deepest sorrow she had ever known and held her to her heart until she was comforted by the sweet influences of love. Oh, this was hard to bear! She bowed her head and stood silent.

"I wish," said Mr. Voss, speaking to Mr. Birtwell, "to get the names of a few of the guests who were here last night. Some of them may have seen Archie go out, or may have gone away at the time he did. I must find some clue to the mystery of his absence."

Mr. Birtwell named over many of his guests, and Mr. Voss made a note of their addresses. The chill went deeper down into the heart of Mrs. Birtwell; and when Mr. Voss, who seemed to grow colder and more constrained every moment, without looking at her, turned to go away, the pang that cut her bosom was sharp and terrible.

"If I can do anything, Mr. Voss, command—" Mr. Birtwell had gone to the door with his visitor, who passed out hastily, not waiting to hear the conclusion of his sentence.

"A little strange in his manner, I should say," remarked Mr. Birtwell as he came back. "One. might infer that he thought us to blame for his son's absence."

"I can't bear this suspense. I must see Frances." It was an hour after Mr. Voss had been there. Mrs. Birtwell rang a bell, and ordering the carriage, made herself ready to go out.

"Mrs. Voss says you must excuse her," said the servant who had taken up Mrs. Birtwell's card. "She is not seeing any but the family," added the man, who saw in the visitor's face the pain of a great disappointment.

Slowly retiring, her head bent forward and her body stooping a little like one pressed down by a burden, Mrs. Birtwell left the house of her oldest and dearest friend with an aching sense of rejection at her heart. In the darkest and saddest hour of her life that friend had turned from the friend who had been to her more than a sister, refusing the sympathy and tears she had come to offer. There was a bitter cup at the lips of both; which was the bitterest it would be hard to tell.

"Not now," Mrs. Voss had said, speaking to her husband; "I cannot meet her now."

"Perhaps you had better see her," returned the latter.

"No, no, no!" Mrs. Voss put up her hands and shivered as she spoke. "I cannot, I cannot! Oh, my boy! my son! my poor Archie! Where are you? Why do you not come home? Hark!"

The bell had rung loudly. They listened, and heard men's voices in the hall below. With face flushing and paling in quick alternations, Mrs. Voss started up in bed and leaned forward, hearkening eagerly. Mr. Voss opened the chamber door and went out. Two policemen had come to report that so far all efforts to find a trace of the young man had been utterly fruitless. Mrs. Voss heard in silence. Slowly the dark lashes fell upon her cheeks, that were white as marble. Her lips were rigid and closely shut, her hands clenched tightly. So she struggled with the fear and agony that were assaulting her life.

T. S. Arthur

CHAPTER V

A HANDSOME man of forty-five stood lingering by the bedside of his wife, whose large tender eyes looked up at him almost wistfully. A baby's head, dark with beautiful hair that curled in scores of silken ringlets, lay close against her bosom. The chamber was not large nor richly furnished, though everything was in good taste and comfortable. A few articles were out of harmony with the rest and hinted at better days. One of these was a large secretary of curious workmanship, inlaid with costly woods and pearl and rich with carvings. Another was a small mantel clock of exquisite beauty. Two or three small but rare pictures hung on the walls.

Looking closely into the man's strong intellectual face, you would have seen something that marred the harmony of its fine features and dimmed its clear expression—something to stir a doubt or awaken a feeling of concern. The eyes, that were deep and intense, had a shadow in them, and the curves of the mouth had suffering and passion and evidences of stern mental conflict in every line. This was no common man, no social drone, but one who in his contact with men was used to making himself felt.

"Come home early, Ralph, won't you?" said his wife.

The man bent down and kissed her, and then pressed his lips to the baby's head.

"Yes, dear; I don't mean to stay late. If it wasn't for the

expectation of meeting General Logan and one or two others that I particularly wish to see, I wouldn't go at all. I have to make good, you know, all the opportunities that come in my way."

"Oh yes, I know. You must go, of course." She had taken her husband's hand, and was holding it with a close pressure. He had to draw it away almost by force.

"Good-night, dear, and God bless you." His voice trembled a little. He stooped and kissed her again. A moment after and she was alone. Then all the light went out of her face and a deep shadow fell quickly over it. She shut her eyes, but not tightly enough to hold back the tears that soon carne creeping slowly out from beneath the closed lashes.

Ralph Ridley was a lawyer of marked ability. A few years before, he had given up a good practice at the bar for an office under the State government. Afterward he was sent to Congress and passed four years in Washington. Like too many of our ablest public men, the temptations of that city were too much for him. It was the old sad story that repeats itself every year. He fell a victim to the drinking customs of our national capital. Everywhere and on all social occasions invitations to wine met him. He drank with a friend on his way to the House, and with another in the Capitol buildings before taking his seat for business. He drank at lunch and at dinner, and he drank more freely at party or levee in the evening. Only in the early morning was he free from the bewildering effects of liquor.

Four years of such a life broke down his manhood. Hard as he sometimes struggled to rise above the debasing appetite that had enslaved him, resolution snapped like thread in a flame with every new temptation. He stood erect and hopeful to-day, and to-morrow lay prone and despairing under the heel of his enemy.

At the end of his second term in Congress the people of his

T. S. Arthur

district rejected him. They could tolerate a certain degree of drunkenness and demoralization in their representative, but Ridley had fallen too low. They would have him no longer, and so he was left out in the party nomination and sent back into private life hurt, humiliated and in debt. No clients awaited his return. His law-office had been closed for years, and there was little encouragement to open it again in the old place. For some weeks after his failure to get the nomination Ridley drank more desperately than ever, and was in a state of intoxication nearly all the while. His poor wife, who clung to him through all with an unwavering fidelity, was nearly broken-hearted. In vain had relatives and friends interposed. No argument nor persuasion could induce her to abandon him. "He is my husband," was her only reply, "and I will not leave him."

One night he was brought home insensible. He had fallen in the street where some repairs were being made, and had received serious injuries which confined him to the house for two or three weeks. This gave time for reflection and repentance. The shame and remorse that filled his soul as he looked at his sad, pale wife and neglected children, and thought of his tarnished name and lost opportunities, spurred him to new and firmer resolves than ever before made. He could go forward no longer without utter ruin. No hope was left but in turning back. He must set his face in a new direction, and he vowed to do so, promising God on his knees in tears and agony to hold, by his vow sacredly.

A new day had dawned. As soon as Mr. Ridley was well enough to be out again he took counsel of friends, and after careful deliberation resolved to leave his native town and remove to the city. A lawyer of fine ability, and known to the public as a clear thinker and an able debater, he had made quite an impression on the country during his first term in Congress; neither he nor his friends had any doubt as to his early success, provided he was able to keep himself free from the thraldom of old habits.

A few old friends and political associates made up a purse to enable him to remove to the city with his family. An office was taken and three rooms rented in a small house, where, with his wife and two children, one daughter in her fourteenth year, life was started anew. There was no room for a servant in this small establishment even if he had been able to pay the hire of one.

So the new beginning was made. A man of Mr. Ridley's talents and reputation could not long remain unemployed. In the very first week he had a client and a retaining fee of twenty-five dollars. The case was an important one, involving some nice questions of mercantile law. It came up for argument in the course of a few weeks, and gave the opportunity he wanted. His management of the case was so superior to that of the opposing counsel, and his citations of law and precedent so cumulative and explicit, that he gained not only an easy victory, but made for himself a very favorable impression.

After that business began gradually to flow in upon him, and he was able to gather in sufficient to keep his family, though for some time only in a very humble way. Having no old acquaintances in the city, Mr. Ridley was comparatively free from temptation. He was promptly at his office in the morning, never leaving it, except to go into court or some of the public offices on business, until the hour arrived for returning home.

A new life had become dominant, a new ambition was ruling him. Hope revived in the heart of his almost despairing wife, and the future looked bright again. His eyes had grown clear and confident once more and his stooping shoulders square and erect. In his bearing you saw the old stateliness and conscious sense of power. Men treated him with deference and respect.

In less than a year Mr. Ridley was able to remove his family into a better house and to afford the expense of a servant. So far they had kept out of the city's social life. Among strangers and living humbly, almost meanly, they neither made nor received calls nor had invitations to evening entertainments; and herein lay Mr. Ridley's safety. It was on his social side that he was weakest. He could hold himself above appetite and deny its cravings if left to the contest alone. The drinking-saloons whose hundred doors he had to pass daily did not tempt him, did not cause his firm steps to pause nor linger. His sorrow and shame for the past and his solemn promises and hopes for the future were potent enough to save him from all such allurements. For him their doors stood open in vain. The path of danger lay in another direction. He would have to be taken unawares. If betrayed at all, it must be, so to speak, in the house of a friend. The Delilah of "good society" must put caution and conscience to sleep and then rob him of his strength.

The rising man at the bar of a great city who had already served two terms in Congress could not long remain in social obscurity; and as it gradually became known in the "best society" that Mrs. Ridley stood connected with some of the "best families" in the State, one and another began to call upon her and to court her acquaintance, even though she was living in comparative obscurity and in a humble way.

At first regrets were returned to all invitations to evening entertainments, large or small. Mr. Ridley very well under-stood why his wife, who was social and naturally fond of company, was so prompt to decline. He knew that the excuse, "We are not able to give parties in return," was not really the true one. He knew that she feared the temptation that would come to him, and he was by no means insensible to the perils that would beset him whenever he found himself in the midst of a convivial company, with the odor of wine heavy on the air and invitations to drink meeting him at every turn.

But this could not always be. Mr. and Mrs. Ridley could not for ever hold themselves away from the social life of a large city among the people of which their acquaintance was gradually extending. Mrs. Ridley would have continued to stand aloof because of the danger she had too good reason to fear, but her husband was growing, she could see, both sensitive and restless. He wanted the professional advantages society would give him, and he wanted, moreover, to prove his manhood and take away the reproach under which he felt himself lying.

Sooner or later he must walk this way of peril, and he felt that he was becoming strong enough and brave enough to meet the old enemy that had vanquished him so many times.

"We will go," he said, on receiving cards of invitation to a party given by a prominent and influential citizen. "People will be there whom I should meet, and people whom I want you to meet."

He saw a shadow creep into his wife's face; Mrs. Ridley saw the shadow reflected almost as a frown from his. She knew what was in her husband's thoughts, knew that he felt hurt and restless under her continued reluctance to have him go into any company where wine and spirits were served to the guests, and feeling that a longer opposition might do more harm than good, answered, with as much heartiness and assent as she could get into her voice:

"Very well, but it will cost you the price of a new dress, for I have nothing fit to appear in."

The shadow swept off Mr. Ridley's face.

"All right," he returned. "I received a fee of fifty dollars to-day, and you shall have every cent; of it."

In the week that intervened Mrs. Ridley made herself ready for the party; but had she been preparing for a funeral, her heart could scarcely have been heavier. Fearful dreams haunted her sleep, and through the day imagination would often draw pictures the sight of which made her cry out in sudden pain and fear. All this she concealed from her husband, and affected to take a pleased interest in the coming entertainment.

T. S. Arthur

Mrs. Ridley was still a handsome woman, and her husband felt the old pride warming his bosom when he saw her again among brilliant and attractive women and noted the impression she made. He watched her with something of the proud interest a mother feels for a beautiful daughter who makes her appearance in society for the first time, and his heart beat with liveliest pleasure as he noticed the many instances in which she attracted and held people by the grace of her manner and the charm of her conversation.

"God bless her!" he said in his heart fervently as the love he bore her warmed into fresher life and moved him with a deeper tenderness, and then he made for her sake a new vow of abstinence and set anew the watch and ward upon his appetite. And he had need of watch and ward. The wine-merchant's bill for that evening's entertainment was over eight hundred dollars, and men and women, girls and boys, all drank in unrestrained freedom.

Mrs. Ridley, without seeming to do so, kept close to her husband while he was in the supper-room, and he, as if feeling the power of her protecting influence, was pleased to have her near. The smell of wine, its sparkle in the glasses, the freedom and apparent safety with which every one drank, the frequent invitations received, and the little banter and half-surprised lifting of the eyebrows that came now and then upon refusal were no light draught on Mr. Ridley's strength.

"Have you tried this sherry, Mr. Ridley?" said the gentlemanly host, taking a bottle from the supper-table and filling two glasses. "It is very choice." He lifted one of the glasses as he spoke and handed it to his guest. There was a flattering cordiality in his manner that made the invitation almost irresistible, and moreover he was a prominent and influential citizen whose favorable consideration Mr. Ridley wished to gain. If his wife had not been standing by his side, he would have accepted the glass, and for what seemed good breeding's sake have sipped a little, just tasting its flavor, so that he could compliment his host upon its rare quality.

"Thank you," Mr. Ridley was able to say, "but I do not take wine." His voice was not clear and manly, but unsteady and weak.

"Oh, excuse me," said the gentleman, setting down the glass quickly. "I was not aware of that." He stood as if slightly embarrassed for a moment, and then, turning to a clergyman who stood close by, said:

"Will you take a glass of wine with me, Mr. Elliott?"

An assenting smile broke into Mr. Elliott's face, and he reached for the glass which Mr. Ridley had just refused.

"Something very choice," said the host.

The clergyman tasted and sipped with the air of a connoisseur.

"Very choice indeed, sir," he replied. "But you always have good wine."

Mrs. Ridley drew her hand in her husband's arm and leaned upon it.

"If it is to be had," returned the host, a little, proudly; "and I generally know where to get it. A good glass of wine I count among the blessings for which one may give thanks—wine, I mean, not drugs."

"Exactly; wine that is pure hurts no one, unless, indeed, his appetite has been vitiated through alcoholic indulgence, and even then I have sometimes thought that the moderate use of strictly pure wine would restore the normal taste and free a man from the tyranny of an enslaving vice."

That sentence took quick hold upon the thought of Mr. Ridley. It gave him a new idea, and he listened with keen interest to what followed.

"You strike the keynote of a true temperance reformation, Mr. Elliott," returned the host. "Give men pure wine instead of the vile stuff that bears its name, and you will soon get rid of drunkenness. I have always preached that doctrine."

"And I imagine you are about right," answered Mr. Elliott. "Wine is one of God's gifts, and must be good. If men abuse it sometimes, it is nothing more than they do with almost every blessing the Father of all mercies bestows upon his children. The abuse of a thing is no argument against its use."

Mrs. Ridley drew upon the arm of her husband. She did not like the tenor of this conversation, and wanted to get him away. But he was interested in what the clergyman was saying, and wished to hear what further he might adduce in favor of the health influence of pure wine.

"I have always used wine, and a little good brandy too, and am as free from any inordinate appetite as your most confirmed abstainer; but then I take especial care to have my liquor pure."

"A thing not easily done," said the clergyman, replying to their host.

"Not easy for every one, but yet possible. I have never found much difficulty."

"There will be less difficulty, I presume," returned Mr. Elliott, "when this country becomes, as it soon will, a large wine producing region. When cheap wines take the place of whisky, we will have a return to temperate habits among the lower classes, and not, I am satisfied, before. There is, and always has been, a craving in the human system for some kind of stimulus. After prolonged effort there is exhaustion and nervous languor that cannot always wait upon the restorative work of nutrition; indeed, the nutritive organs themselves often need stimulation before they can act with due vigor. Isn't that so, Dr. Hillhouse?"

And the clergyman addressed a handsome old man with hair almost as white as snow who stood listening to the conversation. He held a glass of wine in his hand.

"You speak with the precision of a trained pathologist," replied the person addressed, bowing gracefully and with considerable manner as he spoke. "I could not have said it better, Mr. Elliott."

The clergyman received the compliment with a pleased smile and bowed his acknowledgments, then remarked:

"You think as I do about the good effects that must follow a large product of American wines?"

Dr. Hillhouse gave a little shrug.

"Oh, then you don't agree with me?"

"Pure wine is one thing and too much of what is called American wine quite another thing," replied the doctor. "Cheap wine for the people, as matters now stand, is only another name for diluted alcohol. It is better than pure whisky, maybe, though the larger quantity that will naturally be taken must give the common dose of that article and work about the same effect in the end."

"Then you are not in favor of giving the people cheap wines?" said the clergyman.

The doctor shrugged his shoulders again.

"I have been twice to Europe," he replied, "and while there looked a little into the condition of the poorer classes in wine countries. I had been told that there was scarcely any intemperance among them, but I did not find it so. There, as here, the use of alcohol in any form, whether as beer, wine or whisky, produces the same result, varied in its effect upon the individual only by the peculiarity of temperament and national

T. S. Arthur

character of the people. I'll take another glass of that sherry; it's the best I've tasted for a year."

And Dr. Hillhouse held out his glass to be filled by the flattered host, Mr. Elliott doing the same, and physician and clergyman touched their brimming glasses and smiled and bowed "a good health." Before the hour for going home arrived both were freer of tongue and a little wilder in manner than when they came.

"The doctor is unusually brilliant to-night," said one, with just a slight lifting of the eyebrow.

"And so is Mr. Elliott," returned the person addressed, glancing at the clergyman, who, standing in the midst of a group of young men, glass in hand, was telling a story and laughing at his own witticisms.

"Nothing strait-laced about Mr. Elliott," remarked the other. "I like him for that. He doesn't think because he's a clergyman that he must always wear a solemn face and act as if he were conducting a funeral service. Just hear him laugh! It makes you feel good. You can get near to such a man. All the young people in his congregation like him because he doesn't expect them to come up to his official level, but is ever ready to come down to them and enter into their feelings and tastes."

"He likes a good glass of wine," said the first speaker.

"Of course he does. Have you any objection?"

"Shall I tell you what came into my thought just now?"

"Yes."

"What St. Paul said about eating meat."

"Oh!"

"'If meat make my brother to offend, I will eat no flesh while the world standeth, lest I make my brother to offend.' And again: 'Take heed lest by any means this liberty of yours become a stumbling-block to them that are weak.'"

"How does that apply to Mr. Elliott?"

"There are more than one or two young men in the group that surrounds him who need a better example than he is now setting. They need repression in the matter of wine-drinking, not encouragement—a good example of abstinence in their minister, and not enticement to drink through his exhibition of liberty. Do you think that I, church member though I am not, could stand as Mr. Elliott is now standing, glass in hand, gayly talking to young Ellis Whitford, who rarely goes to a party without—poor weak young man!—drinking too much, and so leading him on in the way of destruction instead of seeking in eager haste to draw him back? No sir! It is no light thing, as I regard it, to put a stumbling-block in another's way or to lead the weak or unwary into temptation."

"Perhaps you are right about it," was the answer, "and I must confess that, though not a temperance man myself, I never feel quite comfortable about it when I see clergymen taking wine freely at public dinners and private parties. It is not a good example, to say the least of it; and if there is a class of men in the community to whom we have some right to look for a good example, it is the class chosen and set apart to the work of saving human souls."

T. S. Arthur

CHAPTER VI

MR. RIDLEY went home from that first party with his head as clear and his pulse as cool as when he came. The wine had not tempted him very strongly, though its odor had been fragrant to his nostrils, and the sparkle in the glasses pleasant to his sight. Appetite had not aroused itself nor put on its strength, but lay half asleep, waiting for some better opportunity, when the sentinels should be weaker or off their guard.

It had been much harder for him to refuse the invitation of his host than to deny the solicitations of the old desire. He had been in greater danger from pride than from appetite; and there remained with him a sense of being looked down upon and despised by the wealthy and eminent citizen who had honored him with an invitation, and who doubtless regarded his refusal to take wine with him as little less than a discourtesy. There were moments when he almost regretted that refusal. The wine which had been offered was of the purest quality, and he remembered but too well the theory advanced by Mr. Elliott, that the moderate use of pure wine would restore the normal taste and free a man whose appetite had been vitiated from its enslaving influence. His mind recurred to that thought very often, and the more he dwelt upon it, the more inclined he was to accept it as true. If it were indeed so, then he might be a man among men again.

Mr. Ridley did not feel as comfortable in his mind after as before this party, nor was he as strong as before. The enemy had found a door unguarded, had come in stealthily, and was lying on the alert, waiting for an opportunity.

A few weeks afterward came another invitation. It was accepted. Mrs. Ridley was not really well enough, to go out, but for her husband's sake she went with him, and by her presence and the quiet power she had over him held him back from the peril he might, standing alone, have tempted.

A month later, and cards of invitation were received from Mr. and Mrs. Spencer Birtwell. This was to be among the notable entertainments of the season. Mr. Birtwell was a wealthy banker who, like other men, had his weaknesses, one of which was a love of notoriety and display. He had a showy house and attractive equipages, and managed to get his name frequently chronicled in the newspapers, now as the leader in some public enterprise or charity, now as the possessor of some rare work of art, and now as the princely capitalists whose ability and sagacity had lifted him from obscurity to the proud position he occupied. He built himself a palace for a residence, and when it was completed and furnished issued tickets of admission, that the public might see in what splendor he was going to live. Of course the newspapers described everything with a minuteness of detail and a freedom of remark that made some modest and sensitive people fancy that Mr. Birtwell must be exceedingly annoyed. But he experienced no such feeling. Praise of any kind was pleasant to his ears; you could not give him too much, nor was he over-nice as to the quality. He lived in the eyes of his fellow-citizens, and in all his walk and conversation, he looked to their good opinion.

Such was Mr. Birtwell, at whose house a grand entertainment was to be given. Among the large number of invited guests were included Mr. and Mrs. Ridley. But it so happened that Mrs. Ridley could not go. A few days before the evening on which this party was to be given a new-born babe had been laid on her bosom.

"Good-night, dear, and God bless you!" Mr. Ridley had said, in a voice that was very tender, as he stooped over and kissed his wife. No wonder that all the light went out of her face the moment she was alone, nor that a shadow fell quickly over it, nor that from beneath the fringes of her shut eyelids tears crept slowly and rested upon her cheeks. If her husband had left her for the battlefield, she could not have felt a more dreadful impression of danger, nor have been oppressed by a more terrible fear for his safety. No wonder that her nurse, coming into the chamber a few minutes after Mr. Ridley went out, found her in a nervous chill.

The spacious and elegant drawing-rooms of Mr. and Mrs. Birtwell were crowded with the elite of the city, and the heart of the former swelled with pride as he received his guests and thought of their social, professional or political distinction, the lustre of which he felt to be, for the time, reflected upon himself. It was good to be in such company, and to feel that he was equal with the best. He had not always been the peer of such men. There had been an era of obscurity out of which he had slowly emerged, and therefore he had the larger pride and self-satisfaction in the position he now held.

Mrs. Birtwell was a woman of another order. All her life she had been used to the elegancy that a wealthy parentage gave, and to which her husband had been, until within a few years, an entire stranger. She was "to the manner born," he a parvenu with a restless ambition to outshine. Familiarity with things luxurious and costly had lessened their value in her eyes, and true culture had lifted her above the weakness of resting in or caring much about them, while their newness and novelty to Mr. Birtwell made enjoyment keen, and led him on to extravagant and showy exhibitions of wealth that caused most people to smile at his weakness, and a good many to ask who he was and from whence he came that he carried himself so loftily. Mrs. Birtwell did not like the advanced position to which her husband carried her, but she yielded to his weak love of notoriety and social eclat as gracefully as possible, and did her best to cover his too glaring violations of good taste and conventional refinement. In this she was not always successful.

Of course the best of liquors in lavish abundance were provided by Mr. Birtwell for his guests. Besides the dozen different kinds of wine that were on the supper-table, there was a sideboard for gentlemen, in a room out of common observation, well stocked with brandy, gin and whisky, and it was a little curious to see how quickly this was discovered by certain of the guests, who scented it as truly as a bee scents honey in a clover-field, and extracted its sweets as eagerly.

Of the guests who were present we have now to deal chiefly with Mr. Ridley, and only incidentally with the rest. Dr. Hillhouse was there during the first part of the evening, but went away early—that, is, before twelve o'clock. He remained long enough, however, to do full justice to the supper and wines. His handsome and agreeable young associate, Dr. Angler, a slight acquaintance with whom the reader has already, prolonged his stay to a later hour.

The Rev. Dr. Elliott was also, among the guests, displaying his fine social qualities and attracting about him the young and the old. Everybody liked Dr. Elliott, he was so frank, so cordial, free and sympathetic, and, withal, so intelligent. He did not bring the clergyman with him into a gay drawing-room, nor the ascetic to a feast. He could talk with the banker about finance, with the merchant about trade, with the student or editor about science, literature and the current events of the day, and with young men and maidens about music and the lighter matters in which they happened to be interested. And, moreover, he could enjoy a good supper and knew the flavor of good wine. A man of such rare accomplishments came to be a general favorite, and so you encountered Mr. Elliott at nearly all the fashionable parties.

Mr. Ridley had met the reverend doctor twice, and had been much pleased with him. What he had heard him say about the healthy or rather saving influences of pure wine had taken a strong hold of his thoughts, and he had often wished for an opportunity to talk with him about it. On this evening he found that opportunity. Soon after his arrival at the house of

Mr. Birtwell he saw Mr. Elliott in one of the parlors, and made his way into the little group which had already gathered around the affable clergyman. Joining in the conversation, which was upon some topic of the day, Mr. Ridley, who talked well, was not long in awakening that interest in the mind of Mr. Elliott which one cultivated and intelligent person naturally feels for another; and in a little while, they had the conversation pretty much to themselves. It touched this theme and that, and finally drifted in a direction which enabled Mr. Ridley to refer to what he had heard Mr. Elliott say about the healthy effect of pure wine on the taste of men whose appetites had become morbid, and to ask him if he had any good ground for his belief.

"I do not know that I can bring any proof of my theory," returned Mr. Elliott, "but I hold to it on the ground of an eternal fitness of things. Wine is good, and was given by God to make glad the hearts of men, and is to be used temperately, as are all other gifts. It may be abused, and is abused daily. Men hurt themselves by excess of wine as by excess of food. But the abuse of a thing is no argument against its use. If a man through epicurism or gormandizing has brought on disease, what do you do with him? Deny him all food, or give him of the best in such quantities as his nutritive system can appropriate and change into healthy muscle, nerve and bone? You do the latter, of course, and so would I treat the case of a man who bad hurt himself by excess of wine. I would see that he had only the purest and in diminished quantity, so that his deranged system might not only have time but help in regaining its normal condition."

"And you think this could be safely done?" said Mr. Ridley.

"That is my view of the case."

"Then you do not hold to the entire abstinence theory?"

"No, sir; on that subject our temperance people have run into what we might call fanaticism, and greatly weakened their influence. Men should be taught self-control and moderation in the use of things. If the appetite becomes vitiated through over-indulgence, you do not change its condition by complete denial. What you want for radical cure is the restoration of the old ability to use without abusing. In other words, you want a man made right again as to his rational power of self-control, by which he becomes master of himself in all the degrees of his life, from the highest to the lowest."

"All very well," remarked Dr. Hillhouse, who had joined them while Mr. Elliott was speaking. "But, in my experience, the rational self-control of which you speak is one of the rarest things to be met with in common life, and it may be fair to conclude that the man who cannot exercise it before a dangerous habit has been formed will not be very likely to exercise it afterward when anything is done to favor that habit. Habits, Mr. Elliott, are dreadful hard things to manage, and I do not know a harder one to deal with than the habit of over-indulgence in wine or spirits. I should be seriously afraid of your prescription. The temperate use of wine I hold to be good; but for those who have once lost the power of controlling their appetites I am clear in my opinion there is only one way of safety, and that is the way of entire abstinence from any drink in which there is alcohol, call it by what name you will; and this is the view now held by the most experienced and intelligent men, in our profession."

A movement in the company being observed, Mr. Elliott, instead of replying, stepped toward a lady, and asked the pleasure of escorting her to the supper-room. Dr. Hillhouse was equally courteous, and Mr. Ridley, seeing the wife of General Logan, whom he had often met in Washington, standing a little way off, passed to her side and offered his arm, which was accepted.

There was a crowd and crush upon the stairs, fine gentlemen and ladies seeming to forget their courtesy and good breeding in their haste to be among the earliest who should reach the banqueting-hall. This was long and spacious, having been

T. S. Arthur

planned by Mr. Birtwell with a view to grand entertainments like the one he was now giving. In an almost incredibly short space of time it was filled to suffocation. Those who thought themselves among the first to move were surprised to find the tables already surrounded by young men and women, who had been more interested in the status of the supper-room than in the social enjoyments of the parlors, and who had improved their advanced state of observation by securing precedence of the rest, and stood waiting for the signal to begin.

Mr. Birtwell had a high respect for the Church, and on an occasion like this could do no less than honor one of its dignitaries by requesting him to ask a blessing on the sumptuous repast he had provided—on the rich food and the good wine and brandy he was about dispensing with such a liberal hand. So, in the waiting pause that ensued after the room was well filled, Mr. Elliott was called upon to bless this feast, which he did in a raised, impressive and finely modulated voice. Then came the rattle of plates and the clink of glasses, followed by the popping of champagne and the multitudinous and distracting Babel of tongues.

Mr. Ridley, who felt much inclined to favor the superficial and ill-advised utterances of Mr. Elliott, took scarcely any heed of what Dr. Hillhouse had replied. In fact, knowing that the doctor was free with wine himself, he did not give much weight to what he said, feeling that he was talking more for argument's sake than to express his real sentiments.

A feeling of repression came over Mr. Ridley as he entered the supper-room and his eyes ran down the table. Half of this sumptuous feast was forbidden enjoyment. He must not taste the wine. All were free but him. He could fill a glass for the elegant lady whose hand was still upon his arm, but must not pledge her back except in water. A sense of shame and humiliation crept into his heart. So he felt when, in the stillness that fell upon the company, the voice of Mr. Elliott rose in blessing on the good things now spread for them in such lavish profusion. Only one sentence took hold on, Mr.

Ridley's mind. It was this: "Giver of all natural as well as spiritual good things, of the corn and the wine equally with the bread and the water of life, sanctify these bounties that come from thy beneficent hand, and keep us from any inordinate or hurtful use thereof."

Mr. Ridley drew a deeper breath. A load seemed taken from his bosom. He felt a sense of freedom and safety. If the wine were pure, it was a good gift of God, and could not really do him harm. A priest, claiming to stand as God's representative among men, had invoked a blessing on this juice of the grape, and given it by this act a healthier potency. All this crowded upon him, stifling reason and experience and hushing the voice of prudence.

And now, alas! he was as a feather on the surface of a wind-struck lake, and given up to the spirit and pressure of the hour. The dangerous fallacy to which Mr. Elliott had given utterance held his thoughts to the exclusion of all other considerations. A clear path out of the dreary wilderness in which he had been, straying seemed to open before him, and he resolved to walk therein. Fatal delusion!

As soon as Mr. Ridley had supplied Mrs. General Locran with terrapin and oysters and filled a plate for himself, he poured out two glasses of wine and handed one of them to the lady, then, lifting the other, he bowed a compliment and placed it to his lips. The lady smiled on him graciously, sipping the wine and praising its flavor.

"Pure as nectar," was the mental response of Mr. Ridley as the long-denied palate felt the first thrill of sweet satisfaction. He had taken a single mouthful, but another hand seemed to grasp the one that held the cup of wine and press it back to his lips, from which it was not removed until empty.

The prescription of Mr. Elliott failed. Either the wine was not pure or his theory was at fault. It was but little over an hour from the fatal moment when Mr. Ridley put a glass of wine to

T. S. Arthur

his lips ere he went out alone into the storm of a long-to-be-remembered night in a state of almost helpless intoxication, and staggered off in the blinding snow that soon covered his garments like a winding sheet.

CHAPTER VII

THE nurse of Mrs. Ridley had found her in a nervous chill, at which she was greatly troubled. More clothing was laid upon the bed, and bottles of hot water placed to her feet. To all this Mrs. Ridley made no objection—remained, in fact, entirely passive and irresponsive, like one in a partial stupor, from which she did not, to all appearance, rally even after the chill had subsided.

She lay with her eyes shut, her lips pressed together and her forehead drawn into lines, and an expression of pain on her face, answering only in dull monosyllables to the inquiries made every now and then by her nurse, who hovered about the bed and watched over her with anxious solicitude.

As she feared, fever symptoms began to show themselves. The evening had worn away, and it was past ten o'clock. It would not do to wait until morning in a case like this, and so a servant was sent to the office of Dr. Hillhouse, with a request that he would come immediately. She returned saying that the doctor was not at home.

Mrs. Ridley lay with her eyes shut, but the nurse knew by the expression of her face that she was not asleep. The paleness of her countenance had given way to a fever hue, and she noticed occasional restless movements of the hands, twitches of the eyelids and nervous starts. To her questions the patient gave no satisfactory answers.

T. S. Arthur

An hour elapsed, and still the doctor did not make his appearance. The servant was called and questioned. She was positive about having left word for the doctor to come immediately on returning home.

"Is that snow?" inquired Mrs. Ridley, starting up in bed and listening. The wind had risen suddenly and swept in a gusty dash against the windows, rattling on the glass the fine hard grains which had been falling for some time.

She remained leaning on her arm and listening for some moments, while an almost frightened look came into her face.

"What time is it?" she asked.

"After eleven o'clock," replied the nurse.

All at once the storm seemed to have awakened into a wild fury. More loudly it rushed and roared and dashed its sand-like snow against the windows of Mrs. Ridley's chamber. The sick woman shivered and the fever-flush died out of her face.

"You must lie down!" said the nurse, speaking with decision and putting her hands on Mrs. Ridley to press her back. But the latter resisted.

"Indeed, indeed, ma'am," urged the nurse, showing great anxiety, "you must lie down and keep covered up in bed. It might be the death of you."

"Oh, that's awful!" exclaimed Mrs. Ridley as the wind went howling by and the snow came in heavier gusts against the windows. "Past eleven, did you say?"

"Yes, ma'am, and the doctor ought to have been here long ago. I wonder why he doesn't come?"

"Hark! wasn't that our bell?" cried Mrs. Ridley, bending forward in a listening attitude.

The nurse opened the chamber door and stood hearkening for a moment or two. Not hearing the servant stir, she ran quickly down stairs to the street door and drew it open, but found no one.

There was a look of suspense and fear in Mrs. Ridley's face when the nurse came back:

"Who was it?"

"No one," replied the nurse. "The wind deceived you."

A groan came from Mrs. Ridley's lips as she sank down upon the bed, where, with her face hidden, she lay as still as if sleeping. She did not move nor speak for the space of more than half an hour, and all the while her nurse waited and listened through the weird, incessant noises of the storm for the coming of Dr. Hillhouse, but waited and listened in vain.

All at once, as if transferred to within a few hundred rods of these anxious watchers, the great clock of the city, which in the still hours of a calm night could be heard ringing out clear but afar off, threw a resonant clang upon the air, pealing the first stroke of the hour of twelve. Mrs. Ridley started up in bed with a scared look on her face. Away the sound rolled, borne by the impetuous wind-wave that had caught it up as the old bell shivered it off, and carried it away so swiftly that it seemed to die almost in the moment it was born. The listeners waited, holding their breaths. Then, swept from the course this first peal had taken, the second came to their ears after a long interval muffled and from a distance, followed almost instantly by the third, which went booming past them louder than the first. And so, with strange intervals and variations of time and sound as the wind dashed wildly onward or broke and swerved from its course, the noon of night was struck, and the silence that for a brief time succeeded left a feeling of awe upon the hearts of these lonely women.

To the ears of another had come these strange and solemn

T. S. Arthur

tones, struck out at midnight away up in the clear rush of the tempest, and swept away in a kind of mad sport, and tossed about in the murky sky. To the ears of another, who, struggling and battling with the storm, had made his way with something of a blind instinct to within a short distance of his home, every stroke of the clock seemed to come from a different quarter; and when the last peal rang out, it left him in helpless bewilderment. When he staggered on again, it was in a direction opposite to that in which he had been going. For ten minutes he wrought with the blinding and suffocating snow, which, turn as he would, the wind kept dashing into his face, and then his failing limbs gave out and he sunk benumbed with cold upon the pavement. Half buried in the snow, he was discovered soon afterward and carried to a police station, where he found himself next morning in one of the cells, a wretched, humiliated, despairing man.

"Why, Mr. Ridley! It can't be possible!" It was the exclamation of the police magistrate when this man was brought, soon after daylight, before him.

Ridley stood dumb in presence of the officer, who was touched by the helpless misery of his face.

"You were at Mr. Birtwell's?"

Ridley answered by a silent inclination of his head.

"I do not wonder," said the magistrate, his voice softening, "that, you lost your way in the storm last night. You are not the only one who found himself astray and at fault. Our men had to take care of quite a number of Mr. Birtwell's guests. But I will not detain you, Mr. Ridley. I am sorry this happened. You must be more careful in future."

With slow steps and bowed head Mr. Ridley left the station-house and took his way homeward. How could he meet his wife? What of her? How had she passed the night? Vividly came up the parting scene as she lay with her babe, only a few days old, close against her bosom, her tender eyes, in which he saw shadows of fear, fixed lovingly upon his face.

He had promised to be home soon, and had said a fervent "God bless you!" as he left a kiss warm upon her lips.

And now! He stood still, a groan breaking on the air. Go home! How could he look into the face of his wife again? She had walked with him through the valley of humiliation in sorrow and suffering and shame for years, and now, after going up from this valley and bearing her to a pleasant land of hope and happiness, he had plunged down madly. Then a sudden fear smote his heart. She was in no condition to bear a shock such as his absence all night must have caused. The consequences might be fatal. He started forward at a rapid pace, hurrying along until he came in sight of his house. A carriage stood at the door. What could this mean?

Entering, he was halfway up stairs when, the nurse met him.

"Oh, Mr. Ridley," she exclaimed, "why did you stay away all night? Mrs. Ridley has been so ill, and I couldn't get the doctor. Oh, sir, I don't know what will come of it. She's in a dreadful way—out of her head. I sent for Dr. Hillhouse last night, but he didn't come."

She spoke in a rapid manner, showing much alarm and agitation.

"Is Dr. Hillhouse here now?" asked Mr. Ridley, trying to repress his feelings.

"No, sir. He sent Dr. Angier, but I don't trust much in him. Dr. Hillhouse ought to see her right away. But you do look awful, sir!"

The nurse fixed her eyes upon him in a half-wondering stare.

Mr. Ridley broke from her, and passing up the stairs in two or

T. S. Arthur

three long strides, made his way to the bath-room, where in a few moments he changed as best he could his disordered appearance, and then hurried to his wife's chamber.

A wild cry of joy broke from her lips as she saw him enter; but when he came near, she put up her hands and shrunk away from him, saying in a voice that fairly wailed, it was so full of disappointment:

"I thought it was Ralph—my dear, good Ralph! Why don't he come home?"

Her cheeks were red with fever and her eyes bright and shining. She had started up in bed on hearing her husband's step, but now shrunk down under the clothing and turned her face away.

"Blanche! Blanche!" Mr. Ridley called the name of his wife tenderly as he stood leaning over her.

Moving her head slowly, like one in doubt, she looked at him in a curious, questioning way. Then, closing her eyes, she turned her face from him again.

"Blanche! Blanche!" For all the response that came, Mr. Ridley might as well have spoken to deaf ears. Dr. Angier laid his hand on his arm and drew him away:

"She must have as little to disturb her as possible, Mr. Ridley. The case is serious."

"Where is Dr. Hillhouse? Why did not he come?" demanded Mr. Ridley.

"He will be here after a while. It is too early for him," replied Dr. Angier.

"He must come now. Go for him at once, doctor."

"If you say so," returned Doctor Angier, with some coldness of manner; "but I cannot tell how soon he will be here. He does not go out until after eight or nine o'clock, and there are two or three pressing cases besides this."

"I will go," said Mr. Ridley. "Don't think me rude or uncourteous, Dr. Angier. I am like one distracted. Stay here until I get back. I will bring Dr. Hillhouse."

"Take my carriage—it is at the door; and say to Dr. Hillhouse from me that I would like him to come immediately," Dr. Angier replied to this.

Mr. Ridley ran down stairs, and springing into the carriage, ordered the driver to return with all possible speed to the office. Dr. Hillhouse was in bed, but rose on getting the summons from Dr. Angier and accompanied Mr. Ridley. He did not feel in a pleasant humor. The night's indulgence in wine and other allurements of the table had not left his head clear nor his nerves steady for the morning. A sense of physical discomfort made him impatient and irritable. At first all the conditions of this case were not clear to him; but as his thought went back to the incidents of the night, and he remembered not only seeing Mr. Ridley in considerable excitement from drink, but hearing it remarked upon by one or two persons who were familiar with his life at Washington, the truth dawned upon his mind, and he said abruptly, with considerable sternness of manner and in a quick voice:

"At what time did you get home last night?"

Ridley made no reply.

"Or this morning? It was nearly midnight when *I* left, and you were still there, and, I am sorry to say, not in the best condition for meeting a sick wife at home. If there is anything seriously wrong in this case, the responsibility lies, I am afraid, at your door, sir."

T. S. Arthur

They were in the carriage, moving rapidly. Mr. Ridley sat-with his head drawn down and bent a little forward; not answering, Dr. Hillhouse said no more. On arriving at Mr. Ridley's residence, he met Dr. Angier, with whom he held a brief conference before seeing his patient. He found her in no favorable condition. The fever was not so intense as Dr. Angier had found it on his arrival, but its effect on the brain was more marked.

"Too much time has been lost." Dr. Hillhouse spoke aside to his assistant a's they sat together watching carefully every symptom of their patient.

"I sent for you before ten o'clock last night," said the nurse, who overheard the remark and wished to screen herself from any blame.

Dr. Hillhouse did not reply.

"I knew there was danger," pursued the nurse. "Oh, doctor, if you had only come when I sent for you! I waited and waited until after midnight."

The doctor growled an impatient response, but so muttered and mumbled the words that the nurse could not make them out. Mr. Ridley was in the room, standing with folded arms a little way from the bed, stern and haggard, with wild, congested eyes and closely shut mouth, a picture of anguish, fear and remorse.

The two physicians remained with Mrs. Ridley for over twenty minutes before deciding on their line of treatment. A prescription was then made, and careful instructions given to the nurse.

"I will call again in the course of two or three hours," said Dr. Hillhouse, on going away. "Should any thing unfavorable occur, send to the office immediately."

"Doctor!" Mr. Ridley laid his hand on the arm of Dr. Hillhouse. "What of my wife?" There was a frightened look in his pale, agitated face. His voice shook.

"She is in danger," replied the doctor.

"But you know what to do? You can control the disease? You have had such cases before?"

"I will do my best," answered the doctor, trying to move on; but Mr. Ridley clutched his arm tightly and held him fast:

"Is it—is it—puer-p-p—" His voice shook so that he could not articulate the word that was on his tongue.

"I am afraid so," returned the doctor.

A deep groan broke from the lips of Mr. Ridley. His hand dropped from the arm of Dr. Hillhouse and he stood trembling from head to foot, then cried out in a voice of unutterable despair:

"From heaven down to hell in one wild leap! God help me!"

Dr. Hillhouse was deeply moved at this. He had felt stern and angry, ready each moment to accuse and condemn, but the intense emotion displayed by the husband shocked, subdued and changed his tone of feeling.

"You must calm, yourself, my dear sir," he said. "The case looks bad, but I have seen recovery in worse cases than this. We will do our best. But remember that you have duties and responsibilities that must not fail."

"Whatsoever in me lies, doctor," answered Mr. Ridley, with a sudden calmness that seemed supernatural, "you may count on my doing. If she dies, I am lost." There was a deep solemnity in his tones as he uttered this last sentence. "You see, sir," he added, "what I have at stake."

"Just for the present little more can be done than to follow the prescriptions we have given and watch their effect on the patient," returned Dr. Hillhouse. "If any change occurs, favorable or unfavorable, let us know. If your presence in her room should excite or disturb her in any way, you must prudently abstain from going near her."

The two physicians went away with but little hope in their hearts for the sick woman. Whatever the exciting cause or causes might have been, the disease which had taken hold of her with unusual violence presented already so fatal a type that the issue was very doubtful.

CHAPTER VIII

"IT is too late, I am afraid," said Dr. Hillhouse as the two physicians rode away, "The case ought to have been seen last night. I noticed the call when I came home from Mr. Birtwell's, but the storm was frightful, and I did not feel like going out again. In fact, if the truth must be told, I hardly gave the matter a thought. I saw the call, but its importance did not occur to me. Late hours, suppers and wine do not always leave the head as clear as it should be."

"I do not like the looks of things," returned Dr. Angier. "All the symptoms are bad."

"Yes, very bad. I saw Mrs. Ridley yesterday morning, and found her doing well. No sign of fever or any functional disturbance. She must have had some shock or exposure to cold."

"Her husband was out all night. I learned that much from the nurse," replied Dr. Angier. "When the storm became violent, which was soon after ten o'clock, she grew restless and disturbed, starting up and listening as the snow dashed on the windowpanes and the wind roared angrily. 'I could not keep her down,' said the nurse. 'She would spring up in bed, throw off the clothes and sit listening, with a look of anxiety and dread on her face. The wind came in through every chink and crevice, chilling the room in spite of all I could do to keep it warm. I soon saw, from the color that began coming into her face and from the brightness in her eyes, that fever had set in. I

T. S. Arthur

was alarmed, and sent for the doctor.'"

"And did this go on all night?" asked Dr. Hillhouse.

"Yes. She never closed her eyes except in intervals of feverish stupor, from which she would start up and cry out for her husband, who was, she imagined, in some dreadful peril."

"Bad! bad!" muttered Dr. Hillhouse. "There'll be a death, I fear, laid at Mr. Birtwell's door."

"I don't understand you," said his companion, in a tone of surprise.

"Mr. Ridley, as I have been informed," returned Dr. Hillhouse, has been an intemperate man. After falling very low, he made an earnest effort to reform, and so far got the mastery of his appetite as to hold it in subjection. Such men are always in danger, as you and I very well know. In nine cases out of ten—or, I might say, in ninety-nine cases in a hundred—to taste again is to fall. It is like cutting the chain that holds a wild beast. The bound but not dead appetite springs into full vigor again, and surprised resolution is beaten down and conquered. To invite such a man to, an entertainment where wines and liquors are freely dispensed is to put a human soul in peril."

"Mr. Birtwell may not have known anything about him,' replied Dr. Angier.

"All very true. But there is one thing he did know."

"What?"

"That he could not invite a company of three hundred men and women to his house, though he selected them from the most refined and intelligent circles in our city, and give them intoxicating drinks as freely as he did last night, without serious harm. In such accompany there will be some, like Mr.

Ridley, to whom the cup of wine offered in hospitality will be a cup of cursing. Good resolutions will be snapped like thread in a candle-flame, and men who came sober will go away, as from any other drinking-saloon, drunk, as he went out last night."

"Drinking-saloon! You surprise me, doctor."

"I feel bitter this morning; and when the bitterness prevails, I am apt to call things by strong names. Yes, I say drinking-saloon, Doctor Angier. What matters it in the dispensation whether you give away or sell the liquor, whether it be done over a bar or set out free to every guest in a merchant's elegant banqueting-room? The one is as much a liquor-saloon as the other. Men go away from one, as from the other, with heads confused and steps unsteady and good resolutions wrecked by indulgence. Knowing that such things must follow; that from every fashionable entertainment some men, and women too, go away weaker and in more danger than when they came; that boys and young men are tempted to drink and the feet of some set in the ways of ruin; that health is injured and latent diseases quickened into force; that evil rather than good flows from them,—knowing all this, I say, can any man who so turns his house, for a single evening, into a drinking-saloon—I harp on the words, you see, for I am feeling bitter—escape responsibility? No man goes blindly in this way."

"Taking your view of the case," replied Dr. Angier, "there may be another death laid at the door of Mr. Birtwell."

"Whose?" Dr. Hillhouse turned quickly to his assistant. They had reached home, and were standing in their office.

"Nothing has been heard of Archie Voss since he left Mr. Birtwell's last night, and his poor mother is lying insensible, broken down by her fears."

"Oh, what of her? I was called for in the night, and you went in my place."

"I found Mrs. Voss in a state of coma, from which she had only partially recovered when I left at daylight. Mr. Voss is in great anxiety about his son, who has never stayed away all night before, except with the knowledge of his parents."

"Oh, that will all come right," said Dr. Hillhouse. "The young man went home, probably, with some friend. Had too much to drink, it may be, and wanted to sleep it off before coming into his mother's pressence."

"There is no doubt about his having drank too much," returned Dr. Angier. "I saw him going along the hall toward the street door in rather a bad way. He had his overcoat on and his hat in his hand."

"Was any one with him?"

"I believe not. I think he went out alone."

"Into that dreadful storm?"

"Yes."

The countenance of Dr. Hillhouse became very grave:

"And has not been heard of since?"

"No."

"Have the police been informed about it?"

"Yes. The police have had the matter in hand for several hours, but at the time I left not the smallest clue had been found."

"Rather a bad look," said Dr. Hillhouse. "What does Mr. Voss say about it?"

"His mind seems to dwell on two theories—one that Archie, who had a valuable diamond pin and a gold watch, may have wandered into some evil neighborhood, bewildered by the storm, and there been set upon and robbed—murdered perhaps. The other is that he has fallen in some out-of-the-way place, overcome by the cold, and lies buried in the snow. The fact that no police-officer reports having seen him or any one answering to his description during the night awakens the gravest fears."

"Still," replied Dr. Hillhouse, "it may all come out right. He may have gone to a hotel. There are a dozen theories to set against those of his friends."

After remaining silent for several moments, he said:

"The boy had been drinking too much?"

"Yes; and I judge from, his manner, when I saw him on his way to the street, that he was conscious of his condition and ashamed of it. He went quietly along, evidently trying not to excite observation, but his steps were unsteady and his sight not true, for in trying to thread his way along the hall he ran against one and another, and drew the attention he was seeking to avoid."

"Poor fellow!" said Dr. Hillhouse, with genuine pity. "He was always a nice boy. If anything has happened to him, I wouldn't give a dime for the life of his mother."

"Nor I. And even as it is, the shock already received may prove greater than her exhausted system can bear. I think you had better see her, doctor, as early as possible."

"There were no especially bad symptoms when you left, beyond the state of partial coma?"

"No. Her respiration had become easy, and she presented the appearance of one in a quiet sleep."

"Nature is doing all for her that can be done," returned Dr.

T. S. Arthur

Hillhouse. "I will see her as early as practicable. It's unfortunate that we have these two cases on our hands just at this time, and most unfortunate of all that I should have been compelled to go out so early this morning. That doesn't look right."

And the doctor held up his hand, which showed a nervous unsteadiness.

"It will pass off after you have taken breakfast."

"I hope so. Confound these parties! I should not have gone last night, and if I'd given the matter due consideration would have remained at home."

"Why so?"

"You know what that means as well as I do;" and Dr. Hillhouse held up his tremulous hand again. "We can't take wine freely late at night and have our nerves in good order next morning. A life may depend on a steady hand to-day."

"It will all pass off at breakfast-time. Your good cup of coffee will make everything all right."

"Perhaps yea, perhaps nay," was answered. "I forgot myself last night, and accepted too many wine compliments. It was first this one and then that one, until, strong as my head is, I got more into it than should have gone there. We are apt to forget ourselves on these occasions. If I had only taken a glass or two, it would have made little difference. But my system was stimulated beyond its wont, and, I fear, will not be in the right tone to-day."

"You will have to bring it up, then, doctor," said the assistant. "To touch that work with an unsteady hand might be death."

"A glass or two of wine will do it; but when I operate, I always prefer to have my head clear. Stimulated nerves are not to be depended upon, and the brain that has wine in it is never a sure guide. A surgeon must see at the point of his instrument; and if there be a mote or any obscurity in his mental vision, his hand, instead of working a cure, may bring disaster."

"You operate at twelve?"

"Yes."

"You will be all right enough by that time; but it will not do to visit many patients. I am sorry about this case of child-bed fever; but I will see it again immediately after breakfast, and report."

While they were still talking the bell rang violently, and in a few moments Mr. Ridley came dashing into the office. His face wore a look of the deepest distress.

"Oh, doctor, he exclaimed can't you do something for my wife? She'll die if you don't. Oh, do go to her again!"

"Has any change taken place since we left?" asked Dr. Hillhouse, with a professional calmness it required some effort to assume.

"She is in great distress, moaning and sobbing and crying out as if in dreadful pain, and she doesn't know anything you say to her."

The two physicians looked at each other with sober faces.

"You'd better see her again," said Dr. Hiilhouse, speaking to his assistant.

"No, no, no, Dr. Hillhouse! You must see her yourself. It is a case of life and death!" cried out the distracted husband. "The responsibility is yours, and I must and will hold you to that responsibility. I placed my wife in your charge, not in that of this or any other man."

T. S. Arthur

Mr. Ridley was beside himself with fear. At first Dr. Hillhouse felt like resenting this assault, but he controlled himself.

"You forget yourself, Mr. Ridley," he answered in a repressed voice. We do not help things by passion or intemperance of language. I saw your wife less than half an hour ago, and after giving the utmost care to the examination of her case made the best prescription in my power. There has not been time for the medicines to act yet. I know how troubled you must feel, and can pardon your not very courteous bearing; but there are some things that can and some things that cannot be done. There are good reasons why it will not be right for me to return to your house now—reasons affecting the safety, it may be the life, of another, while my not going back with you can make no difference to Mrs. Ridley. Dr. Angier is fully competent to report on her condition, and I can decide on any change of treatment that may be required as certainly as if I saw her myself. Should he find any change for the worse, I will consider it my duty to see her without delay."

"Don't neglect her, for God's sake, doctor!" answered Mr. Ridley, in a pleading voice. His manner had grown subdued. Forgive my seeming discourtesy. I am wellnigh distracted. If I lose her, I lose my hold on everything. Oh, doctor, you cannot know how much is at stake. God help me if she dies!"

"My dear sir, nothing in our power to do shall be neglected. Dr. Angier will go back with you; and if, on his return, I am satisfied that there is a change for the worse, I will see your wife without a moment's delay. And in the mean time, if you wish to call in another physician, I shall be glad to have you do so. Fix the time for consultation at any hour before half-past ten o'clock, and I will meet him. After that I shall be engaged professionally for two or three hours."

Dr. Angier returned with Mr. Ridley, and Dr. Hillhouse went to his chamber to make ready for breakfast. His hands were so unsteady as he made his toilette for the day that, in the face of what he had said to his assistant only a little while before, he poured himself a glass of wine and drank it off, remarking aloud as he did so, as if apologizing for the act to some one invisibly present:

"I can't let this go on any longer."

The breakfast-bell rang, and the doctor sat down to get the better nerve-sustainer of a good meal. But even as he reached his hand for the fragrant coffee that his wife had poured for him, he felt a single dull throb in one of his temples, and knew too well its meaning. He did not lift the coffee to his mouth, but sat with a grave face and an unusually quiet manner. He had made a serious mistake, and he knew it. That glass of wine had stimulated the relaxed nerves of his stomach too suddenly, and sent a shock to the exhausted brain. A slight feeling of nausea was perceived and then came another throb stronger than the first, and with a faint suggestion of pain. This was followed by a sense of physical depression and discomfort.

"What's the matter, doctor?" asked his wife, who saw something unusual in his manner.

"A feeling here that I don't just like," he replied, touching his temple with a finger.

"Not going to have a headache?"

"I trust not. It would be a bad thing for me today."

He slowly lifted his cup of coffee and sipped a part of it.

"Late suppers and late hours may do for younger people," said Mrs. Hillhouse. "*I* feel wretched this morning, and am not surprised that your nerves are out of order, nor that you should be threatened with headache."

The doctor did not reply. He sipped his coffee again, but without apparent relish, and, instead of eating anything, sat in an unusually quiet manner and with a very sober aspect of countenance.

"I don't want a mouthful of breakfast," said Mrs. Hillhouse, pushing away her plate.

"Nor I," replied the doctor; "but I can't begin to-day on an empty stomach."

And he tried to force himself to take food, but made little progress in the effort.

"It's dreadful about Archie Voss," said Mrs. Hillhouse.

"Oh he'll come up all right," returned her husband, with some impatience in his voice.

"I hope so. But if he were my son, I'd rather see him in his grave than as I saw him last night."

"It's very easy to talk in that way; but if Archie were your son, you'd not be very long in choosing between death and a glass or two of wine more than he had strength to carry."

"If he were my son," replied the doctor's wife, "I would do all in my power to keep him away from entertainments where liquor is served in such profusion. The danger is too great."

"He would have to take his chances with the rest," replied the doctor. "All that we could possibly do would be to teach him moderation and self-denial."

"If there is little moderation and self-denial among the full-grown men and women who are met on these occasions, what can be expected from lads and young men?"

The doctor shrugged his shoulders, but made no reply.

"We cannot shut our eyes to the fact," continued his wife, "that this free dispensation of wine to old and young is an evil of great magnitude, and that it is doing a vast amount of harm."

The doctor still kept silent. He was not in a mood for discussing this or any other social question. His mind was going in another direction, and his thoughts were troubling him. Dr. Hillhouse was a surgeon of great experience, and known throughout the country for his successful operations in some of the most difficult and dangerous cases with which the profession has to deal. On this particular day, at twelve o'clock, he had to perform an operation of the most delicate nature, involving the life or death of a patient.

He might well feel troubled, for he knew, from signs too well understood, that when twelve o'clock came, and his patient lay helpless and unconscious before him, his hand would not be steady nor his brain, clear. Healthy food would not restore the natural vigor which stimulation had weakened, for he had no appetite for food. His stomach turned away from it with loathing.

By this time the throb in his temple had become a stroke of pain. While still sitting at the breakfast-table Dr. Angier returned from his visit to Mrs. Ridley. Dr. Hillhouse saw by the expression of his face that he did not bring a good report.

"How is she?" he asked.

"In a very bad way," replied Dr. Angier.

"New symptoms?"

"Yes."

"What?"

"Intense pain, rigors, hurried respiration and pulse up to a hundred and twenty. It looks like a case of puerperal peritonitis."

T. S. Arthur

Dr. Hillhouse started from the table; the trouble on his face grew deeper.

"You had better see her with as little delay as possible," said Dr. Angier.

"Did you make any new prescription?"

"No."

Dr. Hillhouse shut his lips tightly and knit his brows. He stood irresolute for several moments.

"Most unfortunate!" he ejaculated. Then, going into his office, he rang the bell and ordered his carriage brought round immediately.

Dr. Angier had made no exaggerated report of Mrs. Ridley's condition. Dr. Hillhouse found that serious complications were rapidly taking place, and that all the symptoms indicated inflammation of the peritoneum. The patient was in great pain, though with less cerebral disturbance than when he had seen her last. There was danger, and he knew it. The disease had taken on a form that usually baffles the skill of our most eminent physicians, and Dr. Hillhouse saw little chance of anything but a fatal termination. He could do nothing except to palliate as far as possible the patient's intense suffering and endeavor to check farther complications. But he saw little to give encouragement.

Mr. Ridley, with pale, anxious face, and eyes in which, were pictured the unutterable anguish of his soul, watched Dr. Hillhouse as he sat by his wife's bedside with an eager interest and suspense that was painful to see. He followed him when he left the room, and his hand closed on his arm with a spasm as the door shut behind them.

"How is she, doctor?" he asked, in a hoarse, panting whisper.

"She is very sick, Mr. Ridley," replied Dr. Hillhouse. "It would be wrong to deceive you."

The pale, haggard face of Mr. Ridley grew whiter.

"Oh, doctor," he gasped, "can nothing be done?"

"I think we had better call in another physician," replied the doctor. "In the multitude of counselors there is wisdom. Have you any choice?"

But Mr. Ridley had none.

"Shall it be Dr. Ainsworth? He has large experience in this class of diseases."

"I leave it entirely with you, Dr. Hillhouse. Get the best advice and help the city affords, and for God's sake save my wife."

The doctor went away, and Mr. Ridley, shaking with nervous tremors, dropped weak and helpless into a chair and bending forward until his head rested on his knees, sat crouching down, an image of suffering and despair.

T. S. Arthur

CHAPTER IX

"ELLIS, my son."

There was a little break and tremor in the voice. The young man addressed was passing the door of his mother's room, and paused on hearing his name.

"What is it?" he asked, stepping inside and looking curiously into his mother's face, where he saw a more than usually serious expression.

"Sit down, Ellis; I want to say a word to you before going to Mrs. Birtwell's."

The lady had just completed her toilette, and was elegantly dressed for an evening party. She was a handsome, stately-looking woman, with dark hair through which ran many veins of silver, large, thoughtful eyes and a mouth of peculiar sweetness.

The young man took a chair, and his mother seated herself in front of him.

"Ellis."

The tremor still remained in her voice.

"Well, what is it?"

The young man assumed a careless air, but was not at ease.

"There is a good old adage, my son, the remembrance of which Has saved many a one in the hour of danger: *Forewarned, forearmed.*"

"Oh, then you think we are going into danger to-night?" he answered, in a light tone.

"I am sorry to say that we are going where some will find themselves in great peril," replied the mother, her manner growing more serious; "and it is because of this that I wish to say a word or two now."

"Very well, mother; say on."

He moved uneasily in his chair, and showed signs of impatience.

"You must take it kindly, Ellis, and remember that it is your mother who is speaking, your best and truest friend in all the world."

"Good Heavens, mother! what are you driving at? One would think we were going into a howling wilderness, among savages and wild beasts, instead of into a company of the most cultured and refined people in a Christian city."

"There is danger everywhere, my son," the mother replied, with increasing sobriety of manner, "and the highest civilization of the day has its perils as well as the lowest conditions of society. The enemy hides in ambush everywhere—in the gay drawing-room as well as in the meanest hovel."

She paused, and mother and son looked into each other's faces in silence for several moments. Then the former said:

"I must speak plainly, Ellis. You are not as guarded as you should be on these occasions. You take wine too freely."

"Oh, mother!" His voice was, half surprised, half angry. A red flush mounted to cheeks and forehead. Rising, he walked the room in an agitated manner, and then came and sat down. The color had gone out of his face:

"How could you say so, mother? You do me wrong. It is a mistake."

The lady shook her head:

"No, my son, it is true. A mother's eyes rarely deceive her. You took wine too freely both at Mrs. Judson's and Mrs. Ingersoll's, and acted so little like my gentlemanly, dignified son that my cheeks burned and my heart ached with mortification. I saw in other eyes that looked at you both pity and condemnation. Ah, my son! there was more of bitterness in that for a mother's heart than you will ever comprehend."

Her voice broke into a sob.

"My dear, dear mother," returned the young man, exhibiting much distress, "you and others exaggerated what you saw. I might have been a trifle gay, and who is not after a glass or two of champagne? I was no gayer than the rest. When young people get together, and one spurs another on they are apt to grow a little wild. But to call high spirits, even noisy high spirits, intoxication is unjust. You must not be too hard on me, mother, nor let your care for your son lead you into needless apprehensions. I am in no danger here. Set your heart at rest on that score."

But this was impossible. Mrs. Whitford knew there was danger, and that of the gravest character. Two years before, her son had come home from college, where he had graduated with all the honors her heart could desire, a pure, high-toned young man, possessing talents of no common order. His father wished him to study law; and as his own inclinations led in that direction, he went into the office of one of the best practitioners in the city, and studied for his profession with the same thoroughness that had distinguished him while in college. He had just been admitted to the bar.

For the first year after his return home Mrs. Whitford saw nothing in her son to awaken uneasiness. His cultivated tastes and love of intellectual things held him above the enervating influences of the social life into which he was becoming more and more drawn. Her first feeling of uneasiness came when, at a large party given by one of her most intimate friends, she heard his voice ring out suddenly in the supper-room. Looking down the table, she saw him with a glass of champagne in his hand, which he was flourishing about in rather an excited way. There was a gay group of young girls around him, who laughed merrily at the sport he made. Mrs. Whitford's pleasure was gone for that evening. A shadow came down on the bright future of her son—a future to which her heart had turned with such proud anticipations. She was oppressed by a sense of humiliation. Her son had stepped down from his pedestal of dignified self-respect, and stood among the common herd of vulgar young men to whom in her eyes he had always been superior.

But greater than her humiliation were the fears of Mrs. Whitford. A thoughtful and observant woman, she had reason for magnifying the dangers that lay in the path of her son. The curse of more than one member of both her own and husband's family had been intemperance. While still a young man her father had lost his self-control, and her memory of him was a shadow of pain and sorrow. He died at an early age, the victim of an insatiable and consuming desire for drink. Her husband's father had been what is called a "free liver"—that is, a man who gave free indulgence to his appetites, eating and drinking to excess, and being at all times more or less under the influence of wine or spirits.

It was the hereditary taint that Mrs. Whitford dreaded. Here lay the ground of her deepest anxiety. She had heard and thought enough on this subject to know that parents transmit to their children an inclination to do the things they have done

T. S. Arthur

from habit—strong or weak, according to the power of the habit indulged. If the habit be an evil one, then the children are in more than common danger, and need the wisest care and protection. She knew, also, from reading and observation, that an evil habit of mind or body which did not show itself in the second generation would often be reproduced in the third, and assert a power that it required the utmost strength of will and the greatest watchfulness to subdue.

And so, when her son, replying to her earnest warning, said, "I am in no danger. Set your heart at rest," she knew better—knew that a deadly serpent was in the path he was treading. And she answered him with increasing earnestness:

"The danger may be far greater than you imagine, Ellis. It *is* greater than you imagine."

Her voice changed as she uttered the last sentence into a tone that was almost solemn.

"You are talking wildly," returned the young man, "and pay but a poor compliment to your son's character and strength of will. In danger of becoming a sot!—for that is what you mean. If you were not my mother, I should be angry beyond self-control."

"Ellis," said Mrs. Whitford, laying her hand upon the arm of her son and speaking with slow impressiveness, "I am older than you are by nearly thirty years, have seen more of life than you have, *and know some things that you do not know.* I have your welfare at heart more deeply than any other being except God. I know you better in some things than you know yourself. Love makes me clear-seeing. And this is why I am in such earnest with you to-night. Ellis, I want a promise from you. I ask it in the name of all that is dearest to you—in my name—in the name of Blanche—in the name of God!"

All the color had, gone out of Mrs. Whitford's face, and she stood trembling before her son.

"You frighten me, mother," exclaimed the young man. "What do you mean by all this? Has any one been filling your mind with lies about me?"

"No; none would dare speak to me of you in anything but praise, But I want you to promise to-night, Ellis. I must have that, and then my heart will be at ease. It will be a little thing for you, but for me rest and peace and confidence in the place of terrible anxieties."

"Promise! What? Some wild fancies have taken hold of you."

"No wild fancies, but a fear grounded in things of which I would not speak. Ellis, I want you to give up the use of wine."

The young man did not answer immediately. All the nervous restlessness he had exhibited died out in a moment, and he stood very still, the ruddy marks of excitement going out of his face. His eyes were turned from his mother and cast upon the floor.

"And so it has come to this," he said, huskily, and in a tone of humiliation. "My mother thinks me in danger of becoming a drunkard—thinks me so weak that I cannot be trusted to take even a glass of wine."

"Ellis!" Mrs. Whitford again laid her hand upon the arm of her son. "Ellis," her voice had fallen to deep whisper, "if I must speak, I must. There are ancestors who leave fatal legacies to the generations that come after them, and you are one accursed by such a legacy. There is a taint in your blood, a latent fire that a spark may kindle into a consuming flame."

She panted as she spoke with hurried utterance. "My father!" exclaimed the young man, with an indignant flash in his eyes.

"No, no, no! I don't mean that. But there is a curse that descends to the third and fourth generation," replied Mrs. Whitford, "and you have the legacy of that curse. But it will be harmless unless with your own hand you drag it down, and this is why I ask you to abstain from wine. Others may be safe, but for you there is peril."

"A scarecrow, a mere fancy, a figment of some fanatic's brain;" and Ellis Whitford rejected the idea in a voice full of contempt.

But the pallor and solemnity of his mother's face warned him that such a treatment of her fears could not allay them. Moreover, the hint of ancestral disgrace had shocked his family pride.

"A sad and painful truth," Mrs. Whitford returned, "and one that it will be folly for you to ignore. You do not stand in the same freedom in which many others stand. That is your misfortune. But you can no more disregard the fact than can one born with a hereditary taint of consumption in his blood disregard the loss of health and hope to escape the fatal consequences. There is for every one of us 'a sin that doth easily beset,' a hereditary inclination that must be guarded and denied, or it will grow and strengthen until it becomes a giant to enslave us. Where your danger lies I have said; and if you would be safe, set bars and bolts to the door of appetite, and suffer not your enemy to cross the threshold, of life."

Mrs. Whitford spoke with regaining calmness, but in tones of solemn admonition.

A long silence followed, broken at length by the young man, who said, in a choking, depressed voice that betrayed a quaver of impatience:

"I'm sorry for all this. That your fears are groundless I know, but you are none the less tormented by them. What am I to do? To spare you pain I would sacrifice almost anything, but this humiliation is more than I am strong enough to encounter. If, as you say, there has been intemperance in our family, it is not a secret locked up in your bosom. Society knows all about the ancestry of its members, who and what the fathers and grandfathers were, and we have not escaped investigation. Don't touch wine, you say. Very well. I go to Mrs. Birtwell's to-night. Young and old, men and women, all are partakers, but I stand aloof—I, of all the guests, refuse the hospitality I have pretended to accept. Can I do this without attracting attention or occasioning remark? No; and what will be said? Simply this—that I know my danger and am afraid; that there is in my blood the hereditary taint of drunkenness, and that I dare not touch a glass of wine. Mother, I am not strong enough to brave society on such an issue, and a false one at that. To fear and fly does not belong to my nature. A coward I despise. If there is danger in my way and it is right for me to go forward in that way, I will walk steadily on, and fight if I must. I am not a craven, but a man. If the taint of which you speak is in my blood, I will extinguish it. If I am in danger, I will not save myself by flight, but by conquest. The taint shall not go down to another generation; it shall be removed in this."

He spoke with a fine enthusiasm kindling over his handsome face, and his mother's heart beat with a pride that for the moment was stronger than fear.

"Ask of me anything except to give up my self-respect and my manliness," he added. "Say that you wish me to remain at home, and I will not go to the party."

"No. I do not ask that. I wish you to go. But—"

"If I go, I must do as the rest, and you must have faith in me. Forewarned, forearmed. I will heed your admonition."

So the interview ended, and mother and son went to the grand entertainment at Mr. Birtwell's. Ellis did mean to heed his mother's admonition. What she had said, about the danger in which he stood had made a deeper impression on him than Mrs. Whitford thought. But he did not propose to heed by abstinence, but by moderation. He would be on guard and

T. S. Arthur

always ready for the hidden foe, if such a foe really existed anywhere but in his mother's fancy.

"Ah, Mrs. Whitford! Glad to see you this evening;" and the Rev. Mr. Brantley Elliott gave the lady a graceful and cordial bow. "Had the pleasure of meeting your son a few moments ago—a splendid young man, if you will pardon me for saying so. How much a year has improved him!"

Mrs. Whitford bowed her grateful acknowledgment.

"Just been admitted to the bar, I learn," said Mr. Elliott.

"Yes, sir. He has taken his start in life."

"And will make his mark, or I am mistaken. You have reason to feel proud of him, ma'am."

"That she has," spoke out Dr. Hillhouse, who came up at the moment. "When so many of our young men are content to be idle drones—to let their fathers achieve eminence or move the world by the force of thought and will—it is gratifying to see one of their number taking his place in the ranks and setting his face toward conquest. When the sons of two-thirds of our rich men are forgotten, or remembered only as idlers or nobodies, or worse, your son will stand among the men who leave their mark upon the generations."

"If he escapes the dangers that lie too thickly in the way of all young men," returned Mrs. Whitford, speaking almost involuntarily of what was in her heart, and in a voice that betrayed more concern than she had meant to express.

The doctor gave a little shrug, but replied:

"His earnest purpose in life will be his protection, Mrs. Whitford. Work, ambition, devotion to a science or profession have in them an aegis of safety. The weak and the idle are most in danger."

"It is wrong, I have sometimes thought," said Mrs. Whitford speaking both to the physician and the clergyman, "for society to set so many temptations before its young men—the seed, as some one has forcibly said, of the nation's future harvest."

"Society doesn't care much for anything but its own gratification," replied Dr. Hillhouse, "and says as plainly as actions can do it 'After me the deluge.'"

"Rather hard on society," remarked Mr. Elliott.

"Now take, for instance, its drinking customs, its toleration and participation in the freest public and private dispensation of intoxicating liquors to all classes, weak or strong, young or old. Is there not danger in this—great danger? I think I understand you, Mrs. Whitford."

"Yes, doctor, you understand me;" and dropping her voice to a lower tone, Mrs. Whitford added: "There are wives and mothers and sisters not a few here to-night whose hearts, though they may wear smiles on their faces, are ill at ease, and some of them will go home from these festivities sadder than when they came."

"Right about that," said the doctor to himself as he turned away, a friend of Mrs. Whitford's having come up at the moment and interrupted the conversation—" right about that; and you, I greatly fear, will be one of the number."

"Our friend isn't just herself to-night," remarked Mr. Elliott as he and Dr. Hillhouse moved across the room. "A little dyspeptic, maybe, and so inclined to look on the dark side of things. She has little cause, I should think, to be anxious for her own son or husband. I never saw Mr. Whitford the worse for wine; and as for Ellis, his earnest purpose in life, as you so well said just now, will hold him above the reach of temptation."

"On the contrary, she has cause for great anxiety," returned

Dr. Hillhouse.

"You surprise me. What reason have you for saying this?"

"A professional one—a reason grounded in pathology."

"Ah?" and Mr. Elliott looked gravely curious.

"The young man inherits, I fear, a depraved appetite."

"Oh no. I happen to be too well acquainted with his father to accept that view of the case."

"His father is well enough," replied Dr. Hillhouse, "but as much could not be said of either of his grandfathers while living. Both drank freely, and one of them died a confirmed drunkard."

"If the depraved appetite has not shown itself in the children, it will hardly trouble the grandchildren," said Mr. Elliott. "Your fear is groundless, doctor. If Ellis were my son, I should feel no particular anxiety about him."

"If he were your son," replied Dr. Hillhouse, "I am not so sure about your feeling no concern. Our personal interest in a thing is apt to give it a new importance. But you are mistaken as to the breaking of hereditary influences in the second generation. Often hereditary peculiarities will show themselves in the third and fourth generation. It is no uncommon thing to see the grandmother's red hair reappear in her granddaughter, though her own child's hair was as black as a raven's wing. A crooked toe, a wart, a malformation, an epileptic tendency, a swart or fair complexion, may disappear in all the children of a family, and show itself again in the grand-or great-grandchildren. Mental and moral conditions reappear in like manner. In medical literature we have many curious illustrations of this law of hereditary transmission and its strange freaks and anomalies."

"They are among the curiosities of your literature," said Mr. Elliott, speaking as though not inclined to give much weight to the doctor's views—"the exceptional and abnormal things that come under professional notice."

"The law of hereditary transmission," replied Dr. Hillhouse, "is as certain in its operation as the law of gravity. You may disturb or impede or temporarily suspend the law, but the moment you remove the impediment the normal action goes on, and the result is sure. Like produces like—that is the law. Always the cause is seen in the effect, and its character, quality and good or evil tendencies are sure to have a rebirth and a new life. It is under the action of this law that the child is cursed by the parent with the evil and sensual things he has made a part of himself through long indulgence."

There came at this moment a raid upon Mr. Elliott by three or four ladies, members of his congregation, who surrounded him and Dr. Hillhouse, and cut short their conversation.

Meanwhile, Ellis Whitford had already half forgotten his painful interview with his mother in the pleasure of meeting Blanche Birtwell, to whom he had recently become engaged. She was a pure and lovely young woman, inheriting her mother's personal beauty and refined tastes. She had been carefully educated and kept by her mother as much within the sphere of home as possible and out of society of the hoydenish girls who, moving in the so-called best circles, have the free and easy manners of the denizens of a public garden rather than the modest demeanor of unsullied maidenhood. She was a sweet exception to the loud, womanish, conventional girl we meet everywhere—on the street, in places, of public amusement and in the drawing-room—a fragrant human flower with the bloom of gentle girlhood on every unfolding leaf.

It was no slender tie that bound these lovers together. They had moved toward each other, drawn by an inner attraction that was irresistible to each; and when heart touched heart, their pulses took a common beat. The life of each had become bound up in the other, and their betrothal was no mere outward contract. The manly intellect and the pure heart had recognized each other, tender love had lifted itself to noble thought, and thought had grown stronger and purer as it felt the warmth and life of a new and almost divine inspiration. Ellis Whitford had risen to a higher level by virtue of this betrothal.

They were sitting in a bay-window, out of the crowd of guests, when a movement in the company was observed by Whitford. Knowing what it meant, he arose and offered his arm to Blanche. As he did so he became aware of a change in his companion, felt rather than seen; and yet, if he had looked closely into her face, a change in its expression would have been visible. The smile was still upon her beautiful lips, and the light and tenderness still in her eyes, but from both something had departed. It was as if an almost invisible film of vapor had drifted across the sun of their lives.

In silence they moved on to the supper-room—moved with the light and heavy-hearted, for, as Dr. Hillhouse had intimated, there were some there to whom that supper-room was regarded with anxiety and fear—wives and mothers and sisters who knew, alas! too well that deadly serpents lie hidden among the flowers of every banqueting-room.

How bright and joyous a scene it was! You did not see the trouble that lay hidden in so many hearts; the light and glitter, the flash and brilliancy, were too strong.

Reader, did you ever think of the power of spheres? The influence that goes out from an individual or mass of individuals, we mean—that subtle, invisible power that acts from one upon another, and which when aggregated is almost irresistible? You have felt it in a company moved by a single impulse which carried you for a time with the rest, though all your calmer convictions were in opposition to the movement. It has kept you silent by its oppressive power when you should have spoken out in a ringing protest, and it has borne you away on its swift or turbulent current when you should have stood still and been true to right. Again, in the company of good and true men, moved by the inspiration of some noble cause, how all your weakness and hesitation has died out! and you have felt the influence of that subtle sphere to which we refer.

Everywhere and at all times are we exposed to the action of these mental and moral spheres, which act upon and impress us in thousands of different ways, now carrying us along in some sudden public excitement in which passion drowns the voice of reason, and now causing us to drift in the wake of some stronger nature than our own whose active thought holds ours in a weak, assenting bondage.

You understand what we mean. Now take the pervading sphere of an occasion like the one we are describing, and do you not see that to go against it is possible only to persons of decided convictions and strong individuality? The common mass of men and women are absorbed into or controlled by its subtle power. They can no more set themselves against it, if they would, than against the rush of a swiftly-flowing river. To the young it is irresistible.

As Ellis Whitford, with Blanche leaning on his arm, gained the supper-room, he met the eyes of his mother, who was on the opposite side of the table, and read in them a sign of warning. Did it awaken a sense of danger and put him on his guard? No; it rather stirred a feeling of anger. Could she not trust him among gentlemen and ladies—not trust him with Blanche Birtwell by his side? It hurt his pride and wounded his self-esteem.

He was in the sphere of liberty and social enjoyment and among those who did not believe that wine was a mocker, but something to make glad the heart and give joy to the countenance; and when it began to flow he was among the first to taste its delusive sweets. Blanche, for whom he poured a glass of champagne, took it from his hand, but with only half a smile on her lips, which was veiled by something so like pain or fear that Ellis felt as if the lights about him had suddenly lost a portion of their brilliancy. He stood holding his own glass, after just tasting its contents, waiting for Blanche to raise the sparkling liquor to her lips, but she seemed like one under the influence of a spell, not moving or responding.

CHAPTER X

BLANCHE still held the untasted wine in her hand, when her father, who happened to be near, filled a glass, and said as he bowed to her:

"Your good health, my daughter; and yours, Mr. Whitford," bowing to her companion also.

The momentary spell was broken. Blanche smiled back upon her father and raised the glass to her lips. The lights in the room seemed to Ellis to flash up again and blaze with a higher brilliancy. Never had the taste of wine seemed more delicious. What a warm thrill ran along his nerves! What a fine exhilaration quickened in his brain! The shadow which a moment before had cast a veil over the face of Blanche he saw no longer. It had vanished, or his vision was not now clear enough to discern its subtle texture.

"Take good care of Blanche," said Mr. Birtwell, in a light voice. "And you, pet, see that Mr. Whitford enjoys himself."

Blanche did not reply. Her father turned away. Eyes not veiled as Whitford's now were would have seen that the filmy cloud which had come over her face a little while before was less transparent, and sensibly dimmed its brightness.

Scarcely had Mr. Birtwell left them when Mr. Elliott, who had only a little while before heard of their engagement, said to Blanche in an undertone, and with one of his sweet

T. S. Arthur

paternal smiles:

"I must take a glass of wine with you, dear, in, comme-moration of the happy event."

Mr. Elliott had not meant to include young Whitford in the invitation. The latter had spoken to a lady acquaintance who stood near him, and was saying a few words to her, thus disengaging Blanche. But observing that Mr. Elliott was talking to Blanche, he turned from the lady and joined her again. And, so Mr. Elliott had to say:

"We are going to have a glass of wine in honor of the auspicious event."

Three glasses were filled by the clergyman, and then he stood face to face with the young man and maiden, and each of them, as he said in a low, professional voice, meant for their ears alone, "Peace and blessing, my children!" drank to the sentiment. Whitford drained his glass, but Blanche only tasted the wine in hers.

Mr. Elliott stood for a few moments, conscious that something was out of accord. Then he remembered his conversation with Dr. Hillhouse a little while before, and felt an instant regret. He had noted the manner of Whitford as he drank, and the manner of Blanche as she put the wine to her lips. In the one case was an enjoyable eagerness, and in the other constraint. Something in the expression of the girl's face haunted and troubled him a long time afterward.

"Our young friend is getting rather gay," said Dr. Hillhouse to Mr. Elliott, half an hour afterward. He referred to Ellis Whitford, who was talking and laughing in a way that to some seemed a little too loud and boisterous. "I'm afraid for him." he added.

"Ah, yes! I remember what you were saying about his two grandfathers," returned the clergyman. "And you really think he may inherit something from them?"

"Don't you?" asked the doctor.

"Well, yes, of course. But I mean an inordinate desire for drink, a craving that makes indulgence perilous?"

"Yes; that is just what I do believe."

If that be so, the case is a serious one. In taking wine with him a short time ago I noticed a certain enjoyable eagerness as he held the glass to his lips not often observed in our young men."

"You drank with him?" queried the doctor.

"Yes. He and Blanche Birtwell have recently become engaged, and I took some wine with them in compliment."

The doctor, instead of replying, became silent and thoughtful, and Mr. Elliott moved away among the crowd of guests.

"I am really sorry for Mrs. Whitford," said a lady with whom he soon became engaged in conversation.

"Why so?" asked the clergyman, betraying surprise.

"What's the matter? No family trouble, I hope?"

"Very serious trouble I should call it were it my own," returned the lady.

"I am pained to hear you speak so. What has occurred?"

"Haven't you noticed her son to-night? There! That was his laugh. He's been drinking too much. I saw his mother looking at him a little while ago with eyes so full of sorrow and suffering that it made my heart ache."

T. S. Arthur

"Oh, I hope it's nothing," replied Mr. Elliott. "Young men will become a little gay on these occasions; we must expect that. All of them don't bear wine alike. It's mortifying to Mrs. Whitford, of course, but she's a stately woman, you know, and sensitive about proprieties."

Mr. Elliott did not wait for the lady's answer, but turned to address another person who came forward at the moment to speak to him.

"Sensitive about proprieties," said the lady to herself, with some feeling, as she stood looking down the room to where Ellis Whitford in a group of young men and women was giving vent to his exuberant spirits more noisily than befitted the place and occasion. "Mr. Elliott calls things by dainty names."

"I call that disgraceful," remarked an elderly lady, in a severe tone, as if replying to the other's thought.

"Young men will become a little gay on these occasions," said the person to whom she had spoken, with some irony in her tone. "So Mr. Elliott says."

"Mr. Elliott!" There was a tone of bitterness and rejection in the speaker's voice. "Mr. Elliott had better give our young men a safer example than he does. A little gay! A little drunk would be nearer the truth."

"Oh dear! such a vulgar word! We don't use it in good society, you know. It belongs to taverns and drinking-saloons—to coarse, common people. You must say 'a little excited,' 'a little gay,' but not drunk. That's dreadful!"

"Drunk!" said the other, with emphasis, but speaking low and for the ear only of the lady with whom she was talking. "We understand a great deal better the quality of a thing when we call it by its right name. If a young man drinks wine or brandy until he becomes intoxicated, as Whitford has done to-night, and we say he is drunk instead of exhilarated or a little gay, we do something toward making his conduct odious. We do not excuse, but condemn. We make it disgraceful instead of palliating the offence."

The lady paused, when her companion said:

"Look! Blanche Birtwell is trying to quiet him. Did you know they were engaged?"

"What!"

"Engaged."

"Then I pity her from my heart. A young man who hasn't self-control enough to keep himself sober at an evening party can't be called a very promising subject for a husband."

"She has placed her arm in his and is looking up into his face so sweetly. What a lovely girl she is! There! he's quieter already; and see, she is drawing him out of the group of young men and talking to him in such a bright, animated way."

"Poor child! it makes my eyes wet; and this is her first humiliating and painful duty toward her future husband. God pity and strengthen her is my heartfelt prayer. She will have need, I fear, of more than human help and comfort."

"You take the worst for granted?"

The lady drew a deep sigh:

"I fear the worst, and know something of what the worst means. There are few families of any note in our city," she added, after a slight pause, "in which sorrow has not entered through the door of intemperance. Ah! is not the name of the evil that comes in through this door Legion? and we throw it wide open and invite both young and old to enter. We draw them by various allurements. We make the way of this door

T. S. Arthur

broad and smooth and flowery, full of pleasantness and enticement. We hold out our hands, we smile with encouragement, we step inside of the door to show them the way."

In her ardor the lady half forgot herself, and stopped suddenly as she observed that two or three of the company who stood near had been listening.

Meantime, Blanche Birtwell had managed to get Whitford away from the table, and was trying to induce him to leave the supper-room. She hung on his arm and talked to him in a light, gay manner, as though wholly unconscious of his condition. They had reached the door leading into the hall, when Whitford stopped, and drawing back, said:

"Oh, there's Fred Lovering, my old college friend. I didn't know he was in the city." Then he called out, in a voice so loud as to cause many to turn and look at him, "Fred! Fred! Why, how are you, old boy? This is an unexpected pleasure."

The young man thus spoken to made his way through the crowd of guests, who were closely packed together in that part of the room, some going in and some trying to get out, and grasping the hand of Whitford, shook it with great cordiality.

"Miss Birtwell," said the latter, introducing Blanche. "But you know each other, I see."

"Oh yes, we are old friends. Glad to see you looking so well, Miss Birtwell."

Blanche bowed with cold politeness, drawing a little back as she did so, and tightening her hold on Whitford's arm.

Lovering fixed his eyes on the young lady with an admiring glance, gazing into her face so intently that her color heightened. She turned partly away, an expression of annoyance on her countenance, drawing more firmly on the arm of her companion as she did so, and taking a step toward the door.

But Whitford was no longer passive to her will.

Any one reading the face of Lovering would have seen a change in its expression, the evidence of some quickly formed purpose, and he would have seen also something more than simple admiration of the beautiful girl leaning on the arm of his friend. His manner toward Whitford became more hearty.

"My dear old friend," he said, catching up the hand he had dropped and giving it a tighter grip than before, "this is a pleasure. How it brings back our college days! We must have a glass of wine in memory of the good old times. Come!"

And he moved toward the table. With an impulse she could not restrain, Blanche drew back toward the door, pulling strongly on Whitford's arm:

"Come, Ellis; I am faint with the heat of this room. Take me out, please."

Whitford looked into her face, and saw that it had grown suddenly pale. If his perceptions had not been obscured by drink, he would have taken her out instantly. But his mind was not clear.

"Just a moment, until I can get you a glass of wine," he said, turning hastily from her. Lovering was filling three glasses as he reached the table. Seizing one of them, he went back quickly to Blanche; but she waved her hand, saying: "No, no, Ellis; it isn't wine that I need, only cooler air."

"Don't be foolish," replied Whitford, with visible impatience. "Take a few sips of wine, and you will feel better."

Lovering, with a glass in each hand, now joined them. He saw the change in Blanche's face, and having already observed the exhilarated condition of Whitford, understood its meaning. Handing the latter one of the glasses, he said:

T. S. Arthur

"Here's to your good health, Miss Birtwell, and to yours, Ellis," drinking as he spoke. Whitford drained his glass, but Blanche did not so much as wet her lips. Her face had grown paler.

"If you do not take me out, I must go alone," she said, in a voice that made itself felt. There was in it a quiver of pain and a pulse of indignation.

Lovering lost nothing of this. As his college friend made his way from the room with Blanche on his arm, he stood for a moment in an attitude of deep thought, then nodded two or three times and said to himself:

"That's how the land lies. Wine in and wit out, and Blanche troubled about it already. Engaged, they say. All right. But glass is sharp, and love's fetters are made of silk. Will the edge be duller if the glass is filled with wine? I trow not."

And a gleam of satisfaction lit up the young man's face.

With an effort strong and self-controlling for one so young, Blanche Birtwell laid her hand upon her troubled heart as soon as she was out of the supper-room, and tried to still its agitation. The color came back to her cheeks and some of the lost brightness to her eyes, but she was not long in discovering that the glass of wine taken with his college friend had proved too much for the already confused brain of her lover who began talking foolishly and acting in a way that mortified and pained her exceedingly. She now sought to get him into the library and out of common observation. Her father had just received from France and England some rare books filled with art illustrations, and she invited him to their examination. But he was feeling too social for that.

"Why, no, pet." He made answer with a fond familiarity he would scarcely have used if they had been alone instead of in a crowded drawing-room, touching her cheek playfully with his fingers as he spoke. "Not now. We'll reserve that pleasure for another time. This is good enough for me;" and he swung his arms around and gave a little whoop like an excited rowdy.

A deep crimson dyed for a moment the face of Blanche. In a moment afterward it was pale as ashes. Whitford saw the death-like change, and it partially roused him to a sense of his condition.

"Of course I'll go to the library if your heart's set on it," he said, drawing her arm in his and taking her out of the room with a kind of flourish. Many eyes turned on them. In some was surprise, in some merriment and in some sorrow and pain.

"Now for the books," he cried as he placed Blanche in a large chair at the library-table. "Where are they?"

Self-control has a masterful energy when the demand for its exercise is imperative. The paleness went out of Blanche's face, and a tender light came into her eyes as she looked up at Whitford and smiled on him with loving glances.

"Sit down," she said in a firm, low, gentle voice.

The young man felt the force of her will and sat down by her side, close to the table, on which a number of books were lying.

"I want to show you Dore's illustrations of Don Quixote;" and Blanche opened a large folio volume.

Whitford had grown more passive. He was having a confused impression that all was not just right with him, and that it was better to be in the library looking over books and pictures with Blanche than in the crowded parlors, where there was so much to excite his gayer feelings. So he gave himself up to the will of his betrothed, and tried to feel an interest in the pictures she seemed to admire so much.

They had been so engaged for over twenty minutes, Whitford

T. S. Arthur

beginning to grow dull and heavy as the exhilaration of wine died out, and less responsive to the efforts made by Blanche to keep him interested, when Lovering came into the library, and, seeing them, said, with a spur of banter in his voice:

"Come, come, this will never do! You're a fine fellow, Whitford, and I don't wonder that Miss Birtwell tolerates you, but monopoly is not the word to-night. I claim the privilege of a guest and a word or two with our fair hostess."

And he held out his arm to Blanche, who had risen from the table. She could do no less than take it. He drew her from the room. As they passed out of the door Blanche cast a look back at Whitford. Those who saw it were struck by its deep concern.

"Confound his impudence!" ejaculated Ellis Whitford as he saw Blanche vanish through the library door. Rising from the table he stood with an irresolute air, then went slowly from the apartment and mingled with the company, moving about in an aimless kind of way, until he drifted again into the supper-room, the tables of which the waiters were constantly replenishing, and toward which a stream of guests still flowed. The company here was noisier now than when he left it a short time before. Revelry had taken the place of staid propriety. Glasses clinked like a chime of bells, voices ran up into the higher keys, and the loud musical laugh of girls mingled gaily with the deeper tones of their male companions. Young maidens with glasses of sparkling champagne or rich brown and amber sherry in their hands were calling young men and boys to drink with them, and showing a freedom and abandon of manner that marked the degree of their exhilaration. Wine does not act in one way on the brain of a young man and in another way on the brain of a young woman. Girls of eighteen or twenty will become as wild and free and forgetful of propriety as young men of the same age if you bring them together at a feast and give them wine freely.

We do not exaggerate the scene in Mr. Birtwell's supper-room, but rather subdue the picture. As Whitford drew nigh the supper-room the sounds of boisterous mirth struck on his ears and stirred him like the rattle of a drum. The heaviness went out of his limbs, his pulse beat more quickly, he felt a new life in his veins. As he passed in his name was called in a gay voice that he did not at first recognize, and at the same moment a handsome young girl with flushed face and sparkling eyes came hastily toward him, and drawing her hand in his arm, said, in a loud familiar tone:

"You shall be my knight, Sir Ellis."

And she almost dragged him down the room to where half a dozen girls and young men were having a wordy contest about something. He was in the midst of the group before he really understood who the young lady was that had laid such violent hands upon him. He then recognized her as the daughter of a well-known merchant. He had met her a few times in company, and her bearing toward him had always before been marked by a lady-like dignity and reserve. Now she was altogether another being, loud, free and familiar almost to rudeness.

"You must have some wine, Sir Knight, to give you mettle for the conflict," she said, running to the table and filling a glass, which she handed to him with the air of a Hebe.

Whitford did not hesitate, but raised the glass to his lips and emptied it at a single draught.

"Now for knight or dragon, my lady fair. I am yours to do or die," he exclaimed, drawing up his handsome form with a mock dignity, at which a loud cheer broke out from the group of girls and young men that was far more befitting a tavern-saloon than a gentleman's dining-room.

Louder and noisier this little group became, Whitford, under a fresh supply of wine, leading in the boisterous mirth. One after another, attracted by the gayety and laughter, joined the group, until it numbered fifteen or twenty half-intoxicated young men and women, who lost themselves in a kind of wild saturnalia.

It was past twelve o'clock when Mrs. Whitford entered the dining-room, where the noise and laughter were almost deafening. Her face was pale, her lips closely compressed and her forehead contracted with pain. She stood looking anxiously through the room until she saw her son leaning against the wall, with a young lady standing in front of him holding a glass in her hand which she was trying to induce him to take. One glance at the face of Ellis told her too plainly his sad condition.

To go to him and endeavor to get him away Mrs. Whitford feared might arouse his latent pride and make him stubborn to her wishes.

"You see that young man standing against the wall?" she said to one of the waiters.

"Mr. Whitford do you mean?" asked the waiter.

"Yes," she replied. "Go to him quietly, and say that his mother is going home and wants him. Speak low, if you please."

Mrs. Whitford stood with a throbbing heart as the waiter passed down the room. The tempter was before her son offering the glass of wine, which he yet refused. She saw him start and look disconcerted as the waiter spoke to him, then wave the glass of wine aside. But he did not stir from him place.

The waiter came back to Mrs. Whitford:

"He says don't wait for him, ma'am."

The poor mother felt an icy coldness run along her nerves. For some moments she stood irresolute, and then went back to the parlor. She remained there for a short time, masking her countenance as best she could, and then returned to the dining-room, where noise and merriment still prevailed. She did not at first see her son, though her eyes went quickly from face to face and from form to form. She was about retiring, under the impression that he was not there, when the waiter to whom she had spoken before said to her:

"Are you looking for Mr. Whitford?"

There was something in his voice that made her heart stand still.

"Yes," she replied.

"You will find him at the lower end of the room, just in the corner," said the man.

Mrs. Whitford made her way to the lower end of the room. Ellis was sitting in a chair, stupid and maudlin, and two or three thoughtless girls were around his chair laughing at his drunken efforts to be witty. The shocked mother did not speak to him, but shrunk away and went gliding from the room. At the door she said to the waiter who had followed her out, drawn by a look she gave him:

"I will be ready to go in five minutes, and I want Mr. Whitford to go with me. Get him down to the door as quietly as you can."

The waiter went back into the supper-room, and with a tact that came from experience in cases similar to this managed to get the young man away without arousing his opposition.

Five minutes afterward, as Mrs. Whitford sat in her carriage at the door of Mr. Birtwell's palace home, her son was pushed in, half resisting, by two waiters, so drunk that his wretched mother had to support him with her arm all the way home. Is

T. S. Arthur

it any wonder that in her aching heart the mother cried out, "Oh, that he had died a baby on my breast"?

CHAPTER XI

AMONG the guests at Mr. and Mrs. Birtwell's was an officer holding a high rank in the army, named Abercrombie. He had married, many years before, a lady of fine accomplishments and rare culture who was connected with one of the oldest families in New York. Her grandfather on her mother's side had distinguished himself as an officer in the Revolutionary war; and on her father's side she could count statesmen and lawyers whose names were prominent in the early history of our country.

General Abercrombie while a young man had fallen into the vice of the army, and had acquired the habit of drinking.

The effects of alcohol are various. On some they are seen in the bloated flesh and reddened eyes. Others grow pale, and their skin takes on a dead and ashen hue. With some the whole nervous system becomes shattered; while with others organic derangements, gout, rheumatism and kindred evils attend the assimilation of this poison.

Quite as varied are the moral and mental effects of alcoholic disturbance. Some are mild and weak inebriates, growing passive or stupid in their cups. Others become excited, talkative and intrusive; others good-natured and merry; not a few coarse, arbitrary, brutal and unfeeling; and some jealous, savage and fiend-like.

Of the last-named class was General Abercrombie. When

T. S. Arthur

sober, a kinder, gentler or more considerate man toward his wife could hardly be found; but when intoxicated, he was half a fiend, and seemed to take a devilish delight in tormenting her. It had been no uncommon thing for him to point a loaded pistol at her heart, and threaten to shoot her dead if she moved or cried out; to hold a razor at his own throat, or place the keen edge, close to hers; to open a window at midnight and threaten to fling himself to the ground, or to drag her across the floor, swearing that they should take the leap together.

For years the wretched wife had borne all this, and worse if possible, hiding her dreadful secret as best she could, and doing all in her power to hold her husband, for whom she retained a strong attachment, away from temptation. Friends who only half suspected the truth wondered that Time was so aggressive, taking the flash and merriment out of her beautiful eyes, the color and fullness from her cheeks, the smiles from her lips and the glossy, blackness from her hair.

"Mrs. Abercrombie is such a wreck," one would say on meeting her after a few years. "I would hardly have known her; and she doesn't look at all happy."

"I wonder if the general drinks as hard as ever?" would in all probability be replied to this remark, followed by the response:

"I was not aware that he was a hard drinker. He doesn't look like it."

"No, you would not suspect so much; but I am sorry to say that he has very little control over his appetite."

At which a stronger surprise would be expressed.

General Abercrombie was fifty years old, a large, handsome and agreeable man, and a favorite with his brother officers, who deeply regretted his weakness. As an officer his drinking habits rarely interfered with his duty. Somehow the discipline of the army had gained such a power over him as to hold him repressed and subordinate to its influence. It was only when official restraints were off that the devil had power to enter in and fully possess him.

A year before the time of which we are writing General Abercrombie had been ordered to duty in the north-eastern department. His headquarters were in the city where the characters we have introduced resided. Official standing gave him access to some of the wealthiest and best circles in the city, and his accomplished wife soon became a favorite with all who were fortunate enough to come into close relations with her. Among these was Mrs. Birtwell, the two ladies drawing toward each other with the magnetism of kindred spirits.

A short time before coming to the city General Abercrombie, after having in a fit of drunken insanity come near killing his wife, wholly abandoned the use of intoxicants of every kind. He saw in this his only hope. His efforts to drink guardedly and temperately had been fruitless. The guard was off the moment a single glass of liquor passed his lips, and, he came under the influence of an aroused appetite against which resolution set itself feebly and in vain.

Up to the evening of this party at Mr. Birtwell's General Abercrombie had kept himself free from wine, and people who knew nothing of his history wondered at his abstemiousness. When invited to drink, he declined in a way that left no room for the invitation to be repeated. He never went to private entertainments except in company with his wife, and then he rarely took any other lady to the supper-room.

The new hope born in the sad heart of Mrs. Abercrombie had grown stronger as the weeks and months went by. Never for so long a time had the general stood firm. It looked as, if he had indeed gained the mastery over an appetite which at one time seemed wholly to have enslaved him.

With a lighter heart than usual on such occasions, Mrs.

T. S. Arthur

Abercrombie made ready for the grand entertainment, paying more than ordinary attention to her toilette. Something of her old social and personal pride came back into life, giving her face and bearing the dignity and prestige worn in happier days. As she entered the drawing-room at Mr. and Mrs. Birtwell's, leaning on her husband's arm, a ripple of admiration was seen on many faces, and the question, "Who is she?" was heard on many lips. Mrs. Abercrombie was a centre of attraction that evening, and no husband could have been prouder of such a distinction for his wife than was the general. He, too, found himself an object of interest and attention. Mr. Birtwell was a man who made the most of his guests, and being a genuine *parvenu*, did not fail through any refinement of good breeding in advertising to each other the merits or achievements of those he favored with introductions. If he presented a man of letters to an eminent banker, he informed each in a word or two of the other's distinguished merits. An officer would be complimented on his rank or public service, a scientist on his last book or essay, a leading politician on his statesmanship. At Mr. Birtwell's you always found yourself among men with more in them than you had suspected, and felt half ashamed of your ignorance in regard to their great achievements.

General Abercrombie, like many others that evening, felt unusually well satisfied with himself. Mr. Birtwell complimented him whenever they happened to meet, sometimes on his public services and sometimes on the "sensation" that elegant woman Mrs. Abercrombie was making. He grew in his own estimation under the flattering attentions of his host, and felt a manlier pride swelling in his heart than he had for some time known. His bearing became more self-poised, his innate sense of strength more apparent. Here was a man among men.

This was the general's state of mind when, after an hour, or two of social intercourse, he entered the large supper-room, whither he escorted a lady. He had not seen his wife for half an hour. If she had been, as usual on such occasions, by his side, he would have been on guard. But the lady who leaned on his arm was not his good angel. She was a gay, fashionable woman, and as fond of good eating and drinking as any male epicure there. The general was polite and attentive, and as prompt as any younger gallant in the work of supplying his fair companion with the good things she was so ready to appropriate.

"Will you have a glass of champagne?"

Of course she would. Her eyebrows arched a little in surprise at the question. The general filled a glass and placed it in her hand. Did she raise it to her lips? No; she held it a little extended, looking at him with an expression which said, "I will wait for you."

For an instant General Abercrombie felt as if be were sinking through space. Darkness and fear were upon him. But there was no time for indecision. The lady stood holding her glass and looking at him fixedly. An instant and the struggle was over. He turned to the table and filled another glass. A smile and a bow, and then, a draught that sent the blood leaping along his veins with a hot and startled impulse.

Mrs. Abercrombie, who had entered the room a little while before, and was some distance from the place where her husband stood, felt at the moment a sudden chill and weight fall upon her heart. A gentleman who was talking to her saw her face grow pale and a look that seemed like terror come into he eyes.

"Are you ill, Mrs. Abercrombie?" he asked, in some alarm.

"No," she replied. "Only a slight feeling of faintness. It is gone now;" and she tried to recover herself.

"Shall I take you from the room?" asked the gentleman, seeing that the color did not come back to her face.

"Oh no, thank you."

T. S. Arthur

"Let me give you a glass of wine."

But she waved her hand with a quick motion, saying, "Not wine; but a little ice water."

She drank, but the water did not take the whiteness from her lips nor restore the color to her cheeks. The look of dread or fear kept in her eyes, and her companion saw her glance up and down the room in a furtive way as if in anxious search for some one.

In a few moments Mrs. Abercrombie was able to rise in some small degree above the strange impression which had fallen upon her like the shadow of some passing evil; but the rarely flavored dishes, the choice fruits, confections and ices with which she was supplied scarcely passed her lips. She only pretended to eat. Her ease of manner and fine freedom of conversation were gone, and the gentleman who had been fascinated by her wit, intelligence and frank womanly bearing now felt an almost repellant coldness.

"You cannot feel well, Mrs. Abercrombie," he said. "The air is close and hot. Let me take you back to the parlors."

She did not reply, nor indeed seem to hear him. Her eyes had become suddenly arrested by some object a little way off, and were fixed upon it in a frightened stare. The gentleman turned and saw only her husband in lively conversation with a lady. He had a glass of wine in his hand, and was just raising it to his lips.

"Jealous!" was the thought that flashed through his mind. The position was embarrassing. What could he say? In the next moment intervening forms hid those of General Abercrombie and his fair companion. Still as a statue, with eyes that seemed staring into vacancy, Mrs. Abercrombie remained for some moments, then she drew her hand within the gentleman's arm and said in a low voice that was little more than a hoarse whisper:

"Thank you; yes, I will go back to the parlors."

They retired from the room without attracting notice.

"Can I do anything for you?" asked the gentleman as he seated her on a sofa in one of the bay-windows where she was partially concealed from observation.

"No, thank you," she answered, with regaining self-control. She then insisted on being left alone, and with a decision of manner that gave her attendant no alternative but compliance.

The gentleman immediately returned to the supper-room. As he joined the company there he met a friend to whom he said in a half-confidential way: "Do you know anything about General Abercrombie's relations with his wife?

"What do you mean?" inquired the friend, with evident surprise.

"I saw something just now that looks very suspicious."

"What?"

"I came here with Mrs. Abercrombie a little while ago, and was engaged in helping her, when I saw her face grow deadly pale. Following her eyes, I observed them fixed on the general, who was chatting gayly and taking wine with a lady."

"What! taking wine did you say?"

The gentleman was almost as much surprised at the altered manner of his friend as he had been with that of Mrs. Abercrombie:

"Yes; anything strange in that?"

"Less strange than sad, was replied. "I don't wonder you saw the color go out of Mrs. Abercrombie's face."

T. S. Arthur

"Why so? What does it mean?"

"It means sorrow and heartbreak."

"You surprise and pain me. I thought of the lady by his side, not of the glass of wine in his hand."

The two men left the crowded supper-room in order to be more alone.

"You know something of the general's life and habits?"

"Yes."

"He has not been intemperate, I hope?"

"Yes."

"Oh, I am pained to hear you say so."

"Drink is his besetting sin, the vice that has more than once come near leading to his dismissal from the army. He is one of the men who cannot use wine or spirits in moderation. In consequence of some diseased action of the nutritive organs brought on by drink, he has lost the power of self-control when under the influence of alcoholic stimulation. He is a dypso-maniac. A glass of wine or brandy to him is like the match to a train of powder. I don't wonder, knowing what I do about General Abercrombie, that his wife grew deadly pale to-night when she saw him raise a glass to his lips."

"Has he been abstaining for any length of time?"

"Yes; for many months he has kept himself free. I am intimate with an officer who told me all about him. When not under the influence of drink, the general is one of the kindest-hearted men in the world. To his wife he is tender and indulgent almost to a fault, if that were possible. But liquor seems to put the devil into him. Drink drowns his better nature and changes him into a half-insane fiend. I am told that he came near killing his wife more than once in a drunken phrensy."

"You pain me beyond measure. Poor lady! I don't wonder that the life went out of her so suddenly, nor at the terror I saw in her face. Can nothing be done? Has he no friends here who will draw him out of the supper-room and get him away before he loses control of himself?"

"It is too late. If he has begun to drink, it is all over. You might as well try to draw off a wolf who has tasted blood."

"Does he become violent? Are we going to have a drunken scene?"

"Oh no; we need apprehend nothing of that kind. I never heard of his committing any public folly. The devil that enters into him is not a rioting, boisterous fiend, but quiet, malignant, suspicious and cruel."

"Suspicious? Of what?"

"Of everybody and everything. His brother officers are in league against him; his wife is regarded with jealousy; your frankest speech covers in his view some hidden and sinister meaning. You must be careful of your attentions to Mrs. Abercrombie to-night, for he will construe them adversely, and pour out his wrath on her defenceless head when they are alone."

"This is frightful," was answered. "I never heard of such a case."

"Never heard of a drunken man assaulting his wife when alone with her, beating, maiming or murdering her?"

"Oh yes, among the lowest and vilest. But we are speaking now of people in good society—people of culture and refinement."

T. S. Arthur

"Culture and social refinements have no influence over a man when the fever of intoxication is upon him. He is for the time an insane man, and subject to the influx and control of malignant influences. Hell rules him instead of heaven."

"It is awful to think of. It makes me shudder."

"We know little of what goes on at home after an entertainment like this," said the other. "It all looks so glad and brilliant. Smiles, laughter, gayety, enjoyment, meet you at every turn. Each one is at his or her best. It is a festival of delight. But you cannot at this day give wine and brandy without stint to one or two or three hundred men and women of all ages, habits, temperaments and hereditary moral and physical conditions without the production of many evil consequences. It matters little what the social condition may be; the hurt of drink is the same. The sphere of respectability may and does guard many. Culture and pride of position hold others free from undue sensual indulgence. But with the larger number the enticements of appetite are as strong and enslaving in one grade of society as in another, and the disturbance of normal conditions as great. And so you see that the wife of an intoxicated army officer or lawyer or banker may be in as much danger from his drunken and insane fury, when alone with him and unprotected, as the wife of a street-sweeper or hod-carrier."

"I have never thought of it in that way."

"No, perhaps not. Cases of wife-beating and personal injuries, of savage and frightful assaults, of terrors and sufferings endured among the refined and educated, rarely if ever come to public notice. Family pride, personal delicacy and many other considerations seal the lips in silence. But there are few social circles in which it is not known that some of its members are sad sufferers because of a husband's or a father's intemperance, and there are many, many families, alas! which have always in their homes the shadow of a sorrow that embitters everything. They hide it as best they can, and few know or dream of what they endure."

Dr. Angier joined the two men at this moment, and heard the last remark. The speaker added, addressing him:

"Your professional experience will corroborate this, Dr. Angier."

"Corroborate what?" he asked, with a slight appearance of evasion in his manner.

"We were speaking of the effects of intemperance on the more cultivated and refined classes, and I said that it mattered little as to the social condition; the hurt of drink was the same and the disturbance of normal conditions as great in one class of society as in another, that a confirmed inebriate, when under the influence of intoxicants, lost all idea of respectability or moral responsibility, and would act out his insane passion, whether he were a lawyer, an army officer or a hod-carrier. In other words, that social position gave the wife of an inebriate no immunity from personal violence when alone with her drunken husband."

Dr. Angier did not reply, but his face became thoughtful.

"Have you given much attention to the pathology of drunkenness?" asked one of the gentlemen.

"Some; not a great deal. The subject is one of the most perplexing and difficult we have to deal with."

"You class intemperance with diseases, do you not?"

"Yes; certain forms of it. It may be hereditary or acquired like any other disease. One man may have a pulmonary, another a bilious and another a dypso-maniac diathesis, and an exposure to exciting causes in one case is as fatal to health as in the other. If there exist a predisposition to consumption, the disease will be developed under peculiar morbific influences which would have no deleterious effect upon a subject not so predisposed. The same law operates as unerringly in the inherited predisposition to intemperance. Let the man with a dypso-maniac diathesis indulge in the use of intoxicating liquors, and he will surely become a drunkard. There is no more immunity for him than for the man who with tubercles in his lungs exposes himself to cold, bad air and enervating bodily conditions."

"A more serious view of the case, doctor, than is usually taken."

"I know, but a moment's consideration—to say nothing of observed facts—will satisfy any reasonable man of its truth."

"What do you mean by dypso-mania as a medical term?"

"The word," replied Dr. Angier, "means crazy for drink, and is used in the profession to designate that condition of alcoholic disease in which the subject when under its influence has no power of self-control. It is characterized by an inordinate and irresistible desire for alcoholic liquors, varying in intensity from a slight departure from a normal appetite to the most depraved and entire abandonment to its influence. When this disease becomes developed, its action upon the brain is to deteriorate its quality and impair its functions. All the faculties become more or less weakened. Reason, judgment, perception, memory and understanding lose their vigor and capacity. The will becomes powerless before the strong propensity to drink. The moral sentiments and affections likewise become involved in the general impairment. Conscience, the feeling of accountability, the sense of right and wrong, all become deadened, while the passions are aroused and excited."

"What an awful disease!" exclaimed one of the listeners.

"You may well call it an awful disease," returned the doctor, who, under the influence of a few glasses of wine, was more inclined to talk than usual. "It has been named the mother of diseases. Its death-roll far outnumbers that of any other. When it has fairly seized upon a man, no influence seems able to hold him back from the indulgence of his passion for drink. To gratify this desire he will disregard every consideration affecting his standing in society, his pecuniary interests and his domestic relations, while the most frightful instances of the results of drinking have no power to restrain him. A hundred deaths from this cause, occurring under the most painful and revolting circumstances, fail to impress him with a sense of his own danger. His understanding will be clear as to the cases before him, and he will even condemn the self-destructive acts which he sees in others, but will pass, as it were, over the very bodies of these victims, without a thought of warning or a sense of fear, in order to gratify his own ungovernable propensity. Such is the power of this terrible malady."

"Has the profession found a remedy?"

"No; the profession is almost wholly at fault in its treatment. There are specialists connected with insane and reformatory institutions who have given much attention to the subject, but as yet we have no recorded line of treatment that guarantees a cure."

"Except," said one of his listeners, "the remedy of entire abstinence from drinks in which alcohol is present."

The doctor gave a shrug:

"You do not cure a thirsty man by withholding water."

His mind was a little clouded by the wine he had taken.

"The thirsty man's desire for water is healthy; and if you withhold it, you create a disease that will destroy him," was answered. "Not so the craving for alcohol. With every new supply the craving is increased, and the man becomes more and more helpless in the folds of an enslaving appetite. Is it not true, doctor, that with few exceptions all who have engaged in

T. S. Arthur

treating inebriates agree that only in entire abstinence is cure possible?"

"Well, yes; you are probably right there," Dr. Angler returned, with some professional reserve. "In the most cases isolation and abstinence are no doubt the only remedies, or, to speak more correctly, the only palliatives. As for cure, I am one of the skeptics. If you have the diathesis, you have the danger of exposure always, as in consumption."

"An occasion like this," remarked the other, "is to one with a dypso-maniac diathesis like a draft of cold, damp air on the exposed chest of a delicate girl who has the seeds of consumption in her lungs. Is it not so, doctor?"

"Yes, yes."

"There are over three hundred persons here to-night."

"Not less."

"In so large a company, taking society as we have it to-day, is it likely that we have none here with a hereditary or acquired love of drink?"

"Scarcely possible," replied Dr. Angier.

"How large do you think the percentage?"

"I have no means of knowing; but if we are to judge by the large army of drunkards in the land, it must be fearfully great."

"Then we cannot invite to our houses fifty or a hundred guests, and give them as much wine and spirits as they care to drink, without seriously hurting some of them. I say nothing of the effect upon unvitiated tastes; I refer only to those with diseased appetites who made happen to be present."

"It will be bad for them, certainly. Such people should stay at home."

And saying this, Dr. Angier turned from the two gentlemen to speak with a professional friend who came toward him at the moment.

T. S. Arthur

CHAPTER XII

"THE doctor likes his glass of wine," remarked one of the gentlemen as Dr. Angier left them.

"Is that so?"

"Didn't you observe his heightened color and the gleam in his eyes?"

"I noticed something unusual in his manner, but did not think it the effect of wine."

"He is a reticent man, with considerable of what may be called professional dignity, and doesn't often let himself down to laymen as he did just now."

"There wasn't much letting down, that I could see."

"Perhaps not; but professional pride is reserved and sensitive in some persons. It hasn't much respect for the opinions of non-experts, and is chary of discussion with laymen. Dr. Angier is weak, or peculiar if you please, in this direction. I saw that he was annoyed at your reply to his remark that you do not cure a thirsty man by withholding water. It was a little thing, but it showed his animus. The argument was against him, and it hurt his pride. As I said, he likes his glass of wine, and if he does not take care will come to like it too well. A doctor has no more immunity from dypso-mania than his patient. The former may inherit or acquire the disease as well as the latter."

"How does the doctor know that he has not from some ancestor this fatal diathesis? Children rarely if ever betray to their children a knowledge of the vices or crimes of their parents. The death by consumption, cancer or fever is a part of oral family history, but not so the death from intemperance. Over that is drawn a veil of silence and secresy, and the children and grandchildren rarely if ever know anything about it. There may be in their blood the taint of a disease far more terrible than cancer or consumption, and none to give them warning of the conditions under which its development is certain."

"Is it not strange," was replied, "that, knowing as Dr. Angier certainly does, from what he said just now, that in all classes of society there is a large number who have in their physical constitutions the seeds of this dreadful disease—that, as I have said, knowing this, he should so frequently prescribe wine and whisky to his patients?"

"It is a little surprising. I have noticed, now that you speak of it, his habit in this respect."

"He might as well, on his own theory, prescribe thin clothing and damp air to one whose father or mother had died of consumption as alcoholic stimulants to one, who has the taint of dypso-mania in his blood. In one case as in the other the disease will almost surely be developed. This is common sense, and something that can be understood by all men."

"And yet, strange to say, the very men who have in charge the public health, the very men whose business it is to study the relations between cause and effect in diseases, are the men who in far too many instances are making the worst possible prescriptions for patients in whom even the slightest tendency to inebriety may exist hereditarily. We have, to speak plainly, too many whisky doctors, and the harm they are doing is beyond calculation. A physician takes upon himself a great responsibility when, without any knowledge of the antecedents of a patient or the stock from which he may have come, he prescribes whisky or wine or brandy as a stimulant. I believe thousands of drunkards have been made by these unwise prescriptions, against which I am glad to know some of the most eminent men in the profession, both in this country and Europe, have entered a solemn protest."

"There is one thing in connection with the disease of intemperance," replied the other, "that is very remarkable. It is the only one from which society does not protect itself by quarantine and sanitary restrictions. In cholera, yellow fever and small-pox every effort is made to guard healthy districts from their invasion, and the man who for gain or any other consideration should be detected in the work of introducing infecting agents would be execrated and punished. But society has another way of dealing with the men who are engaged in spreading the disease of intemperance among the people. It enacts laws for their protection, and gives them the largest liberty to get gain in their work of disseminating disease and death, and, what is still more remarkable, actually sells for money the right to do this."

"You put the case sharply."

"Too sharply?"

"Perhaps not. No good ever comes of calling evil things by dainty names or veiling hard truth under mild and conservative phrases. In granting men a license to dispense alcohol in every variety of enticing forms and in a community where a large percentage of the people have a predisposition to intemperance, consequent as well on hereditary taint as unhealthy social conditions, society commits itself to a disastrous error the fruit of which is bitterer to the taste than the ashen core of Dead Sea apples."

"What about Dead Sea apples?" asked Mr. Elliott, who came up at the moment and heard the last remark. The two gentlemen were pew-holders in his church. Mr. Elliott's countenance was radiant. All his fine social feelings were active, and he was enjoying a "flow of soul," if not "a feast of reason." Wine was making glad his heart—not excess of wine, in the ordinary sense, for Mr. Elliott had no morbid desire for stimulants. He was of the number who could take a social glass and not feel a craving for more. He believed in wine as a good thing, only condemning its abuse.

"What were you saying about Dead Sea apples?" Mr. Elliott repeated his question.

"We were speaking of intemperance," replied one of the gentlemen.

"O—h!" in a prolonged and slightly indifferent tone. Mr. Elliott's countenance lost some of its radiance. "And what were you saying about it?"

Common politeness required as much as this, even though the subject was felt to be out of place.

"We were talking with Dr. Angier just now about hereditary drunkenness, or rather the inherited predisposition to that vice—disease, as the doctor calls it. This predisposition he says exists in a large number of persons, and is as well defined pathologically, and as certain to become active, under favoring causes, as any other disease. Alcoholic stimulants are its exciting causes. Let, said the doctor, a man so predisposed indulge in the use of intoxicating liquors, and he will surely become a drunkard. There is no more immunity for him, he added, than for the man who with tubercles in his lungs exposes himself to cold, bad air and enervating bodily conditions. Now, is not this a very serious view to take of the matter?"

"Certainly it is," replied Mr. Elliott. "Intemperance is a sad thing, and a most fearful curse."

He did not look comfortable. It was to him an untimely intrusion of an unpleasant theme. "But what in the world set

T. S. Arthur

the doctor off on this subject?" he asked, trying to make a diversion.

"Occasions are apt to suggest subjects for conversation," answered the gentleman. "One cannot be present at a large social entertainment like this without seeing some things that awaken doubts and questionings. If it be true, as Dr. Angier says, that the disease of intemperance is as surely transmitted, potentially, as the disease of consumption, and will become active under favoring circumstances, then a drinking festival cannot be given without fearful risk to some of the invited guests."

"There is always danger of exciting disease where a predisposition exists," replied Mr. Elliott. "A man can hardly be expected to make himself acquainted with the pathology of his guests before inviting them to a feast. If that is to be the rule, the delicate young lady with the seeds of consumption in her system must be left at home for fear she may come with bare arms and a low-necked dress, and expose herself after being heated with dancing to the draught of an open window. The bilious and dyspeptic must be omitted also, lest by imprudent eating and drinking they make themselves sick. We cannot regulate these things. The best we can do is to warn and admonish. Every individual is responsible for his own moral character, habits and life. Because some may become the slaves of appetite, shall restraint and limitation be placed on those who make no abuse of liberty? We must teach men self-control and self-mastery, if we would truly help and save them. There is some exaggeration, in my opinion, about this disease-theory of intemperance. The deductions of one-idea men are not always to be trusted. They are apt to draw large conclusions from small facts. Man is born a free agent, and all men have power, if they will, to hold their appetites in check. This truth should be strongly impressed upon every one. Your disease-theory takes away moral responsibility. It assumes that a man is no more accountable for getting drunk than for getting the consumption. His diathesis excuses him as much in one case as in the other. Now, I don't believe a word of this. I do not class appetites, however inordinate, with physical diseases over which the will has no control. A man must control his appetite. Reason and conscience require this, and God gives to every one the mastery of himself if he will but use his high prerogative."

Mr. Elliott spoke a little loftily, and in a voice that expressed a settlement of the argument. But one at least of his listeners was feeling too strongly on the subject to let the argument close.

"What," he asked, "if a young man who did not, because he could not, know that he had dypso-mania in his blood were enticed to drink often at parties where wine is freely dispensed? Would he not be taken, so to speak, unawares? Would he be any more responsible for acts that quickened into life an over-mastering appetite than the young girl who, not knowing that she had in her lungs the seeds of a fatal disease, should expose herself to atmospheric changes that were regarded by her companions as harmless, but which, to her were fraught with peril?"

"In both cases," replied Mr. Elliott, "the responsibility to care for the health would come the moment it was found to be in danger."

"The discovery of danger may come, alas! too late for responsible action. We know that it does in most cases with the consumptive, and quite as often, I fear, with the dypso-maniac."

As the gentleman was closing the last sentence he observed a change pass over the face of Mr. Elliott, who was looking across the room. Following the direction of his eyes, he saw General Abercrombie in the act of offering his arm to Mrs. Abercrombie. It was evident, from the expression of his countenance and that of the countenances of all who were near him that something had gone wrong. The general's face was angry and excited. His eyes had a fierce restlessness in them, and glanced from his wife to a gentleman who stood

T. S. Arthur

confronting him and then back to her in a strange and menacing way.

Mrs. Abercrombie's face was deadly pale. She said a few words hurriedly to her husband, and then drew him from the parlor.

"What's the matter?" asked Mr. Elliott, crossing over and speaking to the gentleman against whom the anger of General Abercrombie had seemed to be directed.

"Heaven knows," was answered, "unless he's jealous of his wife."

"Very strange conduct," said one.

"Been drinking too much," remarked another.

"What did he do?" inquired a third.

"Didn't you see it? Mr. Ertsen was promenading with Mrs. Abercrombie, when the general swept down upon them as fierce as a lion and took the lady from his arm."

This was exaggeration. The thing was done more quietly, but still with enough of anger and menace to create something more than a ripple on the surface.

A little while afterward the general and Mrs. Abercrombie were seen coming down stairs and going along the hall. His face was rigid and stern. He looked neither to the right nor the left, but with eyes set forward made his way toward the street door. Those who got a glimpse of Mrs. Abercrombie as she glided past saw a face that haunted them a long time afterward.

CHAPTER XIII

AS General and Mrs. Abercrombie reached the vestibule, and the door shut behind them, the latter, seeing, that her husband was going out into the storm, which was now at its height, drew back, asking at the same time if their carriage had been called.

The only answer made by General Abercrombie was a fiercely-uttered imprecation. Seizing at the same time the arm she had dropped from his, he drew her out of the vestibule and down the snow-covered step with a sudden violence that threw her to the ground. As he dragged her up he cursed her again in a cruel undertone, and then, grasping her arm, moved off in the very teeth of the blinding tempest, going so swiftly that she could not keep pace with him. Before they had gone a dozen steps she fell again.

Struggling to her feet, helped up by the strong grasp of the madman whose hand was upon her arm, Mrs. Abercrombie tried to rally her bewildered thoughts. She knew that her life was in danger, but she knew also that much, if not everything, depended on her own conduct. The very extremity of her peril calmed her thoughts and gave them clearness and decision. Plunging forward as soon as his wife could recover herself again, General Abercrombie strode away with a speed that made it almost impossible for her to move on without falling, especially as the snow was lying deep and unbroken on the pavement, and her long dress, which she had not taken time to loop up before starting, dragged about her feet and impeded

T. S. Arthur

her steps. They had not gone half a block before she fell again. A wild beast could hardly have growled more savagely than did this insane man as he caught her up from the bed of snow into which she had fallen and shook her with fierce passion. A large, strong man, with an influx of demoniac, strength in every muscle, his wife was little more than a child in his hands. He could have crushed the life out of her at a single grip.

Not a word or sound came from Mrs. Abercrombie. The snow that covered the earth was scarcely whiter than her rigid face. Her eyes, as the light of a flickering gas-lamp shone into them, hardly reflected back its gleam, so leaden was their despair.

He shook her fiercely, the tightening grasp on her arms bruising the tender flesh, cursed her, and then, in a blind fury, cast her from him almost into the middle of the street, where she lay motionless, half buried in the snow. For some moments he stood looking at the prostrate form of his wife, on which the snow sifted rapidly down, making the dark garments white in so short a space of time that she seemed to fade from his view. It was this, perhaps, that wrought a sudden change in his feelings, for he sprang toward her, and taking her up in his arms, called her name anxiously. She did not reply by word or sign, He carried her back to the pavement and turned her face to the lamp; it was white and still, the eyes closed, the mouth shut rigidly.

But Mrs. Abercrombie was not unconscious. Every sense was awake.

"Edith! Edith!" her husband cried. His tones, anxious at first, now betrayed alarm. A carriage went by at the moment. He called to the driver, but was unheard or unheeded. Up and down the street, the air of which was so filled with snow that he could see only a short distance, he looked in vain for the form of a policeman or citizen. He was alone in the street at midnight, blocks away from his residence, a fierce storm raging in the air, the cold intense, and his wife apparently insensible in his arms. If anything could free his brain from its illusions, cause enough was here. He shouted aloud for help, but there came no answer on the wild careering winds. Another carriage went by, moving in ghostly silence, but his call to the driver was unheeded, as before.

Feeling the chill of the intensely cold air going deeper and deeper, and conscious of the helplessness of their situation unless she used the strength that yet remained, Mrs. Abercrombie showed symptoms of returning life and power of action. Perceiving this, the general drew an arm around her for support and made a motion to go on again, to which she responded by moving forward, but with slow and not very steady steps. Soon, however, she walked more firmly, and began pressing on with a haste that ill accorded with the apparent condition out of which she had come only a few moments before.

The insane are often singularly quick in perception, and General Abercrombie was for the time being as much insane as any patient of an asylum. It flashed into his mind that his wife had been deceiving him, had been pretending a faint, when she was as strong of limb and clear of intellect as when they left Mr. Birtwell's. At this thought the half-expelled devil that had been controlling him leaped back into his heart, filling it again with evil passions. But the wind was driving the fine, sand-like, sharp-cutting snow into his face with such force and volume as to half suffocate and bewilder him. Turning at this moment a corner of the street that brought him into the clear sweep of the storm, the wind struck him with a force that seemed given by a human hand, and threw him staggering against his wife, both falling.

Struggling to his feet, General Abercrombie cursed his wife as he jerked her from the ground with a sudden force that came near dislocating her arm. She gave no word of remonstrance nor cry of pain or fear, but did all in her power to keep up with her husband as he drove on again with mad precipitation.

How they got home Mrs. Abercrombie hardly knew, but home

they were at last and in their own room, the door closed and locked and the key withdrawn by her husband, out of whose manner all the wild passion had gone. His movements were quiet and his voice when he spoke low, but his wife knew by the gleam of his restless eyes that thought and purpose were active.

Their room was in the third story of a large boarding-house in a fashionable part of the city. The outlook was upon the street. The house was double, a wide hall running through the centre. There were four or five large rooms on this floor, all occupied. In the one adjoining theirs were a lady and gentleman who had been at Mr. and Mrs. Birtwell's party, and who drove up in a carriage just as the general and Mrs. Abercrombie, white with snow, came to the door. They entered together, the lady expressing surprise at their appearance, at which the general growled some incoherent sentences and strode away from them and up the stairs, Mrs. Abercrombie following close after him.

"There's something wrong, I'm afraid," said the gentleman, whose name was Craig, as he and his wife gained their own room. They went in a carriage, I know. What can it mean?"

"I hope the general has not been drinking too much," remarked the wife.

"I'm afraid he has. He used to be very intemperate, I've heard, but reformed a year or two ago, A man with any weakness in this direction would be in danger at an entertainment such as Mr. and Mrs. Birtwell gave to-night."

"I saw the general taking wine with a lady," said Mrs. Craig.

If he took one glass, he would hardly set that as a limit. It were much easier to abstain altogether; and we know that if a man over whom drink has once gained the mastery ventures upon the smallest indulgence of his appetite he is almost sure to give way and to fall again. It's a strange thing, and sad as strange."

"Hark!"

Mr. Craig turned quickly toward the door which when opened made a communication between their apartment and that of General and Mrs. Abercrombie. It was shut, and fastened on both sides, so that it could not be opened by the occupants, of either room.

A low but quickly-stifled cry had struck on the ears of Mr. and Mrs. Craig. They looked at each other with questioning glances for several moments, listening intently, but the cry was not repeated.

"I don't like that," said Mr. Craig. He spoke with concern.

"What can it mean?" asked his wife.

"Heaven knows!" he replied.

They sat silent and listening. A sharp click, which the ear of Mr. Craig detected as the sound made by the cocking of a pistol, struck upon the still air. He sprang to his feet and took a step or two toward the door leading into the hall, but his wife caught his arm and clung to it tightly.

"No, no! Wait! wait!" she cried, in a deep whisper, while her face grew-ashen pale. For some moments they stood with repressed breathing, every instant expecting to hear the loud report of a pistol. But the deep silence remained unbroken for nearly a minute; then a dull movement of feet was heard in the room, and the opening and shutting of a drawer.

"No, general, you will not do that," they heard Mrs. Abercrombie say, in a low, steady tone in which fear struggled with tenderness.

"Why will I not do it?" was sternly demanded.

They were standing near the door, so that their voices could be

T. S. Arthur

heard distinctly in the next room.

"Because you love me too well," was the sweet, quiet answer. The voice of Mrs. Abercrombie did not betray a single tremor.

All was hushed again. Then came another movement in the room, and the sound of a closing drawer. Mr. and Mrs. Craig were beginning to breathe more freely, when the noise as of some one springing suddenly upon another was heard, followed by a struggle and a choking cry. It continued so long that Mr. Craig ran out into the hall and knocked at the door of General Abercrombie's room. As he did so the noise of struggling ceased, and all grew still. The door was not opened to his summons, and after waiting for a little while he went back to his own room.

"This is dreadful," he said. "What can it mean? The general must be insane from drink. Something will have to be done. He may be strangling his poor wife at this very moment. I cannot bear it. I must break open the door."

Mr. Craig started toward the hall, but his wife seized hold of him and held him back.

"No, no, no!" she cried, in a low voice. "Let them alone. It may be her only chance of safety. Hark!"

The silence in General Abercrombie's room was again broken. A man's firm tread was on the floor and it could be heard passing clear across the apartment, then returning and then going from side to side. At length the sound of moving furniture was heard. It was as if a person were lifting a heavy wardrobe or bureau, and getting it with some difficulty from one part of the room to the other.

"What can he be doing?" questioned Mrs. Craig, with great alarm.

"He is going to barricade the door, most likely," replied

her husband.

"Barricade the door? What for? Good heavens, Mr. Craig! He may have killed his wife. She may be lying in there dead at this very moment. Oh, it is fearful! Can nothing be done?"

"Nothing, that I know of, except to break into the room."

"Hadn't you better rouse some of the boarders, or call a waiter and send for the police?"

The voice of Mrs. Abercrombie was heard at this moment. It was calm and clear.

"Let me help you, general," she said.

The noise of moving furniture became instantly still. It seemed as if the madman had turned in surprise from his work and stood confronting his wife, but whether in wrath, or not it was impossible to conjecture. They might hear her fall to the floor, stricken down by her husband, or cry out in mortal agony at any moment. The suspense was dreadful.

"Do it! I am ready."

It was Mrs. Abercrombie speaking again, and in a calm, even voice. They heard once more and with curdling blood, the sharp click of a pistol-lock as the hammer was drawn back. They held their breaths in horror and suspense, not moving lest even the slightest sound they made should precipitate the impending tragedy.

"I have been a good and true wife to you always, and I shall remain so even unto death."

The deep pathos of her quiet voice brought tears to the eyes of Mr. and Mrs. Craig.

"If you are tired of me, I am ready to go. Look into my eyes.

You see that I am not afraid."

It was still as death again. The clear, tender eyes that looked so steadily into those of General Abercrombie held him like a spell, and made his fingers so nerveless that they could not respond to the passion of the murderous fiend that possessed him. That was why the scared listeners did not hear the deadly report of the pistol he was holding within a few inches of his wife's head.

"Let me put it away. It isn't a nice thing to have in a lady's chamber. You know I can't bear the sight of a pistol, and you love me too well to give me the smallest pain or uneasiness. That's a dear, good husband."

They could almost see Mrs. Abercrombie take the deadly weapon from the general's hand. They heard her dress trailing across the room, and heard her open and shut and then lock a drawer. For some time afterward they could hear the low sound of voices, then all became silent again.

"Give me that pistol!" startled them not long afterward in a sudden wild outbreak of frenzied passion.

"What do you want with it?" they heard Mrs. Abercrombie ask. There was no sign of alarm in her tones.

"Give me that pistol, I say!" The general's voice was angry and imperious. "How dared you take, it out of my hand!"

"Oh, I thought you wished it put away because the sight of a pistol is unpleasant to me."

And they heard the dress trailing across the room again.

"Stop!" cried the general, in a commanding tone.

"Just as you please, general. You can have the pistol, if you want it," answered Mrs. Abercrombie, without the smallest tremor in her voice. Shall I get it for you?"

"No!" He flung the word out angrily, giving it emphasis by an imprecation. Then followed a growl as if from an ill-natured beast, and they could hear his heavy tread across the floor.

"Oh, general!" came suddenly from the lips of Mrs. Abercrombie, in a surprised, frightened tone. Then followed the sound of a repressed struggle, of an effort to get free without making a noise or outcry, which continued for a considerable time, accompanied by a low muttering and panting as of a man in some desperate effort.

Mr. and Mrs. Craig stood with pale faces, irresolute and powerless to help, whatever might be the extremity of their neighbor. To attempt a forcible entry into the room was a doubtful expedient, and might be attended with instant fatal consequences. The muttering and panting ceased at length, and so did all signs of struggling and resistance. The madman had wrought his will, whatever that might be. Breathlessly they listened, but not a sound broke the deep silence. Minutes passed, but the stillness reigned.

"He may have killed her," whispered Mrs. Craig, with white lips. Her husband pressed his ear closely to the door.

"Do you hear anything?"

"Yes."

"What?"

They spoke in a low whisper.

"Put your ear against the door."

Mrs. Craig did so, and after a moment or two could hear a faint movement, as of something being pulled across the carpet. The sound was intermittent, now being very distinct

T. S. Arthur

and now ceasing altogether. The direction of the movement was toward that part of the room occupied by the bed. The listeners' strained sense of hearing was so acute that it was able to interpret the meaning of each varying sound. A body had been slowly dragged across the floor, and now, hushed and almost noiselessly as the work went on, they knew that the body was being lifted from the floor and placed upon the bed. For a little while all was quiet, but the movements soon began again, and were confined to the bed. Something was being done with the dead or unconscious body. What, it was impossible to make out or even guess. Mrs. Abercrombie might be lifeless, in a swoon or only feigning unconsciousness.

"It won't do to let this go on any longer," said Mr. Craig as he came back from the door at which he had been listening. "I must call some of the boarders and have a consultation."

He was turning to go out, when a sound as of a falling chair came from General Abercrombie's room, and caused him to stop and turn back, This was followed by the quick tread of heavy feet going up and down the chamber floor, and continuing without intermission for as much as five minutes. It stopped as suddenly as it had begun, and all was silent again. They knew that the general was standing close by the bed.

"My God!" in a tone full, of anguish and fear dropped from his lips. "Edith! Edith! oh, Edith!" he called in a low wail of distress. "Speak to me, Edith! Why don't you speak to me?"

They listened, but heard no answer. General Abercrombie called the name of his wife over and over again, and in terms of endearment, but for all Mr. and Mrs. Craig could tell she gave back no sign.

"O my God! what have I done?" they heard him say, the words followed by a deep groan.

"It is my time now;" and Mr. Craig ran out into the hall as he said this and knocked at the general's door. But no answer came. He knocked again, and louder than at first. After waiting for a short time he heard the key turn in the lock. The door was opened a few inches, and he saw through the aperture the haggard and almost ghastly face of General Abercrombie. His eyes were wild and distended.

"What do you want?" he demanded, impatiently.

"Is Mrs. Abercrombie sick? Can we do anything for you, general?" said Mr. Craig, uttering the sentences that came first to his tongue.

"No!" in angry rejection of the offered service. The door shut with a jar, and the key turned in the lock. Mr. Craig stood for a moment irresolute, and then went back to his wife. Nothing more was heard in the adjoining room. Though they listened for a long time, no voice nor sound of any kind came to their ears. The general had, to all appearance, thrown himself upon the bed and fallen asleep.

It was late on the next morning when Mr. and Mrs. Craig awoke. Their first thought was of their neighbors, General and Mrs. Abercrombie. The profoundest silence reigned in their apartments—a silence death-like and ominous.

"If he has murdered her!" said Mrs. Craig, shivering at the thought as she spoke.

"I hope not, but I shouldn't like to be the first one who goes into that room," replied her husband. Then, after a moment's reflection, he said:

"If anything has gone wrong in there, we must be on our guard and make no admissions. It won't do for us to let it be known that we heard the dreadful things going on there that we did, and yet gave no alarm. I'm not satisfied with myself, and can hardly expect others to excuse where I condemn."

T. S. Arthur

CHAPTER XIV

WHEN Mr. and Mrs. Craig entered the breakfast-room, they saw, to their surprise, General Abercrombie and his wife sitting in their usual places. They bowed to each other, as was their custom on meeting at the table.

The face of Mrs. Abercrombie was pale and her features pinched. She had the appearance of one who had been ill and was just recovering, or of one who had endured exhausting pain of mind or body. She arose from the table soon after Mr. and, Mrs. Craig made their appearance, and retired with her husband from the room.

"The general is all out of sorts this morning," remarked a lady as soon as they were gone.

"And so is Mrs. Abercrombie," said another. "Dissipation does not agree with them. They were at the grand party given last night by Mr. and Mrs. Birtwell. You were among the guests, Mrs. Craig?"

The lady addressed bowed her affirmative.

"A perfect jam, I suppose?"

"Yes."

"Who were there? But I needn't ask. All the world his wife, of course, little bugs and big bugs. How was the entertainment?"

"Splendid! I never saw such a profusion of everything."

"Fools make feasts for wise men to eat," snapped out the sharp voice of a lady whose vinegar face gave little promise of enjoyment of any kind. Nobody thinks any more of them for it. Better have given the money to some charity. There's want and suffering enough about, Heaven knows,"

"I don't imagine that the charity fund has suffered anything in consequence of Mr. Birtwell's costly entertainment," replied Mr. Craig. "If the money spent for last night's feast had not gone to the wine-merchant and the caterer, it would have remained as it was."

The lady with the vinegar face said something about the Dives who have their good things here, adding, with a zest in her voice, that "Riches, thank God! can't be taken over to the other side, and your nabobs will be no better off after they die than the commonest beggars."

"That will depend on something more than the money-aspect of the case," said Mr. Craig. "And as to the cost of giving a feast, what would be extravagance in one might only be a liberal hospitality in another. Cake and ice cream for my friends might be as lavish an expenditure for me as Mr. Birtwell's banquet last night was for him, and as likely to set me among the beggars when I get over to the other side."

"Then you don't believe that God holds rich men to a strict account for the manner in which they spend the money he has placed in their hands? Are they not his almoners?"

"No more than poor men, and not to be held to any stricter accountability," was replied. "Mr. Birtwell does not sin against the poor when he lavishes his hundreds, or it may be thousands, of dollars in the preparation of a feast for his friends any more than you do when you buy a box of French

T. S. Arthur

candies to eat alone in your room or share with your visitors, maybe not so much."

There was a laugh at the expense of the vinegar-faced lady, who did not fail in a sharp retort which was more acid than convincing. The conversation then went back to General Abercrombie and his wife.

"Didn't she look dreadful?" remarked one of the company.

"And her manner toward the general was so singular."

"In what respect?" asked Mrs. Craig.

"She looked at him so strangely, so anxious and scared-like. I never knew him to be so silent. He's social and talkative, you know—such good company. But he hadn't a word to say this morning. Something has gone wrong between him and his wife. I wonder what it can be?"

But Mr. and Mrs. Craig, who were not of the gossiping kind, were disposed to keep their own counsel.

"I thought I heard some unusual noises in their room last night after they came home from the party," said a lady whose chamber was opposite theirs across the hall. "They seemed to be moving furniture about, and twice I thought I heard a scream. But then the storm was so high that one might easily have mistaken a wail of the wind for a cry of distress."

"A cry of distress! You didn't imagine that the general was maltreating his wife?"

"I intimated nothing of the kind," returned the lady.

"But what made you think about a cry of distress?"

"I merely said that I thought I heard a scream; and if you had been awake from twelve to one or two o'clock this morning, you would have thought the air full of wailing voices. The storm chafed about the roof and chimneys in a dreadful way. I never knew a wilder night."

"You saw the general at the party?" said one, addressing Mr. Craig.

"Yes, a few times. But there was a crowd in all the rooms, and the same people were not often thrown together."

"Nothing unusual about him? Hadn't been drinking too much?"

"Not when I observed him. But—" Mr. Craig hesitated a moment, and then went on: "But there's one thing has a strange look. They went in a carriage, I know, but walked home in all that dreadful storm."

"Walked home!" Several pairs of eyes and hands were upraised.

"Yes; they came to the door, white with snow, just as we got home."

"How strange! What could it have meant?"

"It meant," said one, "that their carriage disappointed them— nothing else, of course."

"That will hardly explain it. Such disappointments rarely, if ever, occur," was replied to this.

"Did you say anything to them, Mr. Craig?"

"My wife did, but received only a gruff response from the general. Mrs. Abercrombie made no reply, but, went hastily after her husband. There was something unusual in the manner of both."

While this conversation was going on General Abercrombie

T. S. Arthur

and his wife stood in the hall, she trying, but in vain, to persuade him not to go out. He said but little, answering her kindly, but with a marked decision of manner. Mrs. Abercrombie went up slowly to their room after he left her, walking as one who carried a heavy load. She looked ten years older than on the day previous.

No one saw her during the morning. At dinner-time their places were vacant at the table.

"Where are the general and his wife?" was asked as time passed and they did not make their appearance.

No one had seen either of them since breakfast.

Mrs. Craig knew that Mrs. Abercrombie had not been out of her room all the morning, but she did not feel inclined to take part in the conversation, and so said nothing.

"I saw the general going into the Clarendon about two o'clock," said a gentleman. "He's dining with some friend, most probably."

"I hear," remarked another, "that he acted rather strangely at Mr. Birtwell's last night."

Every ear pricked up at this.

"How?" "In what way?" "Tell us about it," came in quick response to the speaker's words.

"I didn't get anything like a clear story. But there was some trouble about his wife."

"About his wife?" Faces looked eagerly down and across the table.

"What about his wife?" came from half a dozen lips.

"He thought some one too intimate with her, I believe. A brother officer, if I am not mistaken. Some old flame, perhaps. But I couldn't learn any of the particulars."

"Ah! That accounts for their singular conduct this morning. Was there much of a row?" This came from a thin-visaged young man with eye-glasses and a sparse, whitish moustache.

"I didn't say anything about a row," was the rather sharp reply. "I only said that I heard that the general had acted strangely, and that there had been some trouble about his wife."

"What was the trouble?" asked two or three anxious voices—anxious for some racy scandal.

"Couldn't learn any of the particulars, only that he took his wife from a gentleman's arm in a rude kind of way, and left the party."

"Oh! that accounts for their not coming home in a carriage," broke in one of the listeners.

"Perhaps so. But who said they didn't ride home?"

"Mr. Craig. He and Mrs. Craig saw them as they came to the door, covered with snow. They were walking."

"Oh, you were at the party, Mr. Craig? Did you see or hear anything about this affair?"

"Nothing," replied Mr. Craig. "If there had been any trouble, I should most likely have heard something of it."

"I had my information from a gentleman who was there," said the other.

"I don't question that," replied Mr. Craig. "A trifling incident but half understood will often give rise to exaggerated reports —so exaggerated that but little of the original truth remains in them. The general may have done something under the excitement of wine that gave color to the story now in circulation. I think that very possible. But I don't believe the affair to be half so bad as represented."

While this conversation was going on Mrs. Abercrombie sat alone in her room. She had walked the floor restlessly as the time drew near for the general's return, but after the hour went by, and there was no sign of his coming, all the life seemed to go out of her. She was sitting now, or rather crouching down, in a large cushioned chair, her face white and still and her eyes fixed in a kind of frightened stare.

Time passed, but she remained so motionless that but for her wide-open eyes you would have thought her asleep or dead.

No one intruded upon her during the brief afternoon; and when darkness shut in, she was still sitting where she had dropped down nerveless from mental pain. After it grew dark Mrs. Abercrombie arose, lighted the gas and drew the window curtains. She then moved about the room putting things in order. Next she changed her dress and gave some careful attention to her personal appearance. The cold pallor which had been on her face all the afternoon gave way to a faint tinge of color, her eyes lost their stony fixedness and became restless and alert. But the trouble did not go out of her face or eyes; it was only more active in expression, more eager and expectant.

After all the changes in her toilette had been made, Mrs. Abercrombie sat down again, waiting and listening. It was the general's usual time to come home from headquarters. How would he come? or would he come at all? These were the questions that agitated her soul. The sad, troubled humiliating, suffering past, how its records of sorrow and shame and fear kept unrolling themselves before her eyes! There was little if anything in these records to give hope or comfort. Ah! how many times had he fallen from his high estate of manhood, each time sinking lower and lower, and each time recovering himself from the fall with greater difficulty than before! He might never rise again. The chances were largely against him.

How the wretched woman longed for yet dreaded the return of her husband! If he had been drinking again, as she feared, there, was before her a night of anguish and terror—a night which might have for her no awaking in the world. But she had learned to dread some things more than death.

Time wore on until it was past the hour for General Abercrombie's return, and yet there was no sign of his coming. At last the loud clang of the supper-bell ringing through the halls gave her a sudden start. She clasped her hands across her forehead, while a look of anguish convulsed her face, then held them tightly against her heart and groaned aloud.

"God pity us both!" she cried, in a low, wailing voice, striking her hands together and lifting upward her eyes, that were full of the deepest anguish.

For a few moments her eyes were upraised. Then her head sunk forward upon her bosom, and she sat an image of helpless despair.

A knock at the door roused her. She started to her feet and opened it with nervous haste.

"A letter for you," said a servant.

She took it from his hand and shut and locked the door before examining the handwriting on the envelope. It was that of her husband. She tore it open with trembling hand and read:

"DEAR EDITH: An order requiring my presence in Washington to-morrow morning has just reached me, and I have only time to make the train. I shall be gone two or three days."

The deep flush which excitement had spread over the face of Mrs. Abercrombie faded off, and the deadly pallor returned.

T. S. Arthur

Her hands shook so that the letter dropped out of them and fell to the floor. Another groan as of a breaking heart sobbed through her lips as she threw herself in despairing abandonment across the bed and buried her face deep among the pillows.

She needed no interpreter to unfold the true meaning of that letter. Its unsteady and blotted words and its scrawled, uncertain signature told her too well of her husband's sad condition. His old enemy had stricken him down, his old strong, implacable enemy, always armed, always lying in wait for him, and always ready for the unguarded moment.

CHAPTER XV

DOCTOR HILLHOUSE was in his office one morning when a gentleman named Carlton, in whose family he had practiced for two or three years, came in. This was a few weeks before the party at Mr. Birtwell's.

"Doctor"—there was a troubled look on his visitor's face—"I wish you would call in to-day and examine a lump on Mrs. Carlton's neck. It's been coming for two or three months. We thought it only the swelling of a gland at first, and expected it to go away in a little while. But in the last few weeks it has grown perceptibly."

"How large is it?" inquired the doctor.

"About the size of a pigeon's egg."

"Indeed! So large?"

"Yes; and I am beginning to feel very much concerned about it."

"Is there any discoloration?"

"No."

"Any soreness or tenderness to the touch?"

"No; but Mrs. Carlton is beginning to feel a sense of tightness

T. S. Arthur

and oppression, as though the lump, whatever it may be, were beginning to press upon some of the blood-vessels."

"Nothing serious, I imagine," replied Dr. Hillhouse, speaking with a lightness of manner he did not feel. "I will call about twelve o'clock. Tell Mrs. Carlton to expect me at that time."

Mr. Carlton made a movement to go, but came back from the door, and betraying more anxiety of manner than at first, said:

"This may seem a light thing in your eyes, doctor, but I cannot help feeling troubled. I am afraid of a tumor."

"What is the exact location?" asked Dr. Hillhouse.

"On the side of the neck, a little back from the lower edge of the right ear."

The doctor did not reply. After a brief silence Mr. Carlton said:

"Do you think it a regular tumor, doctor?"

"It is difficult to say. I can speak with more certainty after I have made an examination," replied Doctor Hillhouse, his manner showing some reserve.

"If it should prove to be a tumor, cannot its growth be stopped? Is there no relief except through an operation—no curative agents that will restore a healthy action to the parts and cause the tumor to be absorbed?"

"There is a class of tumors," replied the doctor, "that may be absorbed, but the treatment is prejudicial to the general health, and no wise physician will, I think, resort to it instead of a surgical operation, which is usually simple and safe."

"Much depends on the location of a tumor," said Mr. Carlton. "The extirpation may be safe and easy if the operation be in one place, and difficult and dangerous if in another."

"It is the surgeon's business to do his work so well that danger shall not exist in any case," replied Doctor Hillhouse.

"I shall trust her in your hands," said Mr. Carlton, trying to assume a cheerful air. "But I cannot help feeling nervous and extremely anxious."

"You are, of course, over-sensitive about everything that touches one so dear as your wife," replied the doctor. "But do not give yourself needless anxiety. Tumors in the neck are generally of the kind known as 'benignant,' and are easily removed."

Dr. Angier came into the office while they were talking, and heard a part of the conversation. As soon as Mr. Carlton had retired he asked if the tumor were deep-seated or only a wen-like protuberance.

"Deep-seated, I infer, from what Mr. Carlton said," replied Dr. Hillhouse.

"What is her constitution?"

"Not as free from a scrofulous tendency as I should like."

"Then this tumor, if it should really prove to be one, may be of a malignant character."

"That is possible. But I trust to find only a simple cyst, or, at the worst, an adipose or fibrous tumor easy of removal, though I am sorry it is in the neck. I never like to cut in among the large blood-vessels and tendons of that region."

At twelve o'clock Doctor Hillhouse made the promised visit. He found Mrs. Carlton to all appearance quiet and cheerful.

"My husband is apt to worry himself when anything ails me,"

T. S. Arthur

she said, with a faint smile.

The doctor took her hand and felt a low tremor of the nerves that betrayed the nervous anxiety she was trying hard to conceal. His first diagnosis was not satisfactory, and he was not able wholly to conceal his doubts from the keen observation of Mr. Carlton, whose eyes never turned for a moment from the doctor's face. The swelling was clearly outlined, but neither sharp nor protuberant. From the manner of its presentation, and also from the fact that Mrs. Carlton complained of a feeling of pressure on the vessels of the neck, the doctor feared the tumor was larger and more deeply seated than the lady's friends had suspected. But he was most concerned as to its true character. Being hard and nodulated, he feared that it might prove to be of a malignant type, and his apprehensions were increased by the fact that his patient had in her constitution a taint of scrofula. There was no apparent congestion of the veins nor discoloration of the skin around the hard protuberance, no pulsation, elasticity, fluctuation or soreness, only a solid lump which the doctor's sensitive touch recognized as the small section or lobule of a deeply-seated tumor already beginning to press upon and obstruct the blood vessels in its immediate vicinity. Whether it were fibrous or albuminous, "benignant" or "malignant," he was not able in his first diagnosis to determine.

Dr. Hillhouse could not so veil his face as to hide from Mr. Carlton the doubt and concern that were in his mind.

"Deal with me plainly," said the latter as he stood alone with the doctor after the examination was over. "I want the exact truth. Don't conceal anything."

Mr. Carlton's lips trembled.

"Is it a—a tumor?" He got the words out in a low, shaky voice.

"I think so," replied Doctor Hillhouse. He saw the face of Mr. Carlton blanch instantly.

"It presents," added the doctor, "all the indications of what we call a fibrous tumor."

"Is it of a malignant type?" asked Mr. Carlton, with suspended breath.

"No; these tumors are harmless in themselves, but their mechanical pressure on surrounding blood-vessels and tissues renders their removal necessary."

Mr. Carlton caught his breath with a sigh of relief.

"Is their removal attended with danger?" he asked.

"None," replied Dr. Hillhouse.

"Have you ever taken a tumor from the neck?"

"Yes. I have operated in cases of this kind often."

"Were you always successful?"

"Yes; in every instance."

Mr. Carlton breathed more freely. After a pause, he said, his lips growing white as he spoke:

"There will have to be an operation in this case?"

"It cannot, I fear, be avoided," replied the doctor.

"There is one comfort," said Mr. Carlton, rallying and speaking in a more cheerful voice. "The tumor is small and superficial in character. The knife will not have to go very deep among the veins and arteries."

Doctor Hillhouse did not correct his error.

"How long will it take?" queried the anxious husband, to

whom the thought of cutting down into the tender flesh of his wife was so painful that it completely unmanned him.

"Not very long," answered the doctor.

"Ten minutes?"

"Yes, or maybe a little longer."

"She will feel no pain?"

"None."

"Nor be conscious of what you are doing?"

"She will be as much in oblivion as a sleeping infant," replied the doctor.

Mr. Carlton turned from Dr. Hillhouse and walked the whole length of the parlor twice, then stood still, and said, with painful impressiveness:

"Doctor, I place her in your hands. She is ready for anything we may decide upon as best."

He stopped and turned partly away to hide his feelings. But recovering himself, and forcing a smile to his lips, he said:

"To your professional eyes I show unmanly weakness. But you must bear in mind how very dear she is to me. It makes me shiver in every nerve to think of the knife going down into her tender flesh. You might cut me to pieces, doctor, if that would save her."

"Your fears exaggerate everything," returned Doctor Hillhouse, in an assuring voice. "She will go into a tranquil sleep, and while dreaming pleasant dreams we will quickly dissect out the tumor, and leave the freed organs to continue their healthy action under the old laws of unobstructed life."

"When ought it to be done?" asked Mr. Carlton the tremor coming back into his voice.

"The sooner, the better, after an operation is decided upon," answered the doctor. "I will make another examination in about two weeks. The changes that take place in that time will help me to a clearer decision than it is possible to arrive at now."

After a lapse of two weeks Doctor Hillhouse, in company with another surgeon, made a second examination. What his conclusions were will appear in the following conversation held with Dr. Angier.

"The tumor is not of a malignant character," Doctor Hillhouse replied, in answer to his assistant's inquiry. "But it is larger than I at first suspected and is growing very rapidly. From a slight suffusion of Mrs. Carlton's face which I did not observe at any previous visit, it is evident that the tumor is beginning to press upon the carotids. Serious displacements of blood-vessels, nerves, glands and muscles must soon occur if this growth goes on."

"Then her life is in danger?" said Dr. Angier.

"It is assuredly, and nothing but a successful operation can save her."

"What does Doctor Kline think of the case?"

"He agrees with me as to the character of the tumor, but thinks it larger than an orange, deeply cast among the great blood-vessels, and probably so attached to their sheaths as to make its extirpation not only difficult, but dangerous."

"Will he assist you in the operation?"

"Yes."

T. S. Arthur

Dr. Hillhouse became thoughtful and silent. His countenance wore a serious, almost troubled aspect.

"Never before," he said, after a long pause, "have I looked forward to an operation with such a feeling of concern as I look forward to this. Three or four months ago, when there was only a little sack there, it could have been removed without risk. But I greatly fear that in its rapid growth it has become largely attached to the blood-vessels and the sheaths of nerves, and you know how difficult this will make the operation, and that the risk will be largely increased. The fact is, doctor, I am free to say that it would be more agreeable to me if some other surgeon had the responsibility of this case."

"Dr. Kline would, no doubt, be very ready to take it off of your hands."

"If the family were satisfied, I would cheerfully delegate the work to him," said Doctor Hillhouse.

"He's a younger man, and his recent brilliant operations have brought him quite prominently before, the public."

As he spoke Doctor Hillhouse, who was past sixty-five and beginning to feel the effects of over forty years of earnest professional labor, lifted his small hand, the texture of which, was as fine as that of a woman's, and holding it up, looked at it steadily for some moments. It trembled just a little.

"Not quite so firm as it was twenty years ago," he remarked, with a slight depression in his voice.

"But the sight is clearer and the skill greater," said Doctor Angier.

"I don't know about the sight." returned Doctor Hillhouse. "I'm afraid that is no truer than the hand."

"The inner sight, I mean, the perception that comes from

long-applied skill," said Doctor Angier. "That is something in which you have the advantage of younger men."

Doctor Hillhouse made no reply to this, but sat like one in deep and, perplexed thought for a considerable time.

"I must see Doctor Kline and go over the case with him more carefully," he remarked at length. "I shall then be able to see with more clearness what is best. The fact that I feel so averse to operating myself comes almost as a warning; and if no change should occur in my feelings, I shall, with the consent of the family, transfer the knife to Doctor Kline."

T. S. Arthur

CHAPTER XVI

MRS. CARLTON was a favorite in the circle where she moved; and when it became known that she would have to submit to a serious operation in order to save her life, she became an object of painful interest to her many friends. Among the most intimate of these was Mrs. Birtwell, who, as the time approached for the great trial, saw her almost every day.

It was generally understood that Doctor Hillhouse, who was the family physician, would perform the operation. For a long series of years he had held the first rank as a surgeon. But younger men were coming forward in the city, and other reputations were being made that promised to be even more notable than his.

Among those who were steadly achieving success in the walks of surgery was Doctor Kline, now over thirty-five years of age. He held a chair in one of the medical schools, and his name was growing more and more familiar to the public and the profession every year.

The friends of Mrs. Carlton were divided on the question as to who could best perform the operation, some favoring Doctor Kline and some Doctor Hillhouse.

The only objection urged by any one against the latter was on account of his age.

Mr. and Mrs. Carlton had no doubt or hesitation on the subject. Their confidence in the skill of Doctor Hillhouse was complete. As for Doctor Kline, Mr. Carlton, who met him now and then at public dinners or at private social entertainments, had not failed to observe that he was rather free in his use of liquor, drinking so frequently on these occasions as to produce a noticeable exhilaration. He had even remarked upon the fact to gentlemen of his acquaintance, and found that others had noticed this weakness of Doctor Kline as well as himself.

As time wore on Doctor Hillhouse grew more and more undecided. No matter how grave or difficult an operation might be, he had always, when satisfied of its necessity, gone forward, looking neither to the right nor to the left. But so troubled and uncertain did he become as the necessity for fixing an early day for the removal of this tumor became more and more apparent that he at last referred the whole matter to Mr. Carlton, and proposed that Doctor Kline, whose high reputation for surgical skill he knew, should be entrusted with the operation. To this he received an emphatic "No!"

"All the profession award him the highest skill in our city, if not the whole country," said Doctor Hillhouse.

"I have no doubt of his skill," replied Mr. Carlton. "But—"

"What?" asked the doctor, as Mr. Carlton hesitated. "Are you not aware that he uses wine too freely?"

Doctor Hillhouse was taken by surprise at this intimation.

"No, I am not aware of anything of the kind," he replied, almost indignantly. "He is not a teetotaller, of course, any more than you or I. Socially and at dinner he takes his glass of wine, as we do. But to say that he uses liquor too freely. is, I am sure, a mistake."

"Some men, as you know, doctor, cannot use wine without a

T. S. Arthur

steady increase of the appetite until it finally gets the mastery, and I am afraid Doctor Kline is one of them."

"I am greatly astonished to hear you say this," replied Dr. Hillhouse, "and I cannot but hold you mistaken."

"Have you ever met him at a public dinner, at the club or at a private entertainment where there was plenty of wine?"

"Oh yes."

"And observed no unusual exhilaration?"

Dr. Hillhouse became reflective. Now that his attention was called to the matter, some doubts began to intrude themselves.

"We cannot always judge the common life by what we see on convivial occasions," he made answer. "One may take wine freely with his friends and be as abstemious as an anchorite during business-or profession-hours."

"Not at all probable," replied Mr. Carlton, "and not good in my observation. The appetite that leads a man into drinking more when among friends than his brain will carry steadily is not likely to sleep when he is alone. Any over-stimulation, as you know, doctor, leaves in the depressed state that follows a craving for renewed exhilaration. I am very sure that on the morning after one of the occasions to which I have referred Doctor Kline finds himself in no condition for the work of a delicate surgical operation until he has steadied his relaxed nerves with more than a single glass."

He paused for a moment, and then said, with strong emphasis:

"The hand, Doctor Hillhouse, that cuts down into her dear flesh must be steadied by healthy nerves, and not by wine or brandy. No, sir; I will not hear to it. I will not have Doctor Kline. In your hands, and yours alone, I trust my wife in this great extremity."

"That is for you to decide," returned Dr. Hillhouse. "I felt it to be only right to give you an opportunity to avail of Doctor Kline's acknowledged skill. I am sure you can do so safely."

But Mr. Carlton was very emphatic in his rejection of Dr. Kline.

"I may be a little peculiar," he said, "but do you know I never trust any important interest with a man who drinks habitually? —one of your temperate drinkers, I mean, who can take his three or four glasses of wine at dinner, or twice that number, during an evening while playing at whist, but who never debases himself by so low a thing as intoxication."

"Are not you a little peculiar, or, I might say, over-nice, in this?" remarked Doctor Hillhouse.

"No, I am only prudent." Let me give you a fact in my own experience. I had a law-suit several years ago involving many thousands of dollars. My case was good, but some nice points of law were involved, and I needed for success the best talent the bar afforded. A Mr. B——, I will call him, stood very high in the profession, and I chose him for my counsel. He was a man of fine social qualities, and admirable for his after-dinner speeches. You always met him on public occasions. He was one of your good temperate drinkers and not afraid of a glass of wine, or even brandy, and rarely, if ever, refused a friend who asked him to drink.

"He was not an intemperate man, of course." No one dreamed of setting him over among that banned and rejected class of men whom few trust, and against whom all are on guard. He held his place of honor and confidence side by side with the most trusted men in his profession. As a lawyer, interests of vast magnitude were often in his hands, and largely depended on his legal sagacity, clearness of thought and sleepless vigilance. He was usually successful in his cases.

"I felt my cause safe in his hands—that is, as safe as human

T. S. Arthur

care and foresight could make it." But to my surprise and disappointment, his management of the case on the day of trial was faulty and blind. I had gone over all the points with him carefully, and he had seemed to hold them with a masterly hand. He was entirely confident of success, and so was I. But now he seemed to lose his grasp on the best points in the case, and to bring forward his evidence in a way that, in my view, damaged instead of making our side strong. Still, I forced myself to think that he knew best what to do, and that the meaning of his peculiar tactics should soon become apparent. I noticed, as the trial went on, a bearing of the opposing counsel toward Mr. B—that appeared unusual. He seemed bent on annoying him with little side issues and captious objections, not so much showing a disposition to meet him squarely, upon the simple and clearly defined elements of the case, as to draw him away from them and keep them as far out of sight as possible.

"In this he was successful. Mr. B—seemed in his hands more like a bewildered child than a strong, clear-seeing man." When, after all the evidence was in, the arguments on both sides were submitted to the jury, I saw with alarm that Mr. B—had failed signally. His summing up was weak and disjointed, and he did not urge with force and clearness the vital points in the case on which all our hopes depended. The contrast of his closing argument with that of the other side was very great, and I knew when the jury retired from the courtroom that all was lost, and so it proved.

"It was clear to me that I had mistaken my man—that Mr. B—'s reputation was higher than his ability." He was greatly chagrined at the result, and urged me to take an appeal, saying he was confident we could get a reversal of the decision.

"While yet undecided as to whether I would appeal or not," a friend who had been almost as much surprised and disappointed at the result of the trial as I was came to me in considerable excitement of manner, and said:

"I heard something this morning that will surprise you, I think, as much as it has surprised me. Has it never occurred to you that there was something strange about Mr. B——on the day your case was tried?"

"'Yes,' I replied, 'it has often occurred to me; and the more I think about it, the more dissatisfied am with his management of my case. He is urging me to appeal; but should I do so, I have pretty well made up my mind to have other counsel.'"

"'That I should advise by all means,' returned my friend."

"'The thought has come once or twice,' said I, 'that there might have been false play in the case.'"

"'There has been,' returned my friend."

"What!' I exclaimed. 'False play? No, no, I will not believe so base a thing of Mr. B——.'"

"'I do not mean false play on his part,' replied my friend. 'Far be it from me to suggest a thought against his integrity of character. No, no! I believe him to be a man of honor. The false play, if there has been any, has been against him.'"

"'Against him?' I could but respond, with increasing surprise. Then a suspicion of the truth flashed into my mind."

"'He had been drinking too much that morning,' said my friend. 'That was the meaning of his strange and defective management of the case, and of his confusion of ideas when he made his closing argument to the jury.'"

"It was clear to me now, and I wondered that I had not thought of it before. 'But,' I asked, 'what has this to do with foul play? You don't mean to intimate that his liquor was drugged?'"

"'No. The liquor was all right, so far as that goes,' he replied."

T. S. Arthur

The story I heard was this. It came to me in rather a curious way. I was in the reading-room at the League this morning looking over a city paper, when I happened to hear your name spoken by one of two gentlemen who sat a little behind me talking in a confidential way, but in a louder key than they imagined. I could not help hearing what they said. After the mention of your name I listened with close attention, and found that they were talking about the law-suit, and about Mr. B—in connection therewith. "It was a sharp game," one of them said. "How was it done?" inquired the other.

"'I partially held my breath,' continued my friend, 'so as not to lose a word. "Neatly enough," was the reply. "You see our friend the lawyer can't refuse a drink. He's got a strong head, and can take twice as much as the next man without showing it. A single glass makes no impression on him, unless it be to sharpen him up. So a plan was laid to get half a dozen glasses aboard, more or less, before court opened on the morning the case of Walker vs. Carlton was to be called. But not willing to trust to this, we had a wine-supper for his special benefit on the night before, so as to break his nerves a little and make him thirsty next morning. Well, you see, the thing worked, and B—drank his bottle or two, and went to bed pretty mellow. Of course he must tone up in the morning before leaving home, and so come out all right. He would tone up a little more on his way to his office, and then be all ready for business and bright as a new dollar. This would spoil all. So five of us arranged to meet him at as many different points on his way down town and ask him to drink. The thing worked like a charm. We got six glasses into him before he reached his office. I saw as soon as he came into court that it was a gone case for Carlton. B—had lost his head. And so it proved. We had an easy victory."'

"I took the case out of B—'s hands," said Mr. Carlton, "and gained it in a higher court, the costs of both trials falling upon the other side. Since that time, Dr. Hillhouse, I have had some new views on the subject of moderate drinking, as it is called."

"What are they" asked the doctor.

"An experience like this set me to thinking. If, I said to myself, a man uses wine, beer or spirits habitually, is there no danger that at some time when great interests, or even life itself, may be at stake, a glass too much may obscure his clear intellect and make him the instrument of loss or disaster? I pursued the subject, and as I did so was led to this conclusion—that society really suffers more, from what is called moderate drinking than it does from out-and-out drunkenness."

"Few will agree with you in that conclusion," returned Doctor Hillhouse.

"On the contrary," replied Mr. Carlton, "I think that most people, after looking at the subject from the right standpoint, will see it as I do."

"Men who take a glass of wine at dinner and drink with a friend occasionally," remarked Doctor Hillhouse are not given to idleness, waste of property and abuse and neglect of their families, as we find to be the case with common drunkards. They don't fill our prisons and almshouses. Their wives and children do not go to swell the great army of beggars, paupers and criminals. I fear, my friend, that you are looking through the wrong end of your glass."

"No; my glass is all right." The number of drunken men and women in the land is small compared to the number who drink moderately, and very few of them are to be found in places of trust or responsibility. As soon as a man is known to be a drunkard society puts a mark on him and sets him aside. If he is a physician, health and life are no longer entrusted to his care; if a lawyer, no man will give an important case into his hands. A ship-owner will not trust him with his vessel, though a more skilled navigator cannot be found; and he may be the best engineer in the land, yet will no railroad or steam-ship company trust him with life and property. So everywhere the drunkard is ignored. Society will not trust him, and he is

T. S. Arthur

limited in his power to do harm.

"Not so with your moderate drinkers." They fill our highest places and we commit to their care our best and dearest interests. We put the drunkard aside because we know he cannot be trusted, and give to moderate drinkers, a sad percentage of whom are on the way to drunkenness, our unwavering confidence. They sail our ships, they drive our engines, they make and execute our laws, they take our lives in their hands as doctors and surgeons; we trust them to defend or maintain our legal rights, we confide to them our interests in hundreds of different ways that we would never dream of confiding to men who were regarded as intemperate. Is it not fair to conclude, knowing as we do how a glass of wine too much will confuse the brain and obscure the judgment, that society in trusting its great army of moderate drinkers is suffering loss far beyond anything we imagine? A doctor loses his patient, a lawyer his case, an engineer wrecks his ship or train, an agent hurts his principal by a loose or bad bargain, and all because the head had lost for a brief space its normal clearness.

"Men hurt themselves through moderate drinking in thousands of ways," continued Mr. Carlton. "We have but to think for a moment to see this. Many a fatal document has been signed, many a disastrous contract made, many a ruinous bargain consummated, which but for the glass of wine taken at the wrong moment would have been rejected. Men under the excitement of drink often enter into the unwise schemes of designing men only to lose heavily, and sometimes to encounter ruin. The gambler entices his victim to drink, while he keeps his own head clear. He knows the confusing quality of wine."

"You make out rather a strong case," said Doctor Hillhouse.

"Too strong, do you think?"

"Perhaps not. Looking at the thing through your eyes, Mr.

Carlton, moderate drinking is an evil of great magnitude."

"It is assuredly, and far greater, as I have said, than is generally supposed." The children of this world are very wise, and some of them, I am sorry to add, very unscrupulous in gaining their ends. They know the power of all the agencies that are around them, and do not scruple to make use of whatever comes to their hand. Three or four capitalists are invited to meet at a gentleman's house to consider some proposition he has to lay before them. They are liberally supplied with wine, and drink without a lurking suspicion of what the service of good wine means. They see in it only the common hospitality of the day, and fail to notice that one or two of the company never empty their glasses. On the next day these men will most likely feel some doubt as to the prudence of certain large subscriptions made on the previous afternoon or evening, and wonder how they could have been so infatuated as to put money into a scheme that promised little beyond a permanent investment.

"If," added Mr. Carlton, "we could come at any proximate estimate of the loss which falls upon society in consequence of the moderate use of intoxicating drinks, we would find that it exceeded a hundred—nay, a thousand—fold that of the losses sustained through drunkenness. Against the latter society is all the while seeking to guard itself, against the former it has little or no protection—does not, in fact, comprehend the magnitude of its power for evil. But I have wearied you with my talk, and forgotten for the time being the anxiety that lies so near my heart. No, doctor, I will not trust the hand of Doctor Kline, skillful as it may be, to do this work; for I cannot be sure that a glass too much may not have been taken to steady the nerves a night's excess of wine may have left unstrung."

Doctor Hillhouse sat with closely knit brows for some time after Mr. Carlton ceased speaking.

"There is matter for grave consideration in what you have said," he remarked, at length, "though I apprehend your fears

T. S. Arthur

in regard to Doctor Kline are more conjectural than real."

"I hope so," returned Mr. Carlton, "but as a prudent man I will not take needless risk in the face of danger. If an operation cannot be avoided, I will trust that precious life to none but you."

CHAPTER XVII

WE have seen how it was with Doctor Hillhouse on the morning of the day fixed for the operation. The very danger that Mr. Carlton sought to avert in his rejection of Doctor Kline was at his door. Not having attended the party at Mr. and Mrs. Birtwell's, he did not know that Doctor Hillhouse had, with most of the company, indulged freely in wine. If a suspicion of the truth had come to him, he would have refused to let the operation proceed. But like a passenger in some swiftly-moving car who has faith in the clear head and steady hand of the engineer, his confidence in Doctor Hillhouse gave him a feeling of security.

But far from this condition of faith in himself was the eminent surgeon in whom he was reposing his confidence. He had, alas! tarried too long at the feast of wine and fat things dispensed by Mr. Birtwell, and in his effort to restore the relaxed tension of his nerves by stimulation had sent too sudden an impulse to his brain, and roused it to morbid action. His coffee failed to soothe the unquiet nerves, his stomach turned from the food on which he had depended for a restoration of the equipoise which the night's excesses had destroyed. The dangerous condition of Mrs. Ridley and his forced visit to that lady in the early morning, when he should have been free from all unusual effort and excitement, but added to his disturbance.

Doctor Hillhouse knew all about the previous habits of Mr. Ridley, and was much interested in his case. He had seen with hope and pleasure the steadiness with which he was leading his

T. S. Arthur

new life, and was beginning to have strong faith in his future. But when he met him on that morning, he knew by unerring signs that the evening at Mr. Birtwell's had been to him one of debauch instead of restrained conviviality. The extremity of his wife's condition, and his almost insane appeals that he would hold her back from death, shocked still further the doctor's already quivering nerves.

The imminent peril in which Doctor Hillhouse found Mrs. Ridley determined him to call in another physician for consultation. As twelve o'clock on that day had been fixed for the operation on Mrs. Carlton, it was absolutely necessary to get his mind as free as possible from all causes of anxiety or excitement, and the best thing in this extremity was to get his patient into the hands of a brother in the profession who could relieve him temporarily from *all* responsibility, and watch the case with all needed care in its swiftly approaching crisis. So he sent Doctor Angier, immediately on his return from his visit to Mrs. Ridley, with a request to Doctor Ainsworth, a physician of standing and experience, to meet him in consultation at ten o'clock.

Precisely at ten the physicians arrived at the house of Mr. Ridley, and were admitted by that gentleman, whose pale, haggard, frightened face told of his anguish and alarm. They asked him no questions, and he preceded them in silence to the chamber of his sick wife. It needed no second glance at their patient to tell the two doctors that she was in great extremity. Her pinched face was ashen in color and damp with a cold sweat, and her eyes, no longer wild and restless, looked piteous and anxious, as of one in dreadful suffering who pleaded mutely for help. An examination of her pulse showed the beat to be frequent and feeble, and on the slightest movement she gave signs of pain. Her respiration was short and very rapid. Mr. Ridley was present, and standing in a position that enabled him to observe the faces of the two doctors as they proceeded with their examination. Hope died as he saw the significant changes that passed over them. When they left the sick-chamber, he left also, and walked the floor anxiously while they sat in consultation, talking together in low tones. Now and then he caught words, such as "peritoneum," "lesion," "perforation," etc., the fatal meaning of which he more than half guessed.

They were still in consultation when a sudden cry broke from the lips of Mrs. Ridley; and rising hastily, they went back to her chamber. Her face was distorted and her body writhing with pain.

Doctor Hillhouse wrote a prescription hastily, saying to Mr. Ridley as he gave it to him: "Opium, and get it as quickly as you can."

The sick woman had scarcely a moment's freedom from pain of a most excruciating character during the ten minutes that elapsed before her husband's return. The quantity of opium administered was large, and its effects soon apparent in a gradual breaking down of the pains, which had been almost spasmodic in their character.

When Doctor Hillhouse went away, leaving Doctor Ainsworth in charge of his patient, she was sinking: into a quiet sleep. On arriving at his office he found Mr. Wilmer Voss impatiently awaiting his return.

"Doctor," said this gentleman, starting up on seeing him and showing considerable agitation, "you must come to my wife immediately."

Doctor Hillhouse felt stunned for an instant. He drew his hand tightly against his forehead, that was heavy with its dull, half-stupefying pain which, spite of what he could do, still held on. All his nerves were unstrung.

"How is she?" he asked, with the manner of one who had received an unwelcome message. His hand was still held against his forehead.

T. S. Arthur

"She broke all down a little while ago, and now lies moaning and shivering. Oh, doctor, come right away! You know how weak she is. This dreadful suspense will kill her, I'm afraid."

Have you no word of Archie yet?" asked Doctor Hillhouse as he dropped the hand he had been holding against his forehead and temples.

"None! So far, we are without a sign."

"What are you doing?"

"Everything that can be thought of. More than twenty of our friends, in concert with the police, are at work in all conceivable ways to get trace of him, but from the moment he left Mr. Birtwell's he dropped out of sight as completely as if the sea had gone over him. Up to this time not the smallest clue to this dreadful mystery has been found. But come, doctor. Every moment is precious."

Doctor Hillhouse drew out his watch. It was now nearly half-past ten o'clock. His manner was nervous, verging on to excitement. In almost any other case he would have said that it was not possible for him to go. But the exigency and the peculiarly distressing circumstances attending upon this made it next to impossible for him to refuse.

"At twelve o'clock, Mr. Voss, I have a delicate and difficult operation to perform, and I have too short a time now for the preparation I need. I am sure you can rely fully on my assistant, Doctor Angler."

"No, no!" replied Mr. Voss, waving his hand almost impatiently. "I do not want Doctor Angier. You must see Mrs. Voss yourself."

He was imperative, almost angry. What was the delicate and difficult operation to him? What was anything or anybody that stood in the way of succor for his imperiled wife? He could not pause to think of others' needs or danger.

Doctor Hillhouse had to decide quickly, and his decision was on the side where pressure was strongest. He could not deny Mr. Voss.

He found the poor distressed mother in a condition of utter prostration. For a little while after coming out of the swoon into which her first wild fears had thrown her, she had been able to maintain a tolerably calm exterior. But the very effort to do this was a draught on her strength, and in a few hours, under the continued suspense of waiting and hearing nothing from her boy, the overstrained nerves broke down again, and she sunk into a condition of half-conscious suffering that was painful to see.

For such conditions medicine can do but little. All that Doctor Hillhouse ventured to prescribe was a quieting draught. It was after eleven o'clock when he got back to his office, where he found Mr. Ridley waiting for him with a note from Doctor Ainsworth.

"Come for just a single moment," the note said. "There are marked changes in her condition."

"I cannot! It is impossible!" exclaimed Doctor Hillhouse, with an excitement of manner he could not repress. Doctor Ainsworth can do all that it is in the power of medical skill to accomplish. It will not help her for me to go again now, and another life is in my hands. I am sorry, Mr. Ridley, but I cannot see your wife again until this afternoon.

"Oh, doctor, doctor, don't say that!" cried the poor, distressed husband, clasping his hands and looking at Doctor Hillhouse with a pale, imploring face. "Just for single moment, doctor. Postpone your operation. Ten minutes, or even an hour, can be of no consequence. But life or death may depend on your seeing my wife at once. Come, doctor! Come, for God's sake!"

T. S. Arthur

Doctor Hillhouse looked at his watch again, stood in a bewildered, uncertain way for a few moments, and then turned quickly toward the door and went out, Mr. Ridley following.

"Get in," he said, waving his hand in the direction of his carriage, which still remained in front of his office. Mr. Ridley obeyed. Doctor Hillhouse gave the driver a hurried direction, and sprang in after him. They rode in silence for the whole distance to Mr. Ridley's dwelling.

One glance at the face of the sick woman was enough to show Doctor Hillhouse that she was beyond the reach of professional skill. Her disease, as he had before seen, had taken on its worst form, and was running its fatal course with a malignant impetuosity it was impossible to arrest. The wild fever of anxiety occasioned by her husband's absence during that dreadful night, the cold to which, in her delirium of fear, she had exposed herself, the great shock her delicate organism had sustained at a time when even the slightest disturbance might lead to serious consequences,—all these causes combined had so broken down her vitality and poisoned her blood that nature had no force strong enough to rally against the enemies of her life.

A groan that sounded like a wail of desperation broke from Mr. Ridley's lips as he came in with the doctor and looked at the death-stricken countenance of his wife. The two physicians gazed at each other with ominous faces, and stood silent and helpless at the bedside.

When Doctor Hillhouse hurried away ten minutes afterward he knew that he had looked for the last time upon his patient. Mr. Ridley did not attempt to detain him. Hope had expired, and he sat bowed and crushed, wishing that he could die.

The large quantity of opium which had been taken by Mrs. Ridley held all her outward senses locked, and she passed away, soon after Doctor Hillhouse retired, without giving her husband a parting word or even a sign of recognition.

CHAPTER XVIII

WHEN Doctor Hillhouse arrived at his office, it lacked only a quarter of an hour to twelve, the time fixed for the operation on Mrs. Carlton. He found Doctor Kline and Doctor Angier, who were to assist him, both awaiting his return.

"I thought twelve o'clock the hour?" said Doctor Kline as he came in hurriedly.

"So it is. But everything has seemed to work adversely this morning. Mr. Ridley's wife is extremely ill—dying, in fact—and I have had to see her too or three times. Other calls have been imperative, and here I am within a quarter of an hour of the time fixed for a most delicate operation, and my preparations not half completed."

Doctor Kline regarded him for a few moments, and then said:

"This is unfortunate, doctor, and I would advise a postponement until to-morrow. You should have had a morning free from anything but unimportant calls."

"Oh no. I cannot think of a postponement," Doctor Hillhouse replied. "All the arrangements have been made at Mr. Carlton's, and my patient is ready. To put it off for a single day might cause a reaction in her feelings and produce an unfavorable condition. It will have to be done to-day."

"You must not think of keeping your appointment to the

T. S. Arthur

hour," said Doctor Kline, glancing at his watch. "Indeed, that would now be impossible. Doctor Angier had better go and say that we will be there within half an hour. Don't hurry yourself in the slightest degree. Take all the time you need to make yourself ready. I will remain and assist you as best I can."

A clear-seeing and controlling mind was just what Doctor Hillhouse needed at that moment. He saw the value of Doctor Kline's suggestion, and promptly accepted it. Doctor Angier was despatched to the residence of Mr. Carlton to advise that gentleman of the brief delay and to make needed preparations for the work that was to be done.

The very necessity felt by Doctor Hillhouse for a speedy repression of the excitement from which he was suffering helped to increase the disturbance, and it was only after he had used a stimulant stronger than he wished to take that he found his nerves becoming quiet and the hand on whose steadiness so much depended growing firm.

At half-past twelve Doctor Hillhouse, in company with Doctor Kline, arrived at Mr. Carlton's. The white face and scared look of the female servant who admitted them showed how strongly fear and sympathy were at work in the house. She directed them to the room which had been set apart for their use. In the hall above Mr. Carlton met them, and returned with a trembling hand and silent pressure the salutation of the two physicians, who passed into a chamber next to the one occupied by their patient and quickly began the work of making everything ready. Acting from previous concert, they drew the table which had been provided into the best light afforded by the room, and then arranged instruments, bandages and all things needed for the work to be done.

When all these preparations were completed, notice was given to Mrs. Carlton, who immediately entered from the adjoining room. She was a beautiful woman, in the very prime of life, and never had she appeared more beautiful than now. Her strong will had mastered fear, strength, courage and resignation looked out from her clear eyes and rested on her firm lips. She smiled, but did not speak. Doctor Hillhouse took her by the hand and led her to the table on which she was to lie during the operation, saying, as he did so, "It will be over in a few minutes, and you will not feel it as much as the scratch of a pin."

She laid herself down without a moment's hesitation, and as she did so Doctor Angier, according to previous arrangement, presented a sponge saturated with ether to her nostrils, and in two minutes complete anaesthesis was produced. On the instant this took place Doctor Hillhouse made an incision and cut down quickly to the tumor. His hand was steady, and he seemed to be in perfect command of himself. The stimulants he had taken as a last resort were still active on brain and nerves. On reaching the tumor he found it, as he had feared, much larger than its surface presentation indicated. It was a hard, fibrous substance, and deeply seated among the veins, arteries and muscles of the neck. The surgeon's hand retained its firmness; there was a concentration of thought and purpose that gave science and skill their best results. It took over twenty minutes to dissect the tumor away from all the delicate organs upon which it had laid its grasp, and nearly half as long a time to stanch the flow of blood from the many small arteries which had been severed during the operation. One of these, larger than the rest, eluded for a time the efforts of Doctor Hillhouse at ligation, and he felt uncertain about it even after he had stopped the effusion of blood. In fact, his hand had become unsteady and his brain slightly confused. The active stimulant taken half an hour before was losing its effect and his nerves beginning to give way. He was no longer master of the situation, and the last and, as it proved, the most vital thing in the whole operation was done imperfectly.

At the end of thirty-five minutes the patient, still under the influence of ether was carried back to her chamber and laid back upon her bed, quiet as a sleeping infant.

"It is all over," said Doctor Hillhouse as the eyes of Mrs.

T. S. Arthur

Carlton unclosed a little while afterward and she looked up into his face. He was no longer the impassive surgeon, but the tender and sympathizing friend. His voice was flooded with feeling and moisture dimmed his eyes.

What a look of sweet thankfulness came into the face of Mrs. Carlton as she whispered, "And I knew nothing of it!" Then, shutting her eyes and speaking to herself, she said, "It is wonderful. Thank God, thank God!"

It was almost impossible to, restrain Mr. Carlton, so excessive was his delight when the long agony of suspense was over. Doctor Hillhouse had to grasp his arm tightly and hold him back as he stooped down over his wife. In the blindness of his great joy he would have lifted her in his arms.

"Perfect quiet," said the doctor. "There must be nothing to give her heart a quicker pulsation. Doctor Angier will remain for half an hour to see that all goes well."

The two surgeons then retired, Doctor Kline accompanying Doctor Hillhouse to his office. The latter was silent all the way. The strain over and the alcoholic stimulation gone, mind and body had alike lost their abnormal tension.

"I must congratulate you, doctor," said the friendly surgeon who had assisted in the operation. "It was even more difficult than I had imagined. I never saw a case in which the sheathings of the internal jugular vein and carotid artery were so completely involved. The tumor had made its ugly adhesion all around them. I almost held my breath when the blood from a severed artery spurted over your scalpel and hid from sight the keen edge that was cutting around the internal jugular. A false movement of the hand at that instant might have been fatal."

"Yes; and but for the clearness of that inner sight which, in great exigencies, so often supplements the failing natural vision, all might have been lost," replied Doctor Hillhouse, betraying in his unsteady voice the great reaction from which he was suffering. "If I had known," he added, "that the tumor was so large and its adhesion so extensive, I would not have operated to-day. In fact, I was in no condition for the performance of any operation. I committed a great indiscretion in going to Mr. Birtwell's last night. Late suppers and wine do not leave one's nerves in the best condition, as you and I know very well, doctor; and as a preparation for work such as we have had on hand to-day nothing could be worse."

"Didn't I hear something about the disappearance of a young man who left Mr. Birtwell's at a late hour?" asked Doctor Kline.

"Nothing has been heard of the son of Wilmer Voss since he went away from Mr. Birtwell's about one o'clock," replied Doctor Hillhouse, "and his family are in great distress about him. Mrs. Voss, who is one of my patients, is in very delicate health and when I saw her at eleven o'clock to-day was lying in a critical condition."

"There is something singular about that party at Mr. and Mrs. Birtwell's, added Doctor Hillhouse, after a pause. I hardly know what to make of it."

"Singular in what respect?" asked the other.

The face of Doctor Hillhouse grew more serious:

"You know Mr. Ridley, the lawyer? He was in Congress a few years ago."

"Yes."

"He was very intemperate at one time, and fell so low that even his party rejected him. He then reformed and came to this city, where he entered upon the practice of his profession, and has been for a year or two advancing rapidly. I attended his wife a few days ago, and saw her yesterday afternoon, when she was continuing to do well. There were some indications of excitement about her, though whether from mental or physical causes I could not tell, but nothing to awaken concern. This morning I found her in a most critical condition. Puerperal fever had set in, with evident extensive peritoneal involvement. The case was malignant, all the abdominal viscera being more or less affected. I learned from the nurse that Mr. Ridley was away all night, and that Mrs. Ridley, who was restless and feverish through the evening, became agitated and slightly delirious after twelve o'clock, talking about and calling for her husband, whom she imagined dying in the storm, that now raged with dreadful violence. No help could be had all night; and when we saw her this morning, it was too late for medicine to control the fatal disease which was running its course with almost unprecedented rapidity. She was dying when I saw her at half-past eleven this morning. This case and that of Mrs. Voss were the ones that drew so largely on my time this morning, and helped to disturb me so much, and both were in consequence of Mr. Birtwell's party."

"They might have an indirect connection with the party," returned Doctor Kline, "but can hardly be called legitimate consequences."

"They are legitimate consequences of the free wine and brandy dispensed at Mr. Birtwell's," said Doctor Hillhouse. "Tempted by its sparkle and flavor, Archie Voss, as pure and promising a young man as you will find in the city, was lured on until he had taken more than his brain would bear. In this state he went out at midnight alone in a blinding storm and lost his way—how or where is not yet known. He may have been set upon and robbed and murdered in his helpless condition, or he may have fallen into a pit where he lies buried beneath the snow, or he may have wandered in his blind bewilderment to the river and gone down under its chilling waters.

"Mr. Ridley, with his old appetite not dead, but only half asleep and lying in wait for an opportunity, goes also to Mr. Birtwell's, and the sparkle and flavor of wine and the invitations that are pressed upon him from all sides prove too much for his good resolutions. He tastes and falls. He goes in his right mind, and comes away so much intoxicated that he cannot find his way home. How he reached there at last I do not know—he must have been in some station-house until daylight; but when I saw him, his pitiable suffering and alarmed face made my heart ache. He had killed his wife! He, or the wine he found at Mr. Birtwell's? Which?"

Doctor Hillhouse was nervous and excited, using stronger language than was his wont.

"And I," he added, before Doctor Kline could respond—"I went to the party also, and the sparkle and flavor of wine and spirit of conviviality that pervaded the company lured me also—not weak like Archie, nor with a shattered self-control like Mr. Ridley—to drink far beyond the bounds of prudence, as my nervous condition to-day too surely indicates. A kind of fatality seems to have attended this party."

The doctor gave a little shiver, which was observed by Doctor Kline.

"Not a nervous chill?" said the latter, manifesting concern.

"No; a moral chill, if I may use such a term," replied Doctor Hillhouse—"a shudder at the thought of what might have been as one of the consequences of Mr. Birtwell's liberal dispensation of wine."

"The strain of the morning's work has been too much for you, doctor, and given your mind an unhealthy activity," said his companion. You want rest and time for recuperation."

"It would have been nothing except for the baleful effects of that party," answered the doctor, whose thought could not dissever itself from the unhappy consequences which had followed the carousal (is the word too strong?) at Mr. Birtwell's. "If I had not been betrayed into drinking wine

T. S. Arthur

enough to disturb seriously my nervous system and leave it weak and uncertain to-day, if Mr. Ridley had not been tempted to his fall, if poor Archie Voss had been at home last night instead of in the private drinking-saloon of one of our most respected citizens, do you think that hand," holding up his right hand as he spoke, "would have lost for a moment its cunning to-day and put in jeopardy a precious life?"

The doctor rose from his chair in much excitement and walked nervously about the room.

"It did not lose its cunning," said Doctor Kline, in a calm but emphatic voice. I watched you from the moment of the first incision until the last artery was tied, and a truer hand I never saw."

"Thank God that the stimulus which I had to substitute for nervous power held out as long as it did. If it had failed a few moments sooner, I might have—"

Doctor Hillhouse checked himself and gave another little shudder.

"Do you know, doctor," he said, after a pause speaking in a low, half-confidential tone and with great seriousness of manner, "when I severed that small artery as I was cutting close to the internal jugular vein and the jet of blood hid both the knife-points and the surrounding tissues, that for an instant I was in mental darkness and that I did not know whether I should cut to the right or to the left? If in that moment of darkness I had cut to the right, my instrument would have penetrated the jugular vein."

It was several moments before either of the surgeons spoke again. There was a look something like fear in both their faces.

"It is the last time," said Doctor Hillhouse, breaking at length the silence and speaking with unwonted emphasis, "that a drop of wine or brandy shall pass my lips within forty-eight hours of any operation."

"I am not so sure that you will help as much as hurt by this abstinence," replied Doctor Kline. "If you are in the habit of using wine daily, I should say keep to your regular quantity. Any change will be a disturbance and break the fine nervous tension that is required. It is easy to account for your condition to-day. If you had taken only your one or two or three glasses yesterday as the case may be, and kept away from the excitement and—pardon me excesses of last night—anything beyond the ordinary rule in these things is an excess, you know—there would have been no failure of the nerves at a critical juncture."

"Is not the mind clearer and the nerves steadier when sustained by healthy nutrition than when toned up by stimulants?" asked Doctor Hillhouse.

"If stimulants have never been taken, yes. But you know that we all use stimulants in one form or another, and to suddenly remove them is to leave the nerves partially unstrung."

"Which brings us face to face with the question whether or not alcoholic stimulants are hurtful to the delicate and wonderfully complicated machinery of the human body. I say alcoholic, for we know that all the stimulation we get from wine or beer comes from the presence of alcohol."

While Doctor Hillhouse was speaking, the office bell rang violently. As soon as the door was opened a man came in hurriedly and handed him, a slip of paper on which were written these few words:

"An artery has commenced bleeding. Come quickly! ANGIER"

Doctor Hillhouse started to his feet and gave a quick order for his carriage. As it drove up to the office-door soon after, he sprang in, accompanied by Doctor Kline. He had left his case of instruments at the house with Doctor Angier.

Not a word was spoken by either of the two men as they were whirled along over the snow, the wheels of the carriage giving back only a sharp crisping sound, but their faces were very sober.

Mr. Carlton met them, looking greatly alarmed.

"Oh, doctor," he exclaimed as he caught the hand of Doctor Hillhouse, almost crushing it in his grasp, "I am so glad you are here. I was afraid she might bleed to death."

"No danger of that," replied Doctor Hillhouse, trying to look assured and to speak with confidence. "It is only the giving way of some small artery which will have to be tied again."

On reaching his patient, Doctor Hillhouse found that one of the small arteries he had been compelled to sever in his work of cutting the tumor away from the surrounding parts was bleeding freely. Half a dozen handkerchiefs and napkins had already been saturated with blood; and as it still came freely, nothing was left but to reopen the wound and religate the artery.

Ether was promptly given, and as soon as the patient was fairly under its influence the bandages were removed and the sutures by which the wound had been drawn together cut. The cavity left by the tumor was, of course, full of blood. This was taken out with sponges, when at the lower part of the orifice a thin jet of blood was visible. The surrounding parts had swollen, thus embedding the mouth of the artery so deeply that it could not be recovered without again using the knife. What followed will be best understood if given in the doctor's own words in a relation of the circumstances made by him a few years afterward.

"As you will see," he said, "I was in the worst possible condition for an emergency like this. I had used no stimulus since returning from Mr. Carlton's though just going to order wine when the summons from Doctor Angier came. If I had taken a glass or two, it would have been better, but the imperative nature of the summons disconcerted me. I was just in the condition to be disturbed and confused. I remembered when too late the grave omission, and had partly resolved to ask Mr. Carlton for a glass of wine before proceeding to reopen the wound and search for the bleeding artery. But a too vivid recollection of my recent conversation with him about Doctor Kline prevented my doing so.

"I felt my hand tremble as I removed the bandages and opened the deep cavity left by the displaced tumor. After the blood with which it was filled had been removed, I saw at the deepest part of the cavity the point from which the blood was flowing, and made an effort to recover the artery, which, owing to the uncertainty of hand which had followed the loss of stimulation, I had tied imperfectly. But it was soon apparent that the parts had swollen, and that I should have to cut deeper in order to get possession of the artery, which lay in close contact with the internal jugular vein. Doctor Kline was holding the head and shoulders of the patient in such a way as to give tension to all the vessels of the neck, while my assistant held open the lips of the wound, so that I could see well into the cavity."

"My hand did not recover its steadiness. As I began cutting down to find the artery I seemed suddenly to be smitten with blindness and to lose a clear perception of what I was doing. It seemed as if some malignant spirit had for the moment got possession of me, coming in through the disorder wrought in my nervous system by over stimulation, and used the hand I could no longer see to guide the instrument I was holding, for death instead of life. I remember now that a sudden impulse seemed given to my arm as if some one had struck it a blow. Then a sound which it had never before been my misfortune to hear—and I pray God I may never hear it again—startled me to an agonized sense of the disaster I had wrought. Too well I knew the meaning of the lapping, hissing, sucking noise

T. S. Arthur

that instantly smote our ears. I had made a deep cut across the jugular vein, the wound gaping widely in consequence of the tension given to the vein by the position of the patient's head. A large quantity of air rushed in instantly."

"An exclamation of alarm from Doctor Kline, as he changed the position of the patient's neck in order to force the lips of the wound together and stop the fatal influx of air, roused me from a momentary stupor, and I came back into complete self-possession. The fearful exigency of the moment gave to nerve and brain all the stimulus they required. Already there was a struggle for breath, and the face of Mrs. Carlton, which had been slightly suffused with color, became pale and distressed. Sufficient air had entered to change the condition of the blood in the right cavities of the heart, and prevent its free transmission to the lungs. We could hear a churning sound occasioned by the blood and air being whipped together in the heart, and on applying the hand to the chest could feel a strange thrilling or rasping sensation."

"The most eminent surgeons differ in regard to the best treatment in cases like this, which are of very rare occurrence; to save life the promptest action is required. So large an opening as I had unhappily made in this vein could not be quickly closed, and with each inspiration of the patient more. air was sucked in, so that the blood in the right cavities of the heart soon became beaten into a spumous froth that could not be forced except in small quantities through the pulmonary vessels into the lungs."

"The effect of a diminished supply of blood to the brain and nervous centres quickly became apparent in threatened syncope. Our only hope lay in closing the wound so completely that no more air could enter, and then removing from the heart and capillaries of the lungs the air already received, and now hindering the flow of blood to the brain. One mode of treatment recommended by French surgeons consists in introducing the pipe of a catheter through the wound, if in the right jugular vein—or if not, through an opening made for the purpose in that vein—and the withdrawal of the air from the right auricle of the heart by suction."

"Doctor Kline favored this treatment, but I knew that it would be fatal. Any reopening of the wound now partially closed in order to introduce a tube, even if my instrument case had contained one of suitable size and length, must necessarily have admitted a large additional quantity of air, and so made death certain."

"Indecision in a case like this is fatal. Nothing but the right thing done with an instant promptness can save the imperiled life. But what was the right thing? No more air must be permitted to enter, and the blood must be unloaded as quickly as possible of the air now obstructing its way to the lungs, so, that the brain might get a fresh supply before it was too late. We succeeded in the first, but not in the last. Too much air had entered, and my patient was beyond the reach of professional aid. She sank rapidly, and in less than an hour from the time my hand, robbed of its skill by wine, failed in its wonted cunning, she lay white and still before me."

T. S. Arthur

CHAPTER XIX

IT was late in the afternoon when Mrs. Voss came out of the deep sleep into which the quieting draught administered by Doctor Hillhouse had thrown her. She awoke from a dream so vivid that she believed it real.

"Oh, Archie, my precious boy!" she exclaimed, starting up and reaching out her hands, a glad light beaming on her countenance.

While her hands were still outstretched the light began to fade, and then died out as suddenly as when a curtain falls. The boy who stood before her in such clear presence had vanished. Her eyes swept about the room, but he was not there. A deadly pallor on her face, a groan on her lips, she fell back shuddering upon the pillow from which she had risen.

Mr. Voss, who was sitting at the bedside, put his arm under her, and lifting her head, drew it against his breast, holding it there tightly, but not speaking. He had no comfort to give, no assuring word to offer. Not a ray of light had yet come in through the veil of mystery that hung so darkly over the fate of their absent boy. Many minutes passed ere the silence was broken. In that time the mother's heart had grown calmer. She was turning, in her weakness and despair, with religious trust, to the only One who was able to sustain her in this great and crushing sorrow.

"He is in God's hands," she said, in a low voice, lifting her head from her husband's breast and looking into his face.

"And he will take care of him," replied Mr. Voss, falling in with her thought.

"Yes, we must trust him. He is present in every place. He knows where Archie is, and how to shield and succor him. O heavenly Father, protect our boy! If in danger, help and save him. And, O Father, give me strength to bear whatever may come."

The mother closed her eyes and laid her head back upon her husband's bosom. The rigidity and distress went out of her face. In this hour of darkness and distress, God, to whom she looked and prayed for strength, came very close to her, and in his nearer presence there is always comfort.

But as the day declined and the shadows off another dreary winter night began to draw their solemn curtains across the sky the mother's heart failed again, and a wild storm of fear and anguish swept over it. Neither policemen nor friends had been able to discover a trace of the missing young man, and advertisements were given out for the papers next morning offering a large reward for his restoration to his friends if living or for the recovery of his body if dead.

The true cause of Archie's disappearance began to be feared by many of his friends. It did not seem possible that he could have dropped so completely out of sight unless on the theory that he had lost his way in the storm and fallen into the river. This suggestion as soon as it came to Mrs. Voss settled into a conviction. Her imagination brooded over the idea and brought the reality before her mind with such a cruel vividness that she almost saw the tragedy enacted, and heard again that cry of "Mother!" which had seemed to mingle with the wild shrieks of the tempest, but which came only to her inner sense.

She dreamed that night a dream which, though it confirmed all this, tranquilized and comforted her. In a vision her boy stood by her bedside and smiled upon her with his old loving smile. He bent over and kissed her with his wonted tenderness; he laid his hand on her forehead with a soft pressure, and she felt the touch thrilling to her heart in sweet and tender impulses.

"It is all well with me," he said; "I shall wait for you, mother."

And then he bent over and kissed her again, the pressure of his lips bringing an unspeakable joy to her heart. With this joy filling and pervading it, she awoke. From that hour Mrs. Voss never doubted for a single moment that her son was dead, nor that he had come to her in a vision of the night. As a Christian woman with whom faith was no mere ideal thing or vague uncertainty, she accepted her great affliction as within the sphere and permission of a good and wise Providence, and submitted herself to the sad dispensation with a patience that surprised her friends.

Months passed, and yet the mystery was unsolved. The large reward offered by Mr. Voss for the recovery of his son's remains kept hundreds of fishermen and others who frequented the river banks and shores of the bay leading down to the ocean on the alert. As the spring opened and the ice began to give way and float, these men examined every inlet, cove and bar where the tide in its ebb and flow might possibly have left the body for which they were in search; and one day, late in the month of March, they found it, three miles away from the city, where it had drifted by the current.

The long-accepted theory of the young man's death was proved by this recovery of his body. No violence was found upon it. The diamond pin had not been taken from his shirt-bosom, nor the gold watch from his pocket. On the dial of his watch the hands, stopping their movement as the chill of the icy water struck the delicate machinery, had recorded the hour of his death—ten minutes to one o'clock.

It was not possible, under the strain of such an affliction and the wear of a suspense that no human heart was able to endure without waste of life, for one in feeble health like Mrs. Voss to hold her own. Friends read in her patient face and quiet mouth, and eyes that had a far-away look, the signs of a coming change that could not be very far off.

After the sad certainty came and the looking and longing and waiting were over, after the solemn services of the church had been said and the cast-off earthly garments of her precious boy hidden away from sight for ever, the mother's hold upon life grew feebler every day. She was slowly drifting out from the shores of time, and no hand was strong enough to hold her back. A sweet patience smoothed away the lines of suffering which months of sorrow and uncertainty had cut in her brow, the grieving curves of her pale lips were softened by tender submission, the far-off look was still in her eyes, but it was no longer fixed and dreary. Her thought went away from herself to others. The heavenly sphere into which she had come through submission to her Father's will and a humble looking to God for help and comfort began to pervade her soul and fill it with that divine self-forgetting which all who come spiritually near to him must feel.

She could not go out and do strong and widely-felt work for humanity, could not lift up the fallen, nor help the weak, nor visit the sick, nor comfort the prisoner, though often her heart yearned to help and strengthen the suffering and the distressed. But few if any could come into the chamber where most of her days were spent without feeling the sphere of her higher and purer life, and many, influenced thereby, went out to do the good works to which she so longed to put her hands. So from the narrow bounds of her chamber went daily a power for good, and many who knew her not were helped or comforted or lifted into purer and better lives because of her patient submission to God and reception of his love into her soul.

It is not surprising that one thought took a deep hold upon her. The real cause of Archie's death was the wine he had taken in the house of her friend. But for that he could never have lost

T. S. Arthur

his way in the streets of his native city, never have stepped from solid ground into the engulfing water.

The lesson of this disaster was clear, and as Mrs. Voss brooded over it, the folly, the wrong—nay, the crime—of those who pour out wine like water for their guests in social entertainments magnified themselves in her thought, and thought found utterance in speech. Few came into her chamber upon whom she did not press a consideration of this great evil, the magnitude of which became greater as her mind dwelt upon it, and very few of these went away without being disturbed by questions not easily answered.

One day one of her attentive friends who had called on her said:

"I heard a sorrowful story yesterday, and can't get it out of my mind."

Before Mrs. Voss could reply a servant came in with a card.

"Oh, Mrs. Birtwell. Ask her to come up."

The visitor saw a slight shadow creep over her face, and knew its meaning. How could she ever hear the name or look into the face of Mrs. Birtwell without thinking of that dreadful night when her boy passed, almost at a single step, from the light and warmth of her beautiful home into the dark and frozen river? It had cost her a hard and painful struggle to so put down and hold in check her feelings as to be able to meet this friend, who had always been very near and dear to her. For a time, and while her distress of mind was so great as almost to endanger reason, she had refused to see Mrs. Birtwell; but as that lady never failed to call at least once a week to ask after her, always sending up her card and waiting for a reply, Mrs. Voss at last yielded, and the friends met again. Mrs. Birtwell would have thrown her arms about her and clasped her in a passion of tears to her heart, but something stronger than a visible barrier held her off, and she felt that she could never get as near to this beloved friend as of old. The interview was tender though reserved, neither making any reference to the sad event that was never a moment absent from their thoughts.

After this Mrs. Birtwell came often, and a measure of the old feeling returned to Mrs. Voss. Still, the card of Mrs. Birtwell whenever it was placed in her hand by a servant never failed to bring a shadow and sometimes a chill to her heart.

In a few moments Mrs. Birtwell entered the room; and after the usual greetings and some passing remarks, Mrs. Voss said, speaking to the lady with whom she had been conversing:

"What were you going to say—about some sorrowful story, I mean?"

The pleasant light which had come into the lady's face on meeting Mrs. Birtwell, faded out. She did not answer immediately, and showed some signs of embarrassment. But Mrs. Voss, not particularly noticing this, pressed her for the story. After a slight pause she said:

"In visiting a friend yesterday I observed a young girl whom I had never seen at the house before." She was about fifteen or sixteen years of age, and had a face of great refinement and much beauty. But I noticed that it had a sad, shy expression. My friend did not introduce her, but said, turning to the girl a few moments after I came in:

"Go up to the nursery, Ethel, and wait until I am disengaged!"

"As the girl left the room I asked, 'Who is that young lady?' remarking at the same time that there was something peculiarly interesting about her."

"'It's a sad case, remarked my friend, her voice falling to a tone of regret and sympathy. 'And I wish I knew just what to do about it.'"

T. S. Arthur

"'Who is the young girl?' I asked repeating my question."

"'The daughter of a Mr. Ridley,' she replied."

Mrs. Birtwell gave a little start, while an expression of pain crossed her face. The lady did not look at her, but she felt the change her mention of Mr. Ridley had produced.

"'What of him?' I asked; not having heard the name before."

"Oh, I thought you knew about him. He's a lawyer, formerly a member of Congress, and a man of brilliant talents. He distinguished himself at Washington, and for a time attracted much attention there for his ability as well as for his fine personal qualities. But unhappily he became intemperate, and at the end of his second term had fallen so low that his party abandoned him and sent another in his place. After that he reformed and came to this city, bringing his family with him. He had two children, a boy and a girl. His wife was a cultivated and very superior woman. Here he commenced the practice of law, and soon by his talents and devotion to business acquired a good practice and regained the social position he had lost."

"Unhappily, his return to society was his return to the sphere of danger." If invited to dine with a respectable citizen, he had to encounter temptation in one of its most enticing forms. Good wine was poured for him, and both appetite and pride urged him to accept the fatal proffer. If he went to a public or private entertainment, the same perils compassed him about. From all these he is said to have held himself aloof for over a year, but his reputation at the bar and connection with important cases brought him more and more into notice, and he was finally drawn within the circle of danger. Mrs. Ridley's personal accomplishments and relationship with one or two families in the State of high social position brought her calls and invitations, and almost forced her back again into society, much as she would have preferred to remain secluded.

"Mr. Ridley, it is said, felt his danger, and I am told never escorted any lady but his wife to the supper-room at a ball or party, and there you would always see them close together, he not touching wine." But it happened last winter that invitations came, for one of the largest parties of the season, and it happened also that only a few nights before the party a little daughter had been born to Mrs. Ridley. Mr. Ridley went alone. It was a cold and stormy night. The wind blew fiercely, wailing about the roofs and chimneys and dashing the fast-falling snow in its wild passion against the windows of the room in which his sick wife lay. Rest of body and mind was impossible, freedom from anxiety impossible. There was everything to fear, everything to lose. The peril of a soldier going into the hottest of the battle was not greater than the peril that her husband would encounter on that night; and if he fell! The thought chilled her blood, as well it might, and sent a shiver to her heart.

"She was in no condition to bear any shock or strain, much less the shock and strain of a fear like this." As best she could she held her restless anxiety in check, though fever had crept into her blood and an enemy to her life was assaulting its very citadel. But as the hour at which her husband had promised to return passed by and he came not, anxiety gave place to terror. The fever in her blood increased, and sent delirium to her brain. Hours passed, but her husband did not return. Not until the cold dawn of the next sorrowful morning did he make his appearance, and then in such a wretched plight that it was well for his unhappy wife that she could not recognize his condition. He came too late—came from one of the police stations, it is said, having been found in the street too much intoxicated to find his way home, and in danger of perishing in the snow—came to find his wife, dying, and before the sun went down on that day of darkness she was cold and still as marble. Happily for the babe, it went the way its mother had taken, following a few days afterward.

"That was months ago." Alas for the wretched man! He has never risen from that terrible fall, never even made an effort, it

T. S. Arthur

is said, to struggle to his feet again. He gave up in despair.

"His eldest child, Ethel, the young lady you saw just now, was away from home at school when her mother died." Think of what a coming back was hers! My heart grows sick in trying to imagine it. Poor child! she has my deepest sympathy.

"Ethel did not return to school. She was needed at home now. The death of her mother and the unhappy fall of her father brought her face to face with new duties and untried conditions. She had a little brother only six years old to whom she must be a mother as well as sister. Responsibilities from which women of matured years and long experience might well shrink were now at the feet of this tender girl, and there was no escape for her. She must stoop, and with fragile form and hands scarce stronger than a child's lift and bear them up from the ground. Love gave her strength and courage. The woman hidden in the child came forth, and with a self-denial and self-devotion that touches me to tears when I think of it took up the new life and new burdens, and has borne them ever since with a patience that is truly heroic."

"But new duties are now laid upon her. Since her father's fall his practice has been neglected, and few indeed have been willing to entrust him with business. The little he had accumulated is all gone. One article of furniture after another has been sold to buy food and clothing, until scarcely anything is left. And now they occupy three small rooms in an out-of-the-way neighborhood, and Ethel, poor child! is brought face to face with the question of bread."

CHAPTER XX

THE voice of the speaker broke as she uttered the last sentence. A deep silence fell upon the little company. Mrs. Birtwell had turned her face, so that it could not be seen, and tears that she was unable to keep back were falling over it. She was first to speak.

"What," she asked, "was this young lady doing at the house of your friend?"

"She had applied for the situation of day-governess. My friend advertised, and Ethel Ridley, not knowing that the lady had any knowledge of her or her family came and offered herself for the place. Not being able to decide what was best to be done, she requested Ethel to call again on the next day, and I came in while she was there."

"Did your friend engage her?" asked Mrs. Birtwell.

"She had not done so when I saw her yesterday. The question of fitness for the position was one that she had not been able to determine. Ethel is young and inexperienced. But she will do all for her that lies in her power."

"What is your friend's name?" asked Mrs. Birtwell.

"The lady I refer to is Mrs. Sandford. You know her, I believe?"

"Mrs. Sandford? Yes; I know her very well."

By a mutual and tacit consent the subject was here dropped, and soon after Mrs. Birtwell retired. On gaining the street she stood with an air of indetermination for a little while, and then walked slowly away. Once or twice before reaching the end of the block she paused and went back a few steps, turned and moved on again, but still in an undecided manner. At the corner she stopped for several moments, then, as if her mind was made up, walked forward rapidly. By the firm set of her mouth and the contraction of her brows it was evident that some strong purpose was taking shape in her thoughts.

As she was passing a handsome residence before which a carriage was standing a lady came out. She had been making a call. On seeing her Mrs. Birtwell stopped, and reaching out her hand, said:

"Mrs. Sandford! Oh, I'm glad to see you. I was just going to your house."

The lady took her hand, and grasping it warmly, responded:

"And I'm right glad to see you, Mrs. Birtwell. I've been thinking about you all day. Step into the carriage. I shall drive directly home."

Mrs. Birtwell accepted the invitation. As the carriage moved away she said:

"I heard something to-day that troubles me. I am told that Mr. Ridley, since the death of his wife, has become very intemperate, and that his family are destitute—so much so, indeed, that his daughter has applied to you for the situation of day-governess in order to earn something for their support."

"It is too true," replied Mrs. Sandford. "The poor child came to see me in answer to an advertisement."

"Have you engaged her?"

"No. She is too young and inexperienced for the place. But something must be done for her."

"What? Have you thought out anything? You may count on my sympathy and co-operation."

"The first thing to be done," replied Mrs. Sandford, "is to lift her out of her present wretched condition. She must not be left where she is, burdened with the support of her drunken and debased father. She is too weak for that—too young and beautiful and innocent to be left amid the temptations and sorrows of a life such as she must lead if no one comes to her rescue."

"But what will become of her father if you remove his child from him?" asked Mrs. Birtwell.

Her voice betrayed concern. The carriage stopped at the residence of Mrs. Sandford, and the two ladies went in.

"What will become of her wretched father?"

Mrs. Birtwell repeated her question as they entered the parlors.

"He is beyond our reach," was answered. "When a man falls so low, the case is hopeless. He is the slave of an appetite that never gives up its victims. It is a sad and a sorrowful thing, I know, to abandon all efforts to save a human soul, to see it go drafting off into the rapids with the sound of the cataract in your ears, and it is still more sad and sorrowful to be obliged to hold back the loving ones who could only perish in their vain attempts at rescue. So I view the case. Ethel must not be permitted to sacrifice herself for her father."

Mrs. Birtwell sat for a long time without replying. Her eyes were bent upon the floor.

T. S. Arthur

"Hopeless!" she murmured, at length, in a low voice that betrayed the pain she felt. "Surely that cannot be so. While there is life there must be hope. God is not dead."

She uttered the last sentence with a strong rising inflection in her tones.

"But the drunkard seems dead to all the saving influences that God or man can bring to bear upon him," replied Mrs. Sandford.

"No, no, no! I will not believe it," said Mrs. Birtwell, speaking now with great decision of manner. "God can and does save to the uttermost all who come unto him."

"Yes, all who come unto him. But men like Mr. Ridley seem to have lost the power of going to God."

"Then is it not our duty to help them to go? A man with a broken leg cannot walk to the home where love and care await him, but his Good Samaritan neighbor who finds him by the way can help him thither. The traveler benumbed with cold lies helpless in the road, and will perish if some merciful hand does not lift him up and bear him to a place of safety. Even so these unhappy men who, as you say, seem to have lost the power of returning to God, can be lifted up, I am sure, and set down, as it were, in his very presence, there to feel his saving, comforting and renewing power."

"Perhaps so. Nothing is impossible," said Mrs. Sandford, with but little assent in her voice. "But who is to lift them up and where will you take them? Let us instance Mr. Ridley for the sake of illustration. What will you do with him? How will you go about the work of rescue? Tell me."

Mrs. Birtwell had nothing to propose. She only felt an intense yearning to save this man, and in her yearning an undefined confidence had been born. There must be away to save even the most wretched and abandoned of human beings, if we could but find that way, and so she would not give up her hope of Mr. Ridley—nay, her hope grew stronger every moment; and to all the suggestions of Mrs. Sanford looking to help for the daughter she supplemented something that included the father, and so pressed her views that the other became half impatient and exclaimed:

"I will have nothing to do with the miserable wretch!"

Mrs. Birtwell went away with a heavy heart after leaving a small sum of money for Mrs. Sandford to use as her judgment might dictate, saying that she would call and see her again in a few days.

The Rev. Mr. Brantly Elliott was sitting in his pleasant study, engaged in writing, when a servant opened the door and said:

"A gentleman wishes to see you, sir."

"What name?" asked the clergyman.

"He did not give me his name. I asked him, but he said it wasn't any matter. I think he's been drinking, sir."

"Ask him to send his name," said Mr. Elliott, a slight shade of displeasure settling over his pleasant face.

The servant came back with information that the visitor's name was Ridley. At mention of this name the expression on Mr. Elliott's countenance changed:

"Did you say he was in liquor?"

"Yes, sir. Shall I tell him that you cannot see him, sir?"

"No. Is he very much the worse for drink?"

"He's pretty bad, I should say, sir."

T. S. Arthur

Mr. Elliott reflected for a little while, and then said:

"I will see him."

The servant retired. In a few minutes he came back, and opening the door, let the visitor pass in. He stood for a few moments, with his hand on the door, as if unwilling to leave Mr. Elliott alone with the miserable-looking creature he had brought to the study. Observing him hesitate, Mr. Elliott said:

"That will do, Richard."

The servant shut the door, and he was alone with Mr. Ridley. Of the man's sad story he was not altogether ignorant. His fall from the high position to which he had risen in two years and utter abandonment of himself to drink were matters of too much notoriety to have escaped his knowledge. But that he was in the slightest degree responsible for this wreck of a human soul was so far from his imagination as that of his responsibility for the last notorious murder or bank-robbery.

The man who now stood before him was a pitiable-looking object indeed. Not that he was ragged or filthy in attire or person. Though all his garments were poor and threadbare, they were not soiled nor in disorder. Either a natural instinct of personal cleanliness yet remained or a loving hand had cared for him. But he was pitiable in the signs of a wrecked and fallen manhood that were visible everywhere about him. You saw it most in his face, once so full of strength and intelligence, now so weak and dull and disfigured. The mouth so mobile and strong only a few short months before was now drooping and weak, its fine chiseling all obliterated or overlaid with fever crusts. His eyes, once steady and clear as eagles', were now bloodshotten and restless.

He stood looking fixedly at Mr. Elliott, and with a gleam in his eyes that gave the latter a strange feeling of discomfort, if not uneasiness.

"Mr. Ridley" said the clergyman, advancing to his visitor and extending his hand. He spoke kindly, yet with a reserve that could not be laid aside. "What can I do for you?"

A chair was offered, and Mr. Ridley sat down. He had come with a purpose; that was plain from his manner.

"I am sorry to see you in this condition, Mr. Ridley," said the clergyman, who felt it to be his duty to speak a word of reproof.

"In what condition, sir?" demanded the visitor, drawing himself up with an air of offended dignity. "I don't understand you."

"You have been drinking," said Mr. Elliott, in a tone of severity.

"No, sir. I deny it, sir!" and the eyes of Mr. Ridley flashed. "Before Heaven, sir, not a drop has passed my lips to-day!"

His breath, loaded with the fumes of a recent glass of whisky, was filling the clergyman's nostrils. Mr. Elliott was confounded by this denial. What was to be done with such a man?

"Not a drop, sir," repeated Mr. Ridley. "The vile stuff is killing me. I must give it up."

"It is your only hope," said the clergyman. "You must give up the vile stuff, as you call it, or it will indeed kill you."

"That's just why I've come to you, Mr. Elliott. You understand this matter better than most people. I've heard you talk."

"Heard me talk?"

"Yes, sir. It's pure wine that the people want. My sentiments exactly. If we had pure wine, we'd have no drunkenness. You know that as well as I do. I've heard you talk, Mr. Elliott, and

T. S. Arthur

you talk right—yes, right, sir."

"When did you hear me talk?" asked Mr. Elliott, who was beginning to feel worried.

"Oh, at a party last winter. I was there and heard you."

"What did I say?"

"Just these words, and they took right hold of me. You said that 'pure wine could hurt no one, unless indeed his appetite were vitiated by the use of alcohol, and even then you believed that the moderate use of strictly pure wine would restore the normal taste and free a man from the tyranny of an enslaving vice.' That set me to thinking. It sounded just right. And then you were a clergyman, you see, and had studied out these things and so your opinion was worth something. There's no reason in your cold-water men; they don't believe in anything but their patent cut-off. In their eyes wine is an abomination, the mother of all evil, though the Bible doesn't say so, Mr. Elliott, does it?"

At this reference to the Bible in connection with wine, the clergyman's memory supplied a few passages that were not at the moment pleasant to recall. Such as, "Wine is a mocker;' "Look not upon the wine when it is red;" "Who hath woe? who hath sorrow? ... They that tarry long at the wine;" "At last it biteth like a serpent, and stingeth like an adder."

"The Bible speaks often of the misuse of wine," he answered, "and strongly condemns drunkenness."

"Of course it does, and gluttony as well. But against the moderate use of good wine not a word is said. Isn't that so, sir?"

"Six months ago you were a sober man, Mr. Ridley, and a useful and eminent citizen. Why did you not remain so?"

Mr. Elliott almost held his breath for the answer. He had waived the discussion into which his visitor was drifting, and put his question almost desperately.

"Because your remedy failed." Mr. Ridley spoke in a repressed voice, but with a deliberate utterance. There was a glitter in his eyes, out of which looked an evil triumph.

"My remedy? What remedy?"

"The good wine remedy. I tried it at Mr. Birtwell's one night last winter. But it didn't work. *And here I am!*"

Mr. Elliott made no reply. A blow from the arm of a strong man could not have hurt or stunned him more.

"You needn't feel so dreadfully about it," said Mr. Ridley seeing the effect produced on the clergy man. "It wasn't any fault of yours. The prescription was all right, but, you see, the wine wasn't good. If it had been pure, the kind you drink, all would have been well. I should have gained strength instead of having the props knocked from under me."

But Mr. Elliott did not answer. The magnitude of the evil wrought through his unguarded speech appalled him. He had learned, in his profession, to estimate the value of a human soul, or rather to consider it as of priceless value. And here was a human soul cast by his hand into a river whose swift waters were hurrying it on to destruction. The sudden anguish that he felt sent beads of sweat to his forehead and drew his flexible lips into rigid lines.

"Now, don't be troubled about it," urged Mr. Ridley. "You were all right. It was Mr. Birtwell's bad wine that did the mischief."

Then his manner changed, and his voice falling to a tone of solicitation, he said:

"And now, Mr. Elliott, you know good wine—you don't have anything else. I believe in your theory as much as I believe in my existence. It stands to reason. I'm all broken up and run down. Not much left of me, you see. Bad liquor is killing me, and I can't stop. If I do, I shall die. God help me!"

His voice shook now, and the muscles of his face quivered.

"Some good wine—some pure wine, Mr. Elliott!" he went on, his voice rising and his manner becoming more excited. "It's all over with me unless I can get pure wine. Save me, Mr. Elliott, save me, for God's sake!"

The miserable man held out his hands imploringly. There was wild look in his face. He was trembling from head to foot.

"One glass of pure wine, Mr. Elliott—just one glass." Thus he kept on pleading for the stimulant his insatiable appetite was craving. "I'm a drowning man. The floods are about me. I am sinking in dark waters. And you can save me if you will!"

Seeing denial still on the clergyman's face, Mr. Ridley's manner changed, becoming angry and violent.

"You will not?" he cried, starting from the chair in which he had been sitting and advancing toward Mr. Elliott.

"I cannot. I dare not. You have been drinking too much already," replied the clergyman, stepping back as Mr. Ridley came forward until he reached the bell-rope, which he jerked violently. The door of his study opened instantly. His servant. not, liking the visitor's appearance, had remained in the hall outside and came in the moment he heard the bell. On seeing him enter, Mr. Ridley turned from the clergyman and stood like one at bay. His eyes had a fiery gleam; there was anger on his brow and defiance in the hard lines of his mouth. He scowled at the servant threateningly. The latter, a strong and resolute man, only waited for an order to remove the visitor, which he would have done in a very summary way, but Mr.

Elliott wanted no violence.

The group formed a striking tableau, and to any spectator who could have viewed it one of intense interest. For a little while Mr. Ridley and the servant stood scowling at each other. Then came a sudden change. A start, a look of alarm, followed by a low cry of fear, and Mr. Ridley sprang toward the door, and was out of the room and hurrying down stairs before a movement could be made to intercept him, even if there had been on the part of the other two men any wish to do so.

Mr. Elliott stood listening to the sound of his departing feet until the heavy jar of the outer door resounded through the passages and all became still. A motion of his hand caused the servant to retire, As he went out Mr. Elliott sank into a chair. His face had become pale and distressed. He was sick at heart and sorely troubled. What did all this mean? Had his unconsidered words brought forth fruit like this? Was he indeed responsible for the fall of a weak brother and all the sad and sorrowful consequences which had followed? He was overwhelmed, crushed down, agonized by the thought, It was the bitterest moment in all his life.

T. S. Arthur

CHAPTER XXI

MR. ELLIOTT still sat in a kind of helpless maze when his servant came in with the card of Mrs. Spencer Birtwell. He read the name almost with a start. Nothing, it seemed to him, could have been more inopportune, for now he remembered with painful distinctness that it was at the party given by Mr. and Mrs. Birtwell that Ridley had yielded to temptation and fallen, never, he feared, to rise again.

Mrs. Birtwell met him with a very serious aspect.

"I am in trouble," was the first sentence that passed her lips as she took the clergyman's hand and looked into his sober countenance.

"About what?" asked Mr. Elliott.

They sat down, regarding each other earnestly.

"Mr. Elliott," said the lady, with solemn impressiveness, "it is an awful thing to feel that through your act a soul may be lost."

Mrs. Birtwell saw the light go out of her minister's face and a look of pain sweep over it.

"An awful thing indeed," he returned, in a voice that betrayed the agitation from which he was still suffering.

"I want to talk with you about a matter that distresses me deeply," said Mrs. Birtwell, wondering as she spoke at Mr. Elliott's singular betrayal of feeling.

"If I can help you, I shall do so gladly," replied the clergyman. "What is the ground of your trouble?"

"You remember Mr. Ridley?"

Mrs. Birtwell saw the clergyman start and the spasm of pain sweep over his face once more."

"Yes," he replied, in a husky whisper. But he rallied himself with an effort and asked, "What of him?" in a clear and steady voice.

"Mr. Ridley had been intemperate before coming to the city, but after settling here he kept himself free from his old bad habits, and was fast regaining the high position he had lost. I met his wife a number of times. She was a very superior woman; and the more I saw of her, the more I was drawn to her. We sent them cards for our party last winter. Mrs. Ridley was sick and could not come. Mr. Ridley came, and—and—" Mrs. Birtwell lost her voice for a moment, then added: "You know what I would say. We put the cup to his lips, we tempted him with wine, and he fell."

Mrs. Birtwell covered her face with her hands. A few strong sobs shook her frame.

"He fell," she added as soon as she could recover herself," and still lies, prostrate and helpless, in the grasp of a cruel enemy into whose power we betrayed him."

"But you did it ignorantly," said Mr. Elliott.

"There was no intention on your part to betray him. You did not know that your friend was his deadly foe."

T. S. Arthur

"My friend?" queried Mrs. Birtwell. She did not take his meaning.

"The wine, I mean. While to you and me it may be only a pleasant and cheery friend, to one like Mr. Ridley it may be the deadliest of enemies."

"An enemy to most people, I fear," returned Mrs. Birtwell, "and the more dangerous because a hidden foe. In the end it biteth like a serpent and stingeth like an adder."

Her closing sentence cut like a knife, and Mr. Elliott felt the sharp edge.

"He fell," resumed Mrs. Birtwell, "but the hurt was not with him alone. His wife died on the next day, and it has been said that the condition in which he came home from our house gave her a shock that killed her."

Mrs. Birtwell shivered.

"People say a great many things," returned Mr. Elliott, "and this, I doubt not is greatly exaggerated. Have you asked Doctor Hillhouse in regard to the facts in the case? He attended Mrs. Ridley, I think."

"No. I've been afraid to ask him."

"It might relieve your mind."

"Do you think I would feel any better if he said yea instead of nay? No, Mr. Elliott. I am afraid to question him."

"It's a sad affair," remarked the clergyman, gloomily, "and I don't see what is to be done about a it. When a man falls as low as Mr. Ridley has fallen, the case seems hopeless."

"Don't say hopeless, Mr. Elliott." responded Mrs. Birtwell, her voice still more troubled. "Until a man is dead he is not wholly lost. The hand of God is not stayed, and he can save to the uttermost."

"All who come unto him," added the clergyman, in a depressed voice that had in it the knell of a human soul. But these besotted men will not go to him. I am helpless and in despair of salvation, when I stand face to face with a confirmed drunkard. All one's care and thought and effort seem wasted, You lift them up to-day, and they fall to-morrow. Good resolutions, solemn promises, written pledges, go for nothing. They seem to have fallen below the sphere in which God's saving power operates."

"No, no, no, Mr. Elliott. I cannot, I will not, believe it," was the strongly-uttered reply of Mrs. Birtwell. "I do not believe that any man can fall below this potent sphere."

A deep, sigh came from the clergyman's lips, a dreary expression crept into his face. There was a heavy weight upon his heart, and he felt weak and depressed.

"Something must be done." There was the impulse of a strong resolve in Mrs. Birtwell's tones.

"God works by human agencies. If we hold back and let our hands lie idle, he cannot make us his instruments. If we say that this poor fallen fellow-creature cannot be lifted out of his degradation and turn away that he may perish, God is powerless to help him through us. Oh, sir, I cannot do this and be conscience clear. I helped him to fall, and, God giving me strength, I will help him to rise again."

Her closing sentence fell with rebuking force upon the clergyman. He too was oppressed by a heavy weight of responsibility. If the sin of this man's fall was upon the garments of Mrs. Birtwell, his were not stainless. Their condemnation was equal, their duty one.

"Ah!" he said, in tones of deep solicitude, "if we but knew how

T. S. Arthur

to reach and influence him!"

"We can do nothing if we stand afar off, Mr. Elliott," replied Mrs. Birtwell. "We must try to get near him. He must see our outstretched hands and hear our voices calling to him to come back. Oh, sir, my heart tells me that all is not lost. God's loving care is as much over him as it is over you and me, and his providence as active for his salvation."

"How are we to get near him, Mrs. Birtwell? This is our great impediment."

God will show us the way if we desire it. Nay, he is showing us the way, though we sought it not," replied Mrs. Birtwell, her manner becoming more confident.

"How? I cannot see it," answered the clergyman.

"There has come a crisis in his life," said Mrs. Birtwell. "In his downward course he has reached a point where, unless he can be held back and rescued, he will, I fear, drift far out from the reach of human hands. And it has so happened that I am brought to a knowledge of this crisis and the great peril it involves. Is not this God's providence? I verily believe so, Mr. Elliott. In the very depths of my soul I seem to hear a cry urging me to the rescue. And, God giving me strength, I mean to heed the admonition. This is why I have called today. I want your help, and counsel."

"It shall be given," was the clergyman's answer, made in no half-hearted way. "And now tell me all you know about this sad case. What is the nature of the crisis that has come in the life of this unhappy man?"

"I called on Mrs. Sandford this morning," replied Mrs. Birtwell, "and learned that his daughter, who is little more than a child, had applied for the situation of day-governess to her children. From Ethel she ascertained their condition, which is deplorable enough. They have been selling or pawning furniture and clothing in order to get food until but little remains, and the daughter, brought face to face with want, now steps forward to take the position of bread-winner."

"Has Mrs. Sandford engaged her?"

"No."

"Why not?"

"Ethel is scarcely more than a child. Deeply as Mrs. Sandford feels for her, she cannot give her a place of so much responsibility. And besides, she does not think it right to let her remain where she is. The influence upon her life and character cannot be good, to say nothing of the tax and burden far beyond her strength that she will have to bear."

"Does she propose anything?"

"Yes. To save the children and let the father go to destruction."

"She would take them away from him?"

"Yes, thus cutting the last strand of the cord that held him away from utter ruin."

A groan that could not be repressed broke from Mr. Elliott's lips.

This must not be—at least not now," added Mrs. Birtwell, in a firm voice. "It may be possible to save him through his home and children. But if separated from them and cast wholly adrift, what hope is left?"

"None, I fear," replied Mr. Elliott.

"Then on this last hope will I build my faith and work for his rescue," said Mrs. Birtwell, with a solemn determination; "and may I count on your help?"

"To the uttermost in my power." There was nothing half-hearted in Mr. Elliott's reply. He meant to do all that his answer involved.

"Ah!" remarked Mrs. Birtwell as they talked still farther about the unhappy case, "how much easier is prevention than cure! How much easier to keep a stumbling-block out of another's way than to set him on his feet after he has fallen! Oh, this curse of drink!"

"A fearful one indeed," said Mr. Elliott, "and one that is desolating thousands of homes all over the land."

"And yet," replied Mrs. Birtwell, with a bitterness of tone she could not repress, "you and I and some of our best citizens and church people, instead of trying to free the land from this dreadful curse, strike hands with those who are engaged in spreading broadcast through society its baleful infection."

Mr. Elliott dropped his eyes to the floor like one who felt the truth of a stinging accusation, and remained silent. His mind was in great confusion. Never before had his own responsibility for this great evil looked him in the face with such a stern aspect and with such rebuking eyes.

"By example and invitation—nay, by almost irresistible enticements," continued Mrs. Birtwell—"we tempt the weak and lure the unwary and break down the lines of moderation that prudence sets up to limit appetite. I need not describe to you some of our social saturnalias. I use strong language, for I cannot help it. We are all too apt to look on their pleasant side, on the gayety, good cheer and bright reunions by which they are attended, and to excuse the excesses that too often manifest themselves. We do not see as we should beyond the present, and ask ourselves what in natural result is going to be the outcome of all this. We actually shut our eyes and turn ourselves away from the warning signs and stern admonitions that are uplifted before us."

"Is it any matter of surprise, Mr. Elliott, that we should be confronted now and then with some of the dreadful consequences that flow inevitably from the causes to which I refer? or that as individual participants in these things we should find ourselves involved in such direct personal responsibility as to make us actually shudder?"

Mrs. Birtwell did not know how keen an edge these sentences had for Mr. Elliott, nor how, deeply they cut. As for the clergyman, he kept his own counsel.

"What can we do in this sad case?" he asked, after a few assenting remarks on the dangers of social drinking. This is the great question now. I confess to being entirely at a loss. I never felt so helpless in the presence of any duty before."

"I suppose," replied Mrs. Birtwell, "that the way to a knowledge of our whole duty in any came is to begin to do the first thing that we see to be right."

"Granted; and what then? Do you see the first right thing to be done?"

"I believe so."

"What is it?"

"If, as seems plain, the separation of Mr. Ridley from his home and children is to cut the last strand of the cord that holds him away from destruction, then our first work, if we would save him, is to help his daughter to maintain that home."

"Then you would sacrifice the child for the sake of the father?"

"No; I would help the child to save her father. I would help her to keep their little home as pleasant and attractive as possible, and see that in doing so she did not work beyond her strength. This first."

T. S. Arthur

"And what next?" asked Mr. Elliott.

"After I have done so much, I will trust God to show me what next. The path of duty is plain so far. If I enter it in faith and trust and walk whither it leads, I am sure that other ways, leading higher and to regions of safety, will open for my willing feet."

"God grant that it may be so," exclaimed Mr. Elliott, with a fervor that showed how deeply he was interested. "I believe you are right. The slender mooring that holds this wretched man to the shore must not be cut or broken. Sever that, and he is swept, I fear, to hopeless ruin. You will see his daughter?"

"Yes. It is all plain now. I will go to her at once. I will be her fast friend. I will let my heart go out to her as if she were my own child. I will help her to keep the home her tender and loving heart is trying to maintain."

Mrs. Birtwell now spoke with an eager enthusiasm that sent the warm color to her cheeks and made her eyes, so heavy and sorrowful a little while before, bright and full of hope.

On rising to go, Mr. Elliott urged her to do all in her power to save the wretched man who had fallen over the stumbling-block their hands had laid in his way, promising on his part all possible co-operation.

CHAPTER XXII

AS Mrs. Birtwell left the house of Mr. Elliott a slender girl, thinly clad, passed from the beautiful residence of Mrs. Sandford. She had gone in only a little while before with hope in her pale young face; now it had almost a frightened look. Her eyes were wet, and her lips had the curve of one who grieves helplessly and in silence. Her steps, as she moved down the street, were slow and unsteady, like the steps of one who bore a heavy burden or of one weakened by long illness. In her ears was ringing a sentence that had struck upon them like the doom of hope. It was this—and it had fallen from the lips of Mrs. Sandford, spoken with a cold severity that was more assumed than real—

"If you will do as I suggest, I will see that you have a good home; but if you will not, I can do nothing for you."

There was no reply on the part of the young girl, and no sign of doubt or hesitation. All the light—it had been fading slowly as the brief conference between her and Mrs. Sandford had progressed—died out of her face. She shrunk a little in her chair, her head dropping forward. For the space of half a minute she sat with eyes cast down. Both were silent, Mrs. Sandford waiting to see the effect of what she had said, and hoping it would work a change in the girl's purpose. But she was disappointed. After sitting in a stunned kind of way for a short time, she rose, and without trusting herself to speak bowed slightly and left the room. Mrs. Sandford did not call after the girl, but suffered her to go down stairs and leave the

T. S. Arthur

house without an effort to detain her.

"She must gang her ain gait," said the lady, fretfully and with a measure of hardness in her voice.

On reaching the street, Ethel Ridley—the reader has guessed her name—walked away with slow, unsteady steps. She felt helpless and friendless. Mrs. Sandford had offered to find her a home if she would abandon her father and little brother. The latter, as Mrs. Sandford urged, could be sent to his mother's relatives, where he would be much better off than now.

Not for a single instant did Ethel debate the proposition. Heart and soul turned from it. She might die in her effort to keep a home for her wretched father, but not till then had she any thought of giving up.

On leaving the house of Mr. Elliott, Mrs. Birtwell. went home, and after remaining there for a short time ordered her carriage and drove to a part of the town lying at considerable distance from that in which she lived. Before starting she had given her driver the name of the street and number of the house at which she was going to make a call. The neighborhood was thickly settled, and the houses small and poor. The one before which the carriage drew up did not look quite so forlorn as its neighbors; and on glancing up at the second-story windows, Mrs. Birtwell saw two or three flower-pots, in one of which a bright rose was blooming.

"This is the place you gave me, ma'am," said the driver as he held open the door. "Are you sure it is right?"

"I presume so;" and Mrs. Birtwell stepped out, and crossing the pavement to the door, rang the bell. It was opened by a pleasant-looking old woman, who, on being asked if a Miss Ridley lived there, replied in the affirmative.

"You will find her in the front room up stairs, ma'am," she added. "Will you walk up?"

The hall into which Mrs. Birtwell passed was narrow and had a rag carpet on the floor. But the carpet was clean and the atmosphere pure. Ascending the stairs, Mrs. Birtwell knocked at the door, and was answered by a faint "Come in" from a woman's voice.

The room in which she found herself a moment afterward was almost destitute of furniture. There was no carpet nor bureau nor wash-stand, only a bare floor, a very plain bedstead and bed, a square pine table and three chairs. There was not the smallest ornament of any kind on the mantel-shelf but in the windows were three pots of flowers. Everything looked clean. Some work lay upon the table, near which Ethel Ridley was sitting. But she had, turned away from the table, and sat with one pale cheek resting on her open hand. Her face wore a dreary, almost hopeless expression. On seeing Mrs. Birtwell, she started up, the blood leaping in a crimson tide to her neck, cheeks and temples, and stood in mute expectation.

"Miss Ridley?" said her visitor, in a kind voice.

Ethel only bowed. She could not speak in her sudden surprise. But recovering herself in a few moments she offered Mrs. Birtwell a chair.

"Mrs. Sandford spoke to me about you."

As Mrs. Birtwell said this she saw the flush die out of Ethel's face and an expression of pain come over it. Guessing at what this meant, she added, quickly:

"Mrs. Sandford and I do not think alike. You must keep your home, my child."

Ethel gave a start and caught her breath. A look of glad surprise broke into her face.

"Oh, ma'am," she answered, not able to steady her voice or keep the tears out of her eyes, "if I can only do that! I am willing to work if I can find anything to do. But—but—" She broke down, hiding her face in her hands and sobbing.

Mrs. Birtwell was deeply touched. How could she help being so in presence of the desolation and sorrow for which she felt herself and husband to be largely responsible?

"It shall all be made plain and easy for you, my dear child," she answered, taking Ethel's hand and kissing her with almost a mother's tenderness. "It is to tell you this that I have come. You are too young and weak to bear these burdens yourself. But stronger hands shall help you."

It was a long time before Ethel could recover herself from the surprise and joy awakened by so unexpected a declaration. When she comprehended the whole truth, when the full assurance came, the change wrought in her appearance was almost marvelous, and Mrs. Birtwell saw before her a maiden of singular beauty with a grace and sweetness of manner rarely found.

The task she had now to perform Mrs. Birtwell found a delicate one. She soon saw that Ethel had a sensitive feeling of independence, and that in aiding her she would have to devise some means of self-help that would appear to be more largely remunerative than it really was. From a simple gratuity the girl shrank, and it was with some difficulty that she was able to induce her to take a small sum of money as an advance on some almost pretended service, the nature of which she would explain to her on the next day, when Ethel was to call at her house.

So Mrs. Birtwell took her first step in the new path of duty wherein she had set her feet. For the next she would wait and pray for guidance. She had not ventured to say much to Ethel at the first interview about her father. The few questions asked had caused such evident distress of mind that she deemed it best to wait until she saw Ethel again before talking to her more freely on a subject that could not but awaken the keenest suffering.

Mrs. Birtwell's experience was a common one. She had scarcely taken her first step in the path of duty before the next was made plain. In her case this was so marked as to fill her with surprise. She had undertaken to save a human soul wellnigh lost, and was entering upon her work with that singleness of purpose which gives success where success is possible. Such being the case, she was an instrument through which a divine love of saving could operate. She became, as it were, the human hand by which God could reach down and grasp a sinking soul ere the dark waters of sin and sorrow closed over it for ever.

She was sitting alone that evening, her heart full of the work to which she had set her hand and her mind beating about among many suggestions, none of which had any reasonable promise of success, when a call from Mr. Elliott was announced. This was unusual. What could it mean? Naturally she associated it with Mr. Ridley. She hurried down to meet him, her heart beating rapidly. As she entered the parlor Mr. Elliott, who was standing in the centre of the room, advanced quickly toward her and grasped her hand with a strong pressure. His manner was excited and there was a glow of unusual interest on his face:

"I have just heard something that I wish to talk with you about. There is hope for our poor friend."

"For Mr. Ridley?" asked Mrs. Birtwell, catching the excitement of her visitor.

"Yes, and God grant that it may not be a vain hope!" he added, with a prayer in his heart as well as upon his lips.

They sat down and the clergyman went on:

"I have had little or no faith in any of the efforts which have been made to reform drunkenness, for none of them, in my

T. S. Arthur

view, went down to the core of the matter. I know enough of human nature and its depravity, of the power of sensual allurement and corporeal appetite, to be very sure that pledges, and the work usually done for inebriates in the asylums established for their benefit, cannot, except in a few cases, be of any permanent good. No man who has once been enslaved by any inordinate appetite can, in my view, ever get beyond the danger of re-enslavement unless through a change wrought in him by God, and this can only take place after a prayerful submission of himself to God and obedience to his divine laws so far as lies in his power. In other words, Mrs. Birtwell, the Church must come to his aid. It is for this reason that I have never had much faith in temperance societies as agents of personal reformation. To lift up from any evil is the work of the Church, and in her lies the only true power of salvation."

"But," said Mrs. Birtwell, "is not all work which has for its end the saving of man from evil God's work? It is surely not the work of an enemy."

"God forbid that I should say so. Every saving effort, no matter how or when made, is work for God and humanity. Do not misunderstand me. I say nothing against temperance societies. They have done and are still doing much good, and I honor the men who organize and work through them. Their beneficent power is seen in a changed and changing public sentiment, in efforts to reach the sources of a great and destructive evil, and especially in their conservative and restraining influence. But when a man is overcome of the terrible vice against which they stand in battle array, when he is struck down by the enemy and taken prisoner, a stronger hand than theirs is needed to rescue him, even the hand of God; and this is why I hold that, except in the Church, there is little or no hope for the drunkard."

"But we cannot bring these poor fallen creatures into the Church," answered Mrs. Birtwell. "They shun its doors. They stand afar off."

"The Church must go to them," said Mr. Elliott—"go as Christ, the great Head of the Church, himself went to the lowest and the vilest, and lift them up, and not only lift them up, but encompass them round with its saving influences."

"How is this to be done?" asked Mrs. Birtwell.

"That has been our great and difficult problem; but, thank God! it is, I verily believe, now being solved."

"How? Where?" eagerly asked Mrs. Birtwell. "What Church has undertaken the work?"

"A Church not organized for worship and spiritual culture, but with a single purpose to go into the wilderness and desert places in search of lost sheep, and bring them, if possible, back to the fold of God. I heard of it only to-day, though for more than a year it has been at work in our midst. Men and women of nearly every denomination have joined in the organization of this church, and are working together in love and unity. Methodists, Episcopalians, Baptists, Presbyterians, Swedenborgians, Congregationalists, Universalists and Unitarians, so called, here clasp hands in a common Christian brotherhood, and give themselves to the work of saving the lost and lifting up the fallen."

"Why do you call it a Church?" asked Mrs. Birtwell.

"Because it was founded in prayer to God, and with the acknowledgment that all saving power must come from him. Men of deep religious experience whose hearts yearned over the hapless condition of poor drunkards met together and prayed for light and guidance. They were willing to devote themselves to the task of saving these unhappy men if God would show them the way. And I verily believe that he has shown them the way. They have established a *Christian Home*, not a mere inebriate asylum."

As he spoke Mr. Elliott drew a paper from his pocket.

T. S. Arthur

"Let me read you," he said, "a few sentences from an article giving an account of the work of this Church, as I have called it. I only met with it to-day, and I am not sure that it would have taken such a hold upon me had it not been for my concern about Mr. Ridley.

"The writer says, 'In the treatment of drunkenness, we must go deeper than hospital or asylum work. This reaches no farther than the physical condition and moral nature, and can therefore be only temporary in its influence. We must awaken the spiritual consciousness, and lead a man too weak to stand in his own strength when appetite, held only in abeyance, springs back upon him to trust in God as his only hope of permanent reformation. First we must help him physically, we must take him out of his debasement, his foulness and his discomfort, and surround him with the influences of a home. Must get him clothed and in his right mind, and make him feel once more that he has sympathy—is regarded as a man full of the noblest possibilities—and so be stimulated to personal effort. But this is only preliminary work, such as any hospital may do. The real work of salvation goes far beyond this; it must be wrought in a higher degree of the soul—even that which we call spiritual. The man must be taught that only in Heaven-given strength is there any safety. He must be led, in his weakness and sense of degradation, to God as the only one who can lift him up and set his feet in a safe place. Not taught this as from pulpit and platform, but by earnest, self-denying, sympathizing Christian men and women standing face to face with the poor repentant brother, and holding him tightly by the hand lest he stumble and fall in his first weak efforts to walk in a better way. And this is just the work that is now being done in our city by a Heaven-inspired institution not a year old, but with accomplished results that are a matter of wonder to all who are familiar with its operations.'"

Mrs. Birtwell leaned toward Mr. Elliott as he read, the light of a new hope irradiating her countenance.

"Is not this a Church in the highest and best sense?" asked Mr.

Elliott, with a glow of enthusiasm in his voice.

"It is; and if the membership is not full, I am going to join it," replied Mrs. Birtwell, "and do what I can to bring at least one straying sheep out of the wilderness and into its fold."

"And I pray God that your work be not in vain," said the clergyman. "It is that I might lead you to this work that I am now here. Some of the Christian men and women whose names I find here"—Mr. Elliott referred to the paper in his hand—"are well known to me personally, and others by reputation."

He read them over.

"Such names," he added, "give confidence and assurance. In the hands of these men and women, the best that can be done will be done. And what is to hinder if the presence and the power of God be in their work? Whenever two or three meet together in his name, have they not his promise to be with them? and when he is, present, are not all saving influences most active? Present we know him to be everywhere, but his presence and power have a different effect according to the kind and degree of reception. He is present with the evil as well as the good, but he can manifest his love and work of saving far more effectually through the good than he can through the evil.

"And so, because this Home has been made a Christian Home, and its inmates taught to believe that only in coming to God in Christ as their infinite divine Saviour, and touching the hem of his garments, is there any hope of being cured of their infirmity, has its great saving power become manifest."

Just then voices were heard sounding through the hall. Apparently there was an altercation between the waiter and some one at the street door.

"What's that?" asked Mrs Birtwell, a little startled at the

unusual sound.

They listened, and heard the voice of a man saying, in an excited tone:

"I must see her!"

Then came the noise of a struggle, as though the waiter were trying to prevent the forcible entry of some one.

Mrs. Birtwell started to her feet in evident alarm. Mr. Elliott was crossing to the parlor door, when it was thrown open with considerable violence, and he stood face to face with Mr. Ridley.

CHAPTER XXIII

ON leaving the clergyman's residence, baffled in his efforts to get the wine he had hoped to obtain, Mr. Ridley strode hurriedly away, almost running, as though in fear of pursuit. After going for a block or two he stopped suddenly, and stood with an irresolute air for several moments. Then he started forward again, moving with the same rapid speed. His face was strongly agitated and nearly colorless. His eyes were restless, glancing perpetually from side to side.

There was no pause now until he reached the doors of a large hotel in the centre of the city. Entering, he passed first into the reading-room and looked through it carefully, then stood in the office for several minutes, as if waiting for some one. While here a gentleman who had once been a client came in, and was going to the clerk's desk to make some inquiry, when Ridley stepped forward, and calling him by name, reached out his hand. It was not taken, however. The man looked at him with an expression of annoyance and disgust, and then passed him without a word.

A slight tinge of color came into Ridley's pale face. He bit his lips and clenched his hands nervously.

From the office he went to the bar-room. At the door he met a well-known lawyer with whom he had crossed swords many times in forensic battles oftener gaining victory than suffering defeat. There was a look of pity in the eyes of this man when they rested upon him. He suffered his hand to be taken by the

T. S. Arthur

poor wretch, and even spoke to him kindly.

"B——," said Ridley as he held up one of his hands and showed its nerveless condition, "you see where I am going?"

"I do, my poor fellow!" replied the man; "and if you don't stop short, you will be at the end of your journey sooner than you anticipate."

"I can't stop; it's too late. For God's sake get me a glass of brandy! I haven't tasted a drop since morning."

His old friend and associate saw how it was—saw that his over-stimulated nervous system was fast giving way, and that he was on the verge of mania. Without replying the lawyer went back to the bar, at which he had just been drinking. Calling for brandy, he poured a tumbler nearly half full, and after adding a little water gave it to Ridley, who drank the whole of it before withdrawing the glass from his lips.

"It was very kind of you," said the wretched man as he began to feel along his shaking nerves the stimulating power of the draught he had taken. "I was in a desperate bad way."

"And you are not out of that way yet," replied the other. "Why don't you stop this thing while a shadow of hope remains?"

"It's easy enough to say stop"—Ridley spoke in a tone of fretfulness—"and of about as much use as to cry 'Stop!' to a man falling down a precipice or sweeping over a cataract. I can't stop."

His old friend gazed at him pityingly, then, shrugging his shoulders, he bade him good-morning. From the bar Ridley drifted to the reading-room, where he made a feint of looking over the newspapers. What cared he for news? All his interest in the world had become narrowed down to the ways and means of getting daily enough liquor to stupefy his senses and deaden his nerves. He only wanted to rest now, and let the glass of brandy he had taken do its work on his exhausted system. It was not long before he was asleep. How long he remained in this state he did not know. A waiter, rudely shaking him, brought him back to life's dreary consciousness again and an order to leave the reading room sent him out upon the street to go he knew not whither.

Night had come, and Ethel, with a better meal ready for her father than she had been able to prepare for him in many weeks, sat anxiously awaiting his return. Toward her he had always been kind and gentle. No matter how much he might be under the influence of liquor, he had never spoken a harsh word to this patient, loving, much-enduring child. For her sake he had often made feeble efforts at reform, but appetite had gained such mastery; over him that resolution was as flax in the flame.

It was late in the evening when Mr. Ridley returned home. Ethel's quick ears detected something unusual in his steps as he came along the entry. Instead of the stumbling or shuffling noise with which he generally made his way up stairs, she noticed that his footfalls were more distinct and rapid. With partially suspended breath she sat with her eyes upon the door until it was pushed open. The moment she looked into her father's face she saw a change. Something had happened to him. The heavy, besotted look was gone, the dull eyes were lighted up. He shut the door behind him quickly and with the manner of one who had been pursued and now felt himself in a place of safety.

"What's the matter, father dear?" asked Ethel as she started up and laying her hand upon his shoulder looked into his face searchingly.

"Nothing, nothing," he replied. But the nervousness of his manner and the restless glancing of his eyes, now here and now there, and the look of fear in them, contradicted his denial.

"What has happened, father? Are you sick?" inquired Ethel.

"No, dear, nothing has happened. But I feel a little strange."

He spoke with unusual tenderness in his manner, and his voice shook and had a mournful cadence.

"Supper is all ready and waiting. I've got something nice and hot for you. A strong cup of tea will do you good," said Ethel, trying to speak cheerily. She had her father at the table in a few minutes. His hand trembled so in lifting his cup that he spilled some of the contents, but she steadied it for him. He had better control of himself after drinking the tea, and ate a few mouthfuls, but without apparent relish.

"I've got something to tell you," said Ethel, leaning toward her father as they still sat at the table. Mr. Ridley saw a new light in his daughter's face.

"What is it, dear?" he said.

"Mrs. Birtwell was here to-day, and is going—"

The instant change observed in her father's manner arrested the sentence on Ethel's lips. A dark shadow swept across his face and he became visibly agitated.

"Going to do what?" he inquired, betraying some anger.

"Going to help me all she can. She was very kind, and wants me to go and see her to-morrow. I think she's very good, father."

Mr. Ridley dropped his eyes from the flushed, excited face of his child. The frown left his brow. He seemed to lose himself in thought. Leaning forward upon the table, he laid his face down upon his folded arms, hiding it from view.

A sad and painful conflict, precipitated by the remark of his daughter, was going on in the mind of this wretched man. He knew also too well that he was standing on the verge of a dreadful condition from the terrors of which his soul shrunk back in shuddering fear. All day he had felt the coming signs, and the hope of escape had now left him. But love for his daughter was rising above all personal fear and dread. He knew that at any moment the fiend of delirium might spring upon him, and then this tender child would be left alone with him in his awful conflict. The bare possibility of such a thing made him shudder, and all his thought was now directed toward the means of saving her from being a witness of the appalling scene.

The shock and anger produced by the mention of Mrs. Birtwell's name had passed off, and his thought was going out toward her in a vague, groping way, and in a sort of blind faith that through her help in his great extremity might come. It was all folly, he knew. What could she do for a poor wretch in his extremity? He tried to turn his thought from her, but ever as he turned it away it swung back and rested in-this blind faith.

Raising his eyes at last, his mind still in a maze of doubt, he saw just before him an the table a small grinning head. It was only by a strong effort that he could keep from crying out in fear and starting back from the table. A steadier look oblite-rated the head and left a teacup in its place.

No time was now to be lost. At any moment the enemy might be upon him. He must go quickly, but where? A brief struggle against an almost unconquerable reluctance and dread, and then, rising from the table, Mr. Ridley caught up his hat and ran down stairs, Ethel calling after him. He did not heed her anxious cries. It was for her sake that he was going. She heard the street door shut with a jar, and listened to her father's departing feet until the sound died out in the distance.

It was over an hour from this time when Mr. Ridley, forcing his way past the servant who had tried to keep him back, stood confronting Mr. Elliott. A look of disappointment, followed by an angry cloud, came into his face. But seeing Mrs. Birtwell, his countenance brightened; and stepping past the

T. S. Arthur

clergyman, he advanced toward her. She did not retreat from him, but held out her hand, and said, with an earnestness so genuine that it touched his feeling:

"I am glad to see you, Mr. Ridley."

As he took her extended hand Mrs. Birtwell drew him toward a sofa and sat down near him, manifesting the liveliest interest.

"Is there anything I can do for you?" she asked.

"No, ma'am," he replied, in a mournful voice—"not for me. I didn't come for that. But you'll be good to my poor Ethel. won't you, and—and—"

His voice broke into sobs, his weak frame quivered.

"I will, I will!" returned Mrs. Birtwell with prompt assurance.

"Oh, thank you. It's so good of you. My poor girl! I may never see you again."

The start and glance of fear he now threw across the room revealed to Mr. Elliott the true condition of their visitor, and greatly alarmed him. He had never been a witness of the horrors of delirium tremens, and only knew of it by the frightful descriptions he had sometimes read, but he could not mistake the symptoms of the coming attack as now seen in Mr. Ridley, who, on getting from Mrs. Birtwell a repeated and stronger promise to care for Ethel, rose from the sofa and started for the door.

But neither Mr. Elliott nor Mrs. Birtwell could let him go away in this condition. They felt too deeply their responsibility in the case, and felt also that One who cares for all, even the lowliest and most abandoned, had led him thither in his dire extremity.

Following him quickly, Mr. Elliott laid his hand firmly upon his arm.

"Stop a moment, Mr. Ridley," he said, with such manifest interest that the wretched man turned and looked at him half in surprise.

"Where are you going?" asked the clergyman.

"Where?" His voice fell to a deep whisper. There was a look of terror in his eyes. "Where? God only knows. Maybe to hell."

A strong shiver went through his frame.

"The 'Home,' Mr. Elliott! We must get him into the' Home,'" said Mrs. Birtwell, speaking close to the minister's ear.

"What home?" asked Mr. Ridley, turning quickly upon her.

She did not answer him. She feared to say a "Home for inebriates," lest he should break from them in anger.

"What home?" he repeated, in a stronger and more agitated voice; and now both Mr. Elliott and Mrs. Birtwell saw a wild eagerness in his manner.

"A home," replied Mr. Elliott, "where men like you can go and receive help and sympathy. A home where you will find men of large and hopeful nature to take you by the hand and hold you up, and Christian women with hearts full of mother and sister love to comfort, help, encourage and strengthen all your good desires. A home in which men in your unhappy condition are made welcome, and in which they are cared for wisely and tenderly in their greatest extremity."

"Then take me there, for God's sake!" cried out the wretched man, extending his hand eagerly as he spoke.

"Order the carriage immediately," said Mrs. Birtwell to the servant who stood in the half-open parlor door.

T. S. Arthur

Then she drew Mr. Ridley back to the sofa, from which he had started up a little while before, and said, in a voice full of comfort and persuasion:

"You shall go there, and I will come and see you every day; and you needn't have a thought or care for Ethel. All is going to come out right again."

The carriage came in a few minutes. There was no hesitation on the part of Mr. Ridley. The excitement of this new hope breaking in so suddenly upon the midnight of his despair acted as a temporary stimulant and held his nerves steady for a little while longer.

"You are not going?" said Mr. Elliott, seeing that Mrs. Birtwell was making ready to accompany them in the carriage.

"Yes," she replied. "I want to see just what this home is and how Mr. Ridley is going to be received and cared for."

She then directed their man-servant to get into the carriage with them, and they drove away. Mr. Ridley did not stir nor speak, but sat with his head bent down until they arrived at their destination. He left the carriage and went in passively. As they entered a large and pleasant reception-room a gentleman stepped forward, and taking Mr. Elliott by the hand, called him by name in a tone of pleased surprise.

"Oh, Mr. G—!" exclaimed the clergyman. "I am right glad to find you here. I remember seeing your name in the list of directors."

"Yes, I am one of the men engaged in this work," replied Mr. G—. Then, as he looked more closely at Mr. Ridley, he recognized him and saw at a glance his true condition.

"My dear sir," said he, stepping forward and grasping his hand, "I am glad you have come here."

Mr. Ridley looked at, or rather beyond, him in a startled way, and then drew back a few steps. Mr. G—saw him shiver and an expression of fear cross his face. Turning to a man who sat writing at a desk, he called him by name, and with a single glance directed his attention to Mr. Ridley. The man was by his side in a moment, and as Mr. Elliott did not fail to notice all on the alert. He spoke to Mr. Ridley in a kind but firm voice, and drew him a little way toward an adjoining room, the door of which stood partly open.

"Do the best you can for this poor man," said Mrs. Birtwell, now addressing Mr. G—. "I will pay all that is required. You know him, I see."

"Yes, I know him well. A sad case indeed. You may be sure that what can be done will be done."

At this moment Mr. Ridley gave a cry and a spring toward the door. Glancing at him, Mrs. Birtwell saw that his countenance was distorted by terror. Instantly two men came in from the adjoining room and quickly restrained him. After two or three fruitless efforts to break away, he submitted to their control, and was immediately removed to another part of the building.

With white lips and trembling limbs Mrs. Birtwell stood a frightened spectator of the scene. It was over in a moment, but it left her sick at heart.

"What will they do with him?" she asked, her voice husky and choking.

"All that his unhappy case requires," replied Mr. G—. "The man you saw go first to his side can pity him, for he has himself more than once passed through that awful conflict with the power of hell upon which our poor friend has now entered. A year ago he came to this Home in a worse condition than Mr. Ridley begging us for God's sake to take him in. A few weeks saw him, to use sacred words, 'clothed and in his right mind,' and since then he has never gone back a single

T. S. Arthur

step. Glad and grateful for his own rescue, he now devotes his life to the work of saving others. In his hands Mr. Ridley will receive the gentlest treatment consistent with needed restraint. He is better here than he could possibly be anywhere else; and when, as I trust in God the case may be, he comes out of this dreadful ordeal, he will find himself surrounded by friends and in the current of influences all leading him to make a new effort to reform his life. Poor man! You did not get him here a moment too soon."

CHAPTER XXIV

MRS. BIRTWELL slept but little that night and in the brief periods of slumber that came to her she was disturbed by unquiet dreams. The expression of Mr. Ridley's face as the closing door shut it from her sight on the previous evening haunted her like the face of an accusing spectre.

Immediately after breakfast she dressed herself to go out, intending to visit the Home for reforming inebriates and learn something of Mr. Ridley. Just as she came down stairs a servant opened the street door, and she saw the slender figure of Ethel.

"My poor child!" she said, with great kindness of manner, taking her by the hand and drawing her in. "You are frightened about your father."

"Oh yes, ma'am," replied Ethel, with quivering lips. "He didn't come home all night, and I'm so scared about him. I don't know what to do. Maybe you'll think it wrong in me to trouble you about it, but I am in such distress, and don't know where to go.

"No, not wrong, my child, and I'm glad you've come. I ought to have sent you word about him."

"My father! Oh, ma'am, do you know where he is?"

"Yes; he came here last night sick, and I took him in my

T. S. Arthur

carriage to a Home for just such as he is, where he will be kindly taken care of until he gets well."

Ethel's large brown eyes were fixed in a kind of thankful wonder on the face of Mrs. Birtwell. She could not speak. She did not even try to put thought or feeling into words. She only took the hand of Mrs. Birtwell, and after touching it with her lips laid her wet cheek against it and held it there tightly.

"Can I go and see him?" she asked, lifting her face after some moments.

"It will not be best, I think," replied Mrs. Birtwell—"that is, not now. He was very sick when we took him there, and may not be well enough to be seen this morning."

"Very sick! Oh, ma'am!" The face of Ethel grew white and her lips trembled.

"Not dangerously," said Mrs. Birtwell, "but yet quite ill. I am going now to see him; and if you will come here in a couple of hours, when I shall return home—"

"Oh. ma'am, let me go along with you," broke in Ethel. "I won't ask to see him if it isn't thought best, but I'll know how he is without waiting so long."

The fear that Mr. Ridley might die in his delirium had troubled Mrs. Birtwell all night, and it still oppressed her. She would have much preferred to go alone and learn first the good or ill of the case, but Ethel begged so hard to be permitted to accompany her that she could not persist in objection.

On reaching the Home, Mrs. Birtwell found in the office the man in whose care Mr. Ridley had been placed. Remembering what Mr. G—had said of this man, a fresh hope for Ethel's father sprang up in her soul as she looked into his clear eyes and saw his firm mouth and air of conscious poise and strength. She did not see in his manly face a single scar from the old battle out of which he had come at last victorious. Recognizing her, he called her by name, and not waiting for her to ask the question that looked out of her face, said:

"It is all right with him."

A cry of joy that she could not repress broke from Ethel. It was followed by sobbing and tears.

"Can we see him?" asked Mrs. Birtwell.

"The doctor will not think it best," replied the man. "He has had a pretty hard night, but, the worst is over. We must keep him quiet to-day."

"In the morning can I see him?" asked Ethel lifting her eyes, half blinded by tears, to the man's face.

"Yes; I think I can say yes," was the reply.

"How soon?"

"Come at ten o'clock."

"You'll let me call and ask about him this evening, won't you?"

"Oh yes, and you will get a good report, I am sure."

The care and help and wise consideration received in the Home by Mr. Ridley, while passing through the awful stages of his mania, had probably saved his life. The fits of frenzy were violent, so overwhelming him with phantom terrors that in his wild and desperate struggles to escape the fangs of serpents and dragons and the horrid crew of imaginary demons that crowded his room and pressed madly upon him he would, but for the restraint to which he was subjected, have thrown himself headlong from a window or bruised and broken himself against the wall.

T. S. Arthur

It was the morning of the second day after Mr. Ridley entered the Home. He had so far recovered as to be able to sit up in his room, a clean and well ventilated apartment, neatly furnished and with an air of home comfort about it. Two or three pictures hung on the walls, one of them representing a father sitting with a child upon each knee and the happy mother standing beside them. He had looked at this picture until his eyes grew dim. Near it was an illuminated text: "WITHOUT ME YE CAN DO NOTHING."

There came, as he sat gazing at the sweet home-scene, the beauty and tenderness of which had gone down into his heart, troubling its waters deeply, a knock at the door. Then the matron, accompanied by one of the lady managers of the institution, came in and made kind inquiries as to his condition. He soon saw that this lady was a refined and cultivated Christian woman, and it was not long before he felt himself coming under a new influence and all the old desires and purposes long ago cast away warming again into life and gathering up their feeble strength.

Gradually the lady led him on to talk to her of himself as he would have talked to his mother or his sister. She asked him of his family, and got the story of his bereavement, his despair and his helplessness. Then she sought to inspire him with new resolutions, and to lead him to make a new effort.

"I will be a man again," he exclaimed, at last, rising to this declaration under the uplifting and stimulating influences that were around him.

Then the lady answered him in a low, earnest, tender voice that trembled with the burden of its great concern:

"Not in your own strength. That is impossible."

His lips dropped apart. He looked at her strangely.

"Not in your own strength, but in God's," she said reverently.

"You have tried your own strength many times, but it has failed as often. But his strength never fails."

She lifted her finger and pointed to the text on the wall, "Without me ye can do nothing," then added: "But in him we can do all things. Trusting in yourself, my friend, you will go forth from here to an unequal combat, but trusting in him your victory is assured. You shall go among lions and they will have no power to harm you, and stand in the very furnace flame of temptation without even the smell of fire being left upon your garments."

"Ah, ma'am, you are doubtless right in what you say," Mr. Ridley answered, all the enthusiasm dying out of his countenance. But I am not a religious man. I have never trusted in God."

"That is no reason why you should not trust in him now," she answered, quickly. "All other hope for you is vain, but in God there is safety. Will you not go to him now?"

There came a quick, nervous rap upon the door; then it was flung open, and Ethel, with a cry of "Oh, father, my father, my father!" sprang across the room and threw herself into Mr. Ridley's arms.

With an answering cry of "Oh, Ethel, my child, my child!" Mr. Ridley drew her to his bosom, clasped her slender form to his heart and laid his face, over which tears were flowing, down among the thick masses of her golden hair.

"Let us pray," fell the sweet, solemn voice of the lady manager on the deep stillness that followed. All knelt, Mr. Ridley with his arm drawn tightly around his daughter. Then in tender, earnest supplication did this Christian woman offer her prayers for help.

"Dear Lord and Saviour," she said, in hushed, pleading tones, "whose love goes yearning after the lost and straying ones,

T. S. Arthur

open the eyes of this man, one of thy sick and suffering children, that he may see the tender beauty of thy countenance. Touch his heart, that he may feel the sweetness of thy love. Draw him to come unto thee, and to trust and confide in thee as his ever-present and unfailing Friend. In thee is safety, in thee is peace, and nowhere else."

God could answer this prayer through its influence upon the mind of him for whom it was offered. It was the ladder on which his soul climbed upward. The thought of God and of his love and mercy with which it filled all his consciousness inspired him with hope. He saw his own utter helplessness, and felt the peril and disaster that were before him when his frail little vessel of human resolution again met the fierce storms and angry billows of temptation; and so, in despairing abandonment of all human strength, he lifted his thoughts to God and cried out for the help and strength he needed.

And then, for he was deeply and solemnly in earnest, there was a new birth in his soul—the birth of a new life of spiritual forces in which God could be so present with him as to give him power to conquer when evil assailed him. It was not a life of his own, but a new life from God—not a self-acting life by which he was to be taken over the sea of temptation like one in a boat rowed by a strong oarsman, but a power he must use for himself, and one that would grow by use, gaining more and more strength, until it subdued and subordinated every natural desire to the rule of heavenly principles, and yet it was a life that, if not cherished and made active, would die.

There was a new expression in Mr. Ridley's face when he rose from his knees. It was calmer and stronger.

"God being your helper," said the lady manager, impressively, "victory is sure, and he will help you and overcome for you if you will let him. Do not trust to any mere personal motives or considerations. You have tried to stand by these over and over again, and every time you have fallen their power to help you has become less. Pride, ambition, even love, have failed. But the strength that God will give you, if you make his divine laws the rule of your life, cannot fail. Go to him in childlike trust. Tell him as you would tell a loving father of your sin and sorrow and helplessness, and ask of him the strength you need. Read every morning a portion of his holy word, and lay the divine precepts up in your heart. He is himself the word of life, and is therefore present in a more real and saving way to those who reverence and obey this word than it is possible for him to be to those who do not.

"Herein will lie your strength. Hence will come your deliverance. Take hold upon God our Saviour, my friend, and all the powers of hell shall not prevail against you. You will be tempted, but in the moment you hear the voice of the tempter look to God and ask him for strength, and it will surely come. Don't parley, for a single moment. Let no feeling of security lead you to test your own poor strength in any combat with the old appetite, for that would be an encounter full of peril. Trust in God, and all will be safe. But remember that there is no real trust in God without a life in harmony with his commandments. All-abiding spiritual strength comes through obedience only."

Mr. Ridley listened with deep attention, and when the lady ceased speaking said:

"Of myself I can do nothing. Long ago I saw that, and gave up the struggle in despair. If help comes now, it must come from God. No power but his can save me."

"Will you not, then, go to him?"

"How am I to go? What am I to do? What will God require of me?"

He spoke hurriedly and with the manner of one who felt himself in imminent danger and looked anxiously for a way of escape.

T. S. Arthur

"To do justly, to love mercy and to walk humbly before him; he requires nothing more," was the calmly spoken reply.

A light broke into Mr. Ridley's face.

"You cannot be just and merciful if you touch the accursed thing, for that would destroy your power to be so. To touch it, then, will be to sin against God and hurt your neighbor. Just here, then, must your religious life be in. For you to taste any kind of intoxicating drink would be a sin. God cannot help you, unless you shun this evil as a sin against him, and he will give you the power to shun it if, whenever you feel the desire to drink, you resist that desire and pray for strength by which to gain a victory.

"Every time you do this you will receive new spiritual strength, and be so much nearer the ark of safety. So resisting day by day, always in a humble acknowledgment that every good gift comes from a loving Father in heaven, the time is not far distant when your feet will be on the neck of the enemy that has ruled over you so long. God, even our God, will surely bring you off conqueror."

Mr. Ridley on whose calmer face the light of a new confidence now rested, drew his arm closely about Ethel, who was leaning against him, and said:

"Take heart, darling. If God is for us, who shall be against us? Henceforth I will trust in him."

Ethel put her arms about his neck, weeping silently. The matron and lady manager went out and left them alone.

Mrs. Birtwell did not visit the Home on this morning to see how it fared with Mr. Ridley as she had intended doing. The shadow of a great evil had fallen upon her house. For some time she had seen its approaches and felt the gathering gloom. If the reader will go back over the incidents and characters of this story, he will recall a scene between Mrs. Whitford and her son Ellis, the accepted lover of Blanche Birtwell, and will remember with what earnestness the mother sought to awaken in the mind of the young man a sense of danger, going so far as to uncover a family secret and warn him of a taint in his blood. It will also be remembered how the proud, self-confident young man rejected, her warnings and entreaties, and how wine betrayed him.

The humiliation that followed was deep, but not effective to save him. Wine to his inherited appetite was like blood to the wolf-nature. To touch it was to quicken into life an irrepressible desire for more. But his pride fought against any acknowledgment of his weakness, and particularly against so public an acknowledgment as abstinence when all around him were taking wine. Every time he went to a dinner or evening-party, or to any entertainment where wine was to be served, he would go self-admonished to be on guard against excess, but rarely was the admonition heeded. A single glass so weakened his power of restraint that he could not hold back his hand; and if it so happened that from any cause this limit was forced upon him, as in making a morning or an evening call, the stimulated appetite would surely draw his feet to the bar of some fashionable saloon or hotel in order that it might secure a deeper satisfaction.

It was not possible, so impelled by appetite and so indulging its demands, for Ellis Whitford to keep from drifting out into the fatal current on whose troubled waters thousands are yearly borne to destruction.

After her humiliation at Mrs. Birtwell's, a smile was never seen upon the mother's face. All that she deemed it wise to say to her son when he awoke in shame next morning she said in tears that she had no power to hold back. He promised with solemn asseverations that he would never again so debase himself, and he meant to keep his promise. Hope stirred feebly in his mother's heart, but died when, in answer to her injunction, "Touch not, taste not, handle not, my son. Herein lies your only chance of safety," he replied coldly and with irritation:

"I will be a man, and not a slave. I will walk in freedom among my associates, not holding up manacled wrists."

Alas! he did not walk in freedom. Appetite had already forged invisible chains that held him in a fatal bondage. It was not yet too late. With a single strong effort he could have rent these bonds asunder, freeing himself for ever. But pride and a false shame held him back, from making this effort, and all the while appetite kept silently strengthening every link and steadily forging new chains. Day by day he grew feebler as to will-power and less clear in judgment. His fine ambition, that once promised to lift him into the highest ranks of his profession, began to lose its stimulating influence.

None but his mother knew how swiftly this sad demoralization was progressing, through others were aware of the fact that he indulged too freely in wine.

With a charity that in too many instances was self-excusing, not a few of his friends and acquaintances made light of his excesses, saying:

"Oh, he'll get over it;" or, "Young blood is hot and boils up sometimes;" or, "He'll steady himself, never fear."

The engagement between Ellis and Blanche still existed, though Mr. and Mrs. Birtwell were beginning to feel very much concerned about the future of their daughter, and were seriously considering the propriety of taking steps to have the engagement broken off. The young man often came to their house so much under the influence of drink that there was no mistaking his condition; but if any remark was made about it, Blanche not only exhibited annoyance, but excused and defended him, not unfrequently denying the fact that was apparent to all.

One day—it was several months from the date of that fatal

party out of which so many disasters came, as if another Pandora's box had been opened—the card of Mrs. Whitford was placed in the hands of Mrs. Birtwell.

"Say that I will be down in a moment."

But the servant who had brought up the card answered:

"The lady wished me to say that she would like to see you alone in your own room, and would come up if it was agreeable."

"Oh. certainly. Tell her to come right up."

Wondering a little at this request, Mrs. Birtwell waited for Mrs. Whitford's appearance, rising and advancing toward the door as she heard her steps approaching. Mrs. Whitford's veil was down as she entered, and she did not draw it aside until she had shut the door behind her. Then she pushed it away.

An exclamation of painful surprise fell from the lips of Mrs. Birtwell the moment she saw the face of her visitor. It was pale and wretched beyond description, but wore the look of one who had resolved to perform some painful duty, though it cost her the intensest suffering.

T. S. Arthur

CHAPTER XXV

"I HAVE come," said Mrs. Whitford, after she was seated and had composed herself, "to perform the saddest duty of my whole life."

She paused, her white lips quivering, then rallied her strength and went on:

"Even to dishonor my son."

She caught her breath with a great sob, and remained silent for nearly half a minute, sitting so still that she seemed like one dead. In that brief time she had chained down her over-wrought feelings and could speak without a tremor in her voice.

"I have come to say," she now went on, "that this marriage must not take place. Its consummation would be a great wrong, and entail upon your daughter a life of misery. My son is falling into habits that will, I sadly fear, drag him down to hopeless ruin. I have watched the formation and growth of this habit with a solicitude that has for a long time robbed my life of its sweetness. All the while I see him drifting away from me, and I am powerless to hold him back. Every day he gets farther off, and every day my heart grows heavier with sorrow. Can nothing be done? Alas! nothing, I fear; and I must tell you why, Mrs. Birtwell. It is best that you should see the case as hopeless, and save your daughter if you can."

She paused again for a few moments, and then continued:

"It is not with my son as with most young men. He has something more to guard against than the ordinary temptations of society. There is, as you may possibly know, a taint in his blood—the taint of hereditary intemperance. I warned him of this and implored him to abjure wine and all other drinks that intoxicate, but he was proud and sensitive as well as confident in his own strength. He began to imagine that everybody knew the family secret I had revealed to him, and that if he refused wine in public it would be attributed to his fear of arousing a sleeping appetite which when fully awake and active might prove too strong for him, and so he often drank in a kind of bravado spirit. He would be a man and let every one see that he could hold the mastery over himself. It was a dangerous experiment for him, as I knew it would be, and has failed."

Mrs. Whitford broke down and sobbed in an uncontrollable passion of grief. Then, rising, she said:

"I have done a simple duty, Mrs. Birtwell. How hard the task has been you can never know, for through a trial like mine you will never have to pass. It now remains for you to do the best to save your child from the great peril that lies before her. I wish that I could say, 'Tell Blanche of our interview and of my solemn warning.' But I cannot, I dare not do so, for it would be to cast up a wall between me and my son and to throw him beyond the circle of my influence. It would turn his heart against his mother, and that is a calamity from the very thought of which I shrink with a sickening fear."

The two women, sad partners in a grief that time might intensify, instead of making less, stood each leaning her face down upon the other's shoulder and wept silently, then raised their eyes and looked wistfully at each other.

"The path of duty is very rough sometimes; but if we must walk it to save another, we cannot stay our feet and be guiltless

T. S. Arthur

before God," said Mrs. Whitford. "It has taken many days since I saw this path of suffering and humiliation open its dreary course for me to gather up the strength required to walk in it with steady feet. Every day for more than a week I have started out resolved to see you, but every day my heart has failed. Twice I stood at your door with my hand on the bell, then turned, and went away. But the task is over, the duty done, and I pray that it may not be in vain."

What was now to be done? When Mr. Birtwell was informed of this interview, he became greatly excited, declaring that he should forbid any further intercourse between the young people. The engagement, he insisted, should be broken off at once. But Mrs. Birtwell was wiser than her husband, and knew better than he did the heart of their daughter.

Blanche had taken more from her mother than from her father, and the current of her life ran far deeper than that of most of the frivolous girls around her. Love with her could not be a mere sentiment, but a deep and all-pervading passion. Such a passion she felt for Ellis Whitford, and she was ready to link her destinies with his, whether the promise were for good or for evil. To forbid Ellis the house and lay upon her any interdictions, in regard to him would, the mother knew, precipitate the catastrophe they were anxious to avert.

It was not possible for either Mr. or Mrs. Birtwell to conceal from their daughter the state of feeling into which the visit of Mrs. Whitford had thrown them, nor long to remain passive. The work of separation must be commenced without delay. Blanche saw the change in her parents, and felt an instinct of danger; and when the first intimations of a decided purpose to make a breach between her and Ellis came, she set her face like flint against them, not in any passionate outbreak, but with a calm assertion of her undying love and her readiness to accept the destiny that lay before her. To the declaration of her mother that Ellis was doomed by inheritance to the life of a drunkard, she replied:

"Then he will only the more need my love and care."

Persuasion, appeal, remonstrance, were useless. Then Mr. Birtwell interposed with authority. Ellis was denied the house and Blanche forbidden to see him.

This was the condition of affairs at the time Mrs. Birtwell became so deeply interested in Mr. Ridley and his family. Blanche had risen, in a measure, above the deep depression of spirits consequent on the attitude of her parents toward her betrothed husband, and while showing no change in her feelings toward him seemed content to wait for what might come. Still, there was something in her manner that Mrs. Birtwell did not understand, and that occasioned at times a feeling of doubt and uneasiness.

"Where is Blanche?" asked Mr. Birtwell. It was the evening following that on which Mr. Ridley bad been taken to the Home for inebriates. He was sitting at the tea-table with his wife.

"She is in her room," replied Mrs. Birtwell.

"Are you sure?" inquired her husband.

Mrs. Birtwell noticed something in his voice that made her say quickly:

"Why do you ask?"

"For no particular reason, only she's not down to tea."

Mr. Birtwell's face had grown very serious.

"She'll be along in a few moments," returned Mrs. Birtwell.

But several minutes elapsed, and still she did not make her appearance.

T. S. Arthur

"Go up and knock at Miss Blanche's door," said Mrs. Birtwell to the waiter. "She may have fallen asleep."

The man left the room.

"I feel a little nervous," said Mr. Birtwell, setting down his cup, the moment they were alone. Has Blanche been out since dinner?"

"No."

"All right, then. It was only a fancy, as I knew it to be at the time. But it gave me a start."

"What gave you a start?" asked Mrs. Birtwell.

"A face in a carriage. I saw it for an instant only."

"Whose face?"

"I thought for the moment it was that of Blanche."

Mrs. Birtwell grew very pale, leaned back in her chair and turned her head listening for the waiter. Neither of them spoke until he returned.

"Miss Blanche is not there."

Both started from the table and left the room, the waiter looking after them in surprise. They were not long in suspense. A letter from Blanche, addressed to her mother, which was found lying on her bureau, told the sad story of her perilous life-venture, and overwhelmed her parents with sorrow and dismay. It read:

"MY DEAR FATHER AND MOTHER: When you receive this, I shall be married to Ellis Whitford. There is nothing that I can say to break for you the pain of this intelligence. If there was, oh how gladly would I say it! My destiny is on me, and I must walk in the way it leads. It is not that I love you less that I go away from you, but because I feel the voice of duty which is calling to me to be the voice of God. Another life and another destiny are bound up in mine, and there is no help for me. God bless you and comfort you, and keep your hearts from turning against your loving

BLANCHE."

In all their fond looks forward to the day when their beautiful child should stand in bridal robes—and what parents with lovely daughters springing up toward womanhood do not thus look forward and see such visions?—no darkly, brooding fancy had conceived of anything like this. The voice that fell upon their ears was not the song of a happy bride going joyously to the altar, but the cry of their pet lamb bound for the sacrifice.

"Oh, madness, madness!" exclaimed Mr. Birtwell, in anger and dismay.

"My poor unhappy child! God pity her! "sobbed the white-lipped mother, tearless under the sudden shock of this great disaster that seemed as if it would beat out her life.

There was no help, no remedy. The fatal step had been taken, and henceforth the destiny of their child was bound up with that of one whose inherited desire for drink had already debased his manhood. For loving parents we can scarcely imagine a drearier outlook upon life than this.

The anger of Mr. Birtwell soon wasted its strength amid the shallows of his weaker character, but the pain and hopeless sorrow grew stronger and went deeper down into the heart of Mrs. Birtwell day by day. Their action in the case was such as became wise and loving parents. What was done was done, and angry scenes, coldness and repulsion could now only prove hurtful. As soon as Blanche returned from a short bridal-tour the doors of her father's house were thrown open for her and her husband to come in. But the sensitive, high-spirited young

T. S. Arthur

man said, "No." He could not deceive himself in regard to the estimation in which he was held by Mr. and Mrs. Birtwell, and was not willing to encounter the humiliation of living under their roof and coming in daily but restrained contact with them. So he took his bride to his mother's house, and Mrs. Birtwell had no alternative but to submit, hard as the trial was, to this separation from her child.

This was the shadow of the great evil in which Mrs. Birtwell was sitting on the day Mr. Ridley found himself amid the new influences and new friends that were to give him another start in life and another chance to redeem himself. She had passed a night of tears and agony, and though suffering deeply had gained a calm exterior. Ethel, after leaving the Home, came with a heart full of new hope and joy to see Mrs. Birtwell and tell her about her father.

The first impulse of the unhappy mother, sitting in the shadows of her own great sorrow, was to send the girl away with a simple denial.

"Say that I cannot see her this morning," she said coldly. But before the servant could leave the room she repented of this denial.

"Stay!" she called. Then, while the servant paused, she let her thoughts go from herself to, Ethel and her father.

"Tell the young lady to wait for a little while," she said. "I will ring for you in a few minutes." The servant went out, and Mrs. Birtwell turned to her secretary and wrote a few lines, saying that she was not feeling well and could not see Miss Ridley then, but would be glad to have her call in two or three days. Placing this with a bank-bill in an envelope, she rang for the servant, who took the letter down stairs and gave it to Ethel.

But Mrs. Birtwell did not feel as though she had done her whole duty in the case. A pressure was left upon her feelings. What of the father? How was it faring with him? She hesitated about recalling the servant until it was too late. Ethel took the letter, and without opening it went away.

A new disquiet came from this cause, and Mrs. Birtwell could not shake it off. Happily for her relief, Mr. Elliott, whose interest in the fallen man was deep enough to take him to the Home that morning, called upon her with the most gratifying intelligence. He had seen Mr. Ridley and held a long interview with him, the result of which was a strong belief that the new influences under which he had been brought would be effectual in saving him.

"I have faith in these influences," said the clergyman, "because I understand their ground and force. Peter would have gone down hopelessly in the Sea of Galilee if he had depended on himself alone. Only the divine Saviour, on whom he called and in whom he trusted, could save him; and so it is in the case of men like Mr. Ridley who try to walk over the sea of temptation. Peter's despairing cry of 'Save, Lord, or I perish,' must be theirs also if they would keep from sinking beneath the angry waters, and no one ever calls sincerely upon God for help without receiving it. That Mr. Ridley is sincere I have no doubt, and herein lies my great confidence."

At the end of a week Blanche returned from her wedding-tour, and was received by her parents with love and tenderness instead of reproaches. These last, besides being utterly useless, would have pushed the young husband away from them and out of the reach of any saving influences it might be in their power to exercise.

The hardest trial now for Mrs. Birtwell was the separation from Blanche, whose daily visits were a poor substitute for the old constant and close companionship. If there had not been a cloud in the sky of her child's future, with its shadow already dimming the brightness of her young life, the mother's heart would have still felt an aching and a void, would have been a mourner for love's lost delights and possessions that could nevermore return. But to all this was added a fear and, dread

T. S. Arthur

that made her soul grow faint when thought cast itself forward into the coming time.

The Rev. Mr. Brantley Elliott was a wiser and truer man than some who read him superficially imagined. His churchmanship was sometimes narrower than his humanity, while the social element in his character, which was very strong, often led him to forget in mixed companies that much of what he might say or do would be judged of by the clerical and not the personal standard, and his acts and words set down at times as favoring worldliness and self-indulgence. Harm not unfrequently came of this. But he was a sincere Christian man, deeply impressed with the sacredness of his calling and earnest in his desire to lead heavenward the people to whom he ministered.

The case of Mr. Ridley had not only startled and distressed him, but filled him with a painful concern lest other weak and tempted ones might have fallen through his unguarded utterance or been bereaved through his freedom. The declaration of Paul came to him with a new force: "Wherefore, if meat make my brother to offend, I will eat no meat while the world standeth, lest I make my brother to offend;" and he resolved not only to abstain from wine hereafter in mixed companies, but to use his influence to discourage a social custom fraught, as he was now beginning to see, with the most disastrous consequences.

The deep concern felt for Mr. Ridley by Mr. Elliott and Mrs. Birtwell drew them oftener together now, and took them frequently to the Home for inebriates, in which both took a deep interest. For over three weeks Mr. Ridley remained at the institution, its religious influences growing deeper and deeper every day. He met there several men who had fallen from as high an estate as himself—men of cultured intellect, force of character and large ability—and a feeling of brotherhood grew up between them. They helped and strengthened each other, entering into a league offensive and defensive, and pledging themselves to an undying antagonism toward every form of intemperance.

When Mr. Ridley returned to his home, he found it replete with many comforts not there when love and despair sent him forth to die, for aught he knew, amid nameless horrors. An office had been rented for him, and Mr. Birtwell had a case of considerable importance to place in his hands. It was a memorable occasion in the Court of Common Pleas when, with the old clear light in his eyes and bearing of conscious power, he stood among his former associates, and in the firm, ringing voice which had echoed there so many times before, made an argument for his client that held both court and jury almost spellbound for an hour.

CHAPTER XXVI

THE seed and the harvest are alike in quality. Between cause and effect there is an unchanging and eternal relation. Men never find grapes on thorns nor figs on thistles.

As an aggregate man, society has no escape from this law. It must reap as it sows. If its customs be safe and good, its members, so far as they are influenced by these customs, will be temperate, orderly and virtuous; but if its tone be depraved and its customs evil or dangerous, moral and physical ruin must; in too many sad cases be the inevitable result.

It is needless to press this view, for it is self-evident and no one calls it in question. Its truth has daily and sorrowful confirmation in the wan faces and dreary eyes and wrecks of a once noble and promising manhood one meets at every turn.

The thorn and the thistle harvest that society reaps every year is fearfully great, and the seed from which too large a portion of this harvest comes is its drinking customs. Men of observation and intelligence everywhere give this testimony with one consent. All around us, day and night, year by year, in palace and hovel, the gathering of this sad and bitter harvest goes on—the harvest of broken hearts and ruined lives. And still the hand of the sower is not stayed. Refined and lovely women and men of low and brutal instincts, church members and scoffers at religion, stately gentlemen and vulgar clowns, are all at work sowing the baleful seed that ripens, alas! too quickly its fruit of woe. The *home saloon* vies with the common licensed saloon in its allurements and attractions, and men who would think themselves degraded by contact with those who for gain dispense liquor from a bar have a sense of increased respectability as they preside over the good wine and pure spirits they offer to their guests in palace homes free of cost.

We are not indulging in forms of rhetoric. To do so would only weaken the force of our warning. What we have written is no mere fancy work. The pictures thrown upon our canvas with all the power of vivid portraiture that we possess are but feeble representations of the tragic scenes that are enacted in society year by year, and for which every, member of society who does not put his hand to the work of reform is in some degree responsible.

We are not developing a romance, but trying, as just said, to give from real life some warning pictures. Our task is nearly done. A few more scenes, and then our work will be laid for the present aside.

There are men who never seem to comprehend the lesson of events or to feel the pressure of personal responsibility. They drift with the tide, doing as their neighbors do, and resting satisfied. The heroism of self-sacrifice or self-denial is something to which they cannot rise. Nothing is farther from their ambition than the role of a reformer. Comfortable, self-indulgent, placid, they move with the current and manage to keep away from its eddies. Such a man was Mr. Birtwell. He knew of some of the disasters that followed so closely upon his grand entertainment, but refused to connect therewith any personal responsibility. It was unfortunate, of course, that these things should have happened with him, but he was no more to blame for them than if they had happened with his neighbor across the way. So he regarded the matter. But not so Mrs. Birtwell. As we have seen, a painful sense of responsibility lay heavily upon her heart.

The winter that followed was a gay one, and many lag

entertainments were given. The Birtwells always had a party, and this party was generally the event of the season, for Mr. Birtwell liked *eclat* and would get it if possible. Time passed, and Mrs. Birtwell, who had sent regrets to more than half the entertainments to which they received invitations said nothing.

"When are we going to have our party?" asked Mr. Birtwell of his wife as they sat alone one evening. He saw her countenance change. After a few moments she replied in a low but very firm and decided voice:

"Whenever we can have it without wine."

"Then we'll never have it," exclaimed Mr. Birtwell, in considerable excitement.

"It will be better so," returned his wife, "than again to lay stumbling-blocks at the feet of our neighbors."

There came a sad undertone in her voice that her husband did not fail to perceive.

"We don't agree in this thing," said Mr. Birtwell, with some irritation of manner.

"Then will it not be best to let the party go over until we can agree? No harm can come of that, and harm might come, as it did last year, from turning our house into a drinking-saloon."

The sting of these closing words was sharp. It was not the first time Mr. Birtwell had heard his wife use them, and they never failed to shock his fine sense of respectability.

"For Heaven's sake, Margaret," he broke out, in a passion he could not control, "don't say that again! It's an outrage. You'll give mortal offence if you use such language."

"It is best to call things by their right names," replied Mrs. Birtwell, in no way disturbed by her husband's weak anger. "As names signify qualities, we should be very careful how we deceive others by the use of wrong ones. To call a lion a lamb might betray a blind or careless person into the jaws of a ferocious monster, or to speak of the fruit of the deadly nightshade as a cherry might deceive a child into eating it."

"You are incorrigible," said Mr. Birtwell, his anger subsiding. It never went very deep, for his nature was shallow.

"No, not incorrigible, but right," returned Mrs. Birtwell.

"Then we are not to have a party this winter?"

"I did not say so. On the contrary, I am ready to entertain our friends, but the party I give must be one in which no wine or brandy is served."

"Preposterous!" ejaculated Mr. Birtwell. "We'd make ourselves the laughing-stock of the city."

"Perhaps not," returned his wife.

Mr. Birtwell shook his head and shut his mouth tightly:

"There's no use in talking about it if the thing can't be done right, it can't be done at all."

"So say I. Still, I would do it right and show society a better way if you were brave enough to stand by my side. But as you are not, our party must go by default this winter."

Mrs. Birtwell smiled faintly to soften the rebuke of her words. They had reached this point in their conversation when Mr. Elliott, their clergyman, called. His interest in the Home for inebriates had increased instead of abating, and he now held the place of an active member in the board of directors. Mrs. Birtwell had, months before, given in her adhesion to the cause of reform, and the board of lady managers, who had a close supervision of the internal arrangements of the Home, had few

T. S. Arthur

more efficient workers.

In the beginning Mr. Birtwell had "pooh-poohed" at his wife's infatuation, as he called it, and prophesied an early collapse of the whole affair. "The best thing to do with a drunkard," he would say, with mocking levity, "is to let him die. The sooner he is out of the way, the better for himself and society." But of late he had given the matter a more respectful consideration. Still, he would have his light word and pleasant banter both with his wife and Mr. Elliott, who often dropped in to discuss with Mrs. Birtwell the interests of the Home.

"Just in the nick of time," exclaimed Mr. Birtwell, smiling, as he took the clergyman's hand.

"My wife and I have had a disagreement—we quarrel dreadfully, you know—and you must decide between us."

"Indeed! What's the trouble now?" said Mr. Elliott, looking from one to the other.

"Well, you see, we've been discussing the party question, and are at daggers' points."

The light which had spread over Mr. Elliott's countenance faded off quickly, and Mr. Birtwell saw it assume a very grave aspect. But he kept on:

"You never heard anything so preposterous. Mrs. Birtwell actually proposes that we give a coldwater-and-lemonade entertainment. Ha! ha!"

The smile he had expected to provoke by this sally did not break into the clergyman's face.

"But I say," Mr. Birtwell added, "do the thing right, or don't do it all."

"What do you call right?" asked Mr. Elliott.

"The way it is done by other people—as we did it last year, for instance."

"I should be sorry to see last year's entertainment repeated if like consequences must follow," replied Mr. Elliott, becoming still more serious.

Mr. Birtwell showed considerable annoyance at: this.

"I have just come from a visit to your friend Mrs. Voss," said the clergyman.

"How is she?" Mrs. Birtwell asked, anxiously.

"I do not think she can last much longer," was replied.

Tears came into Mrs. Birtwell's eyes and fell over her cheeks.

"A few days at most—a few hours, maybe—and she will be at rest. She spoke of you very tenderly, and I think would like to see you."

"Then I will go to her immediately," said Mrs. Birtwell, rising. "You must excuse me, Mr. Elliott. I will take the carriage and go alone," she added, glancing toward her husband.

The two men on being left alone remained silent for a while. Mr. Birtwell was first to speak.

"I have always felt badly," he said, "about the death of Archie Voss. No blame attaches to us of course, but it was unfortunate that he had been at our house."

"Yes, very unfortunate," responded the clergyman. Something in his voice as well as in his manner awakened an uncomfortable feeling in the mind of Mr. Birtwell.

They were silent again, neither of them seeming at his ease.

"I had hoped," said Mr. Elliott, breaking at length this silence, "to find you by this time over upon our side."

"The cold-water side, you mean?" There was perceptible annoyance in Mr. Birtwell's tone.

"On the side of some reform in our social customs. Why can't you join with your excellent wife in taking the initiative? You may count on me to endorse the movement and give it my countenance and support."

"Thank you, Mr. Elliott, but I'm not your man," returned Mr. Birtwell. He spoke with decision. "I have no desire to be counted in with reformers."

"Think of the good you might do."

"I am not a philanthropist."

"Then think of the evil you might prevent."

"The good or the evil resulting from my action, take which side I may, will be very small," said Mr. Birtwell, with an indifference of manner that showed his desire to drop the subject. But Mr. Elliott was only leading the way for some plainer talk, and did not mean to lose his opportunity.

"It is an error," he said, "to make light of our personal influence or the consequences that may flow from what we do. The hand of a child is not too weak to hold the match that fires a cannon. When evil elements are aggregated, the force required to release them is often very small. We may purpose no wrong to our neighbor in the indulgence of a freedom that leads him into fiery temptation; but if we know that our freedom must of necessity do this, can we escape responsibility if we do not deny ourselves?"

"It is easy to ask questions and to generalize," returned Mr. Birtwell, not hiding the annoyance he felt.

"Shall I come down to particulars and deal in facts?" asked Mr. Elliott.

"If you care to do so."

"I have some facts—very sad and sorrowful ones. You may or may not know them—at least not all. But you should know them, Mr. Birtwell."

There was no escape now.

"You half frighten me, Mr. Elliott. What are you driving at?"

"I need not refer," said the clergyman, "to the cases of Archie Voss and Mr. Ridley."

Mr. Birtwell raised his hands in deprecation.

"Happily," continued Mr. Elliott, "Mr. Ridley has risen from his fall, and now stands firmer, I trust, than ever, and farther away from the reach of temptation, resting not in human but in divine strength. Archie is in heaven, where before many days his mother will join him."

"Why are you saying this?" demanded Mr. Birtwell. "You are going too far." His face had grown a little pale.

"I say it as leading to something more," replied the clergyman. "If there had been no more bitter fruit than this, no more lives sacrificed, it would have been sad enough. But—"

"Sir, you are trifling," exclaimed Mr. Birtwell, starting from his chair. "I cannot admit your right to talk to me in this way."

"Be calm, my dear sir," answered Mr. Elliott, laying his hand upon his companion. "I am not trifling with you. As your warm personal friend as well as your spiritual counselor, I am here to-night to give a solemn admonition, and I can best do this through the communication of facts—facts that stand on

T. S. Arthur

record for ever unchangeable whether you know them or not. Better that you should know them."

Mr. Birtwell sat down, passive now, his hand grasping the arms of his chair like one bracing himself for a shock.

"You remember General Abercrombie?"

"Yes."

"Do you know what has become of him?"

"No. I heard something about his having been dismissed from the army."

"Did you hear the cause?"

"It was drunkenness, I believe."

"Yes, that was the cause. He was a fine officer and a man of high character, but fell into habits of intemperance. Seeing himself drifting to certain ruin, he made a vigorous effort to reform his life. Experience told him that his only safety lay in complete abstinence, and this rule he adopted. For many months he remained firm. But he fell at your house. The odor of wine that pervaded all the air and stirred within him the long-sleeping appetite, the freedom he saw around him, the invitations that met him from distinguished men and beautiful women, the pressure of a hundred influences upon his quickened desires, bore him down at last, and he fell.

"I heard the whole sad story to-day," continued Mr. Elliott. He did not even attempt to struggle up again, but abandoned himself to his fate. Soon after, he was removed from the command of this department and sent off to the Western frontier, and finally court-martialed and dismissed from the army.

"To his wife, who was deeply attached to him, General

Abercrombie was when sober one of the kindest and most devoted of husbands, but a crazy and cruel fiend when drunk. It is said that on the night he went home from your house last winter strange noises and sudden cries of fear were heard in their room, and that Mrs. Abercrombie when seen next morning looked as if she had just come from a bed of sickness. She accompanied him to the West, but I learned today that since his dismissal from the army his treatment of her has been so outrageous and cruel that she has had to leave him in fear of her life, and is now with her friends, a poor broken-hearted woman. As for the general, no one seems to know what has become of him."

"And the responsibility of all this you would lay at my door?" said Mr. Birtwell, in a husky voice, through which quivered a tone of anger. "But I reject your view of the case entirely. General Abercrombie fell because he had no strength of purpose and no control of his appetite. He happened to trip at my house—that is all. He would have fallen sooner or later somewhere."

"Happened to trip! Yes, that is it, Mr. Birtwell; you use the right word. He tripped at your house. But who laid the stone of stumbling in his path? Suppose there had been no wine, served to your guests, would he have stumbled on that fatal night? If there had been no wine served, would Archie Voss have lost his way in the storm or perished in the icy waters? No, my friend, no; and if there had been no wine served at your board that night, three human lives which have, alas! been hidden from us by death's eclipse would be shedding light and warmth upon many hearts now sorrowful and desolate. Three human lives, and a fourth just going out. There is responsibility, and neither you nor I can escape it, Mr. Birtwell, if through indifference or design we permit ourselves to become the instruments of such dire calamities."

Mr. Birtwell had partly risen from his chair in making the weak defence to which this was a reply, but now sunk back with an expression that was half bewilderment and half terror on his countenance.

"In Heaven's name, Mr. Elliott, what does all this mean?" he cried. "Three lives and a fourth going out, and the responsibility laid at my door!"

"It is much easier to let loose an evil power than to stay its progress," said Mr. Elliott. "The near and more apparent effects we may see, rarely the remote and secondary. But we know that the action of all forces, good or evil, is like that of expanding wave-circles, and reaches far beyond, our sight. It has done so in this case. Yes, Mr. Birtwell, three lives, and a fourth now flickering like an expiring candle.

"I would spare you all this if I dared, if I could be conscience-clear," continued Mr. Elliott. "But I would be faithless to my duty if I kept silent. You know the sad case of Mrs. Carlton?"

"You don't mean to lay that, too, at my door!" exclaimed Mr. Birtwell.

"Not directly; it was one of the secondary effects. I had a long conversation with Dr. Hillhouse to-day. His health has failed rapidly for some months past, and he is now much broken down. You know that he performed the operation which cost Mrs. Carlton her life? Well, the doctor has never got over the shock of that catastrophe. It has preyed upon his mind ever since, and is one of the causes of his impaired health."

"I should call that a weakness," returned Mr. Birtwell. "He did his best. No one is safe from accidents or malign influences. I never heard that Mr. Carlton blamed him."

"Ah, these malign influences!" said the clergyman. "They meet us everywhere and hurt us at every turn, and yet not one of them could reach and affect our lives if some human hand did not set them free and send them forth among men to, hurt and to destroy. And now let me tell you of the interview I had with Dr. Hillhouse to-day. He has given his consent, but with this injunction: we cannot speak of it to others."

"I will faithfully respect his wishes," said Mr. Birtwell.

"This morning," resumed Mr. Elliott, "I received a note from the doctor, asking me to call and see him." He was much depressed, and said he had long wanted to have a talk with me about something that weighed heavily on his mind. Let me give you his own words as nearly as I am able to remember them. After some remarks about personal influence and our social responsibilities, he said:

"There is one thing, Mr. Elliott, in which you and I and a great many others I could name have not only been derelict of duty, but serious wrongdoers. There is an evil in society that more than all others is eating out its life, and you and I have encouraged that evil even by our own example, calling it innocent, and so leading the weak astray and the unwary into temptation."

"I understood what he meant, and the shock of his including accusation, his 'Thou art the man,' sent a throb of pain to my heart. That I had already seen my false position and changed front did not lessen the shock, for I was only the more sensitive to pain."

"'Happily for you, Mr. Elliott,' he went on. 'no such bitter fruit has been plucked by your hands as by mine, and I pray God that it may never be. For a long time I have carried a heavy load here'—he drew his hand against his breast—'heavier than I have strength to bear. Its weight is breaking me down. It is no light thing, sir, to feel at times that you are a murderer.'"

"He shivered, and there passed across his face a look of horror. But it was gone in a moment, though an expression of suffering remained."

"'My dear doctor.' I interposed, 'you have permitted yourself

T. S. Arthur

to fall into a morbid state. This is not well. You are over-worked and need change and relaxation.'"

"'Yes,' he replied, a little mournfully 'I am overworked and morbid and all that, I know, and I must have change and relaxation or I shall die. Ah, if I could get rid of this heavy weight!' He laid his hand upon his breast again, and drew a deep inspiration. 'But that is impossible.' I must tell you all about it, but place upon you at the same time an injunction of silence, except in the case of one man, Mr. Spencer Birtwell. He is honorable and he should know, and I can trust him."

"'You remember, of course, the entertainment he gave last winter and some, of the unhappy effects that came of it, but you do not know all. I was there and enjoyed the evening, and you were there, Mr. Elliott, and I am afraid led some into temptation through our freedom. Forgive me for saying so, but the truth is best.'"

"'Wine was free as water—good wine, tempting to the taste. I meant to be very guarded, to take only a glass or two, for on the next day I had a delicate and dangerous operation to perform, and needed steady nerves. But the wine was good, and my one or two glasses only made way for three or four. The temptation of the hour were too much for my habitual self-restraint. I took a glass of wine with you, Mr. Elliott, after I had already taken more than was prudent under the circumstances another with Mr. Birtwell, another with General Abercrombie—alas for him! he fell that night so low that he has never risen again—and another with some one else. It was almost impossible to put a restraint upon yourself. Invitation and solicitation met you at every turn. The sphere of self-indulgence was so strong that it carried almost every one a little too far, and many into excess and debauch. I was told afterward that at a late hour the scene in the supper-room was simply disgraceful. Boys and men, and sadder still, young women, were more than half drunk, and behaved most unseemly. I can believe this, for I have seen such things too often.'"

"As I went out from Mr. Birtwell's that night, and the cold, snow-laden air struck into my face on crossing the pavement to my carriage, cooling my blood and clearing my brain, I thought of Mrs. Carlton and the life that had been placed in my hands, and a feeling of concern dropped into my heart. A night's indulgence in wine-drinking was a poor preparation for the work before me, in which a clear head and steady nerves were absolutely essential. How would I be in the morning? The question thrust itself into my thoughts and troubled me. My apprehensions were not groundless. Morning found me with unsteady nerves. But this was not all. From the moment I left my bed until within half an hour of the time when the operation was to begin, I was under much excitement and deeply anxious about two of my patients, Mrs. Voss and Mrs. Ridley, both dangerously ill, Mrs. Voss, as you know, in consequence of her alarm about her son, and Mrs. Ridley— But you have heard all about her case and its fatal termination, and understand in what way it was connected with the party at Mr. and Mrs. Birtwell's. The consequence of that night's excesses met me at every turn. The unusual calls, the imminent danger in which I found Mrs. Ridley and the almost insane demands made upon me by her despairing husband, all conspired to break down my unsteady nerves and unfit me for the work I had to do. When the time came, there was only one desperate expedient left, and that was the use of a strong stimulant, under the effect of which I was able to extract the tumor from Mrs. Carlton's neck."

"Alas for the too temporary support of my stimulant! It failed me at the last moment. My sight was not clear nor my hand steady as I tied the small arteries which had been cut during the operation. One of these, ligated imperfectly, commenced bleeding soon after I left the house. A hurried summons reached me almost immediately on my return home, and before I had steadied my exhausted nerves with a glass of wine. Hurrying back, I found the wound bleeding freely. Prompt treatment was required. Ether was again administered. But you know the rest, Mr. Elliott. It is all too dreadful, and I cannot go over it again. Mrs. Carlton fell another victim to excess in wine. This is the true story. I was not blamed by the husband. The real cause of the great calamity that fell upon him he does not know to this day, and I trust will never know. But I have not since been able to look steadily into his dreary eyes. A guilty sense of wrong oppresses me whenever I come near him. As I said before, this thing is breaking me down. It has robbed me, I know, of many years of professional usefulness to which I had looked forward, and left a bitter thought in my mind and a shadow on my feelings that can never pass away."

"'Mr. Elliott,' he continued, 'you have a position of sacred trust. Your influence is large. Set yourself, I pray you, against the evil which has wrought these great disasters. Set yourself against the dangerous self-indulgence called "moderate drinking." It is doing far more injury to society than open drunkenness, more a hundred—nay, a thousand—fold. If I had been a drunkard, no such catastrophe as this I have mentioned could have happened in my practice, for Mr. Carlton would not then have trusted his wife in my hands. My drunkenness would have stood as a warning against me. But I was a respectable moderate drinker, and could take my wine without seeming to be in any way affected by it. But see how it betrayed me at last.'"

Mr. Birtwell had been sitting during this relation with his head bowed upon his breast. When Mr. Elliott ceased speaking, he raised himself up in a slow, weary sort of way, like one oppressed by fatigue or weak from illness.

"Dreadful, dreadful!" he ejaculated. "I never dreamed of anything like this. Poor Carlton!"

"You see," remarked Mr. Elliott, "how easily a thing like this may happen." A man cannot go to one of these evening entertainments and indulge with anything like the freedom to which he is invited and be in a condition to do his best work on the day following. Some of your iron-nerved men may claim an exemption here, but we know that all over-stimulation must leave the body in some degree unstrung when the excitement dies out, and they suffer loss with the rest—a loss the aggregate of which makes itself felt in the end. We have to think for a moment only to satisfy ourselves that the wine-and brandy-drinking into which men and women are enticed at dinner-parties and fashionable entertainments is a fruitful source of evil. The effect upon body and mind after the indulgence is over is seen in headaches, clouded brain, nervous irritation, lassitude, inability to think, and sometimes in a general demoralization of both the physical and mental economy. Where there is any chronic or organic ailment the morbid condition is increased and sometimes severe attacks of illness follow.

"Are our merchants, bankers, lawyers, doctors and men holding responsible trusts as fit for duty after a social debauch—is the word too strong?—as before? If we reflect for a moment—you see, Mr. Birtwell, in what current my thoughts have been running—it must be clear to us that after every great entertainment such as you and other good citizens are in the habit of giving many business and professional mistakes must follow, some of them of a serious character. All this crowds upon and oppresses me, and my wonder is that it did not long ago so crowd upon and oppress me. It seems as though scales had dropped suddenly from my eyes and things I had never seen before stood out in clearest vision."

T. S. Arthur

CHAPTER XXVII

THEY were still in conversation when Mrs. Birtwell returned. Her eyes were wet and her face pale and sorrowful. She sat down beside her husband, and without speaking laid her head against him and sobbed violently. Mr. Birtwell feared to ask the question whose answer he guessed too well.

"How is it with our friend?" Mr. Elliott inquired as Mrs. Birtwell grew calmer. She looked up, answering sorrowfully:

"It is all over," then hid her face again, borne down by excessive emotion.

"The Lord bless and comfort his stricken ones," said the minister as he arose and stood for a few moments with his hand resting on the bowed head of Mrs. Birtwell. "The Lord make us wiser, more self-denying and more loyal to duty. Out of sorrow let joy come, out of trouble peace; out of suffering and affliction a higher, purer and nobler life for us all. We are in his merciful hands, and he will make us instruments of blessing if we but walk in the ways he would lead us. Alas that we have turned from him so often to walk in our own paths and follow the devices of our own hearts! His ways are way of pleasantness and his paths are peace, but ours wind too often among thorns and briars, or go down into the gloomy valley and shadow of death."

A solemn silence followed, and in that deep hush vows were

made that are yet unbroken.

"If any have stumbled through us and fallen by the way," said Mr. Elliott, "let us here consecrate ourselves to the work of saving them if possible."

He reached his hand toward Mr. Birtwell. The banker did not hesitate, but took the minister's extended hand and grasped it with a vigor that expressed the strength of his new-formed purpose. Light broke through the tears that blinded the eyes of Mrs. Birtwell. Clasping both of her hands over those of her husband and Mr. Elliott, she cried out with irrepressible emotion:

"I give myself to God also in this solemn consecration!"

"The blessing of our Lord Jesus Christ rest upon it, and make us true and faithful," dropped reverentially from the minister's lips.

Somewhere this panorama of life must close. Scene after scene might still be given; but if those already presented have failed to stir the hearts and quicken the consciences of many who have looked upon them, rousing some to a sense of danger and others to a sense of duty, it were vain to display another canvas; and so we leave our work as it stands, but in the faith that it will do good.

Hereafter we may take it up again and bring into view once more some of the actors in whom it is impossible not to feel a strong interest. Life goes on, though the record of events be not given,—life, with its joys and sorrows, its tempests of passion and its sweet calms, its successes and its failures, its all of good and evil; goes on though we drop the pencil and leave our canvas blank.

It is no pleasant task to paint as we have been painting, nor as we must still paint should the work now dropped ever be resumed. But as we take a last look at some of the scenes over

T. S. Arthur

which we now draw the curtain we see strong points of light and a promise of good shining clear through the shadows of the evil.

Choose from Thousands of 1stWorldLibrary Classics By

A. M. Barnard
Ada Leverson
Adolphus William Ward
Aesop
Agatha Christie
Alexander Aaronsohn
Alexander Kielland
Alexandre Dumas
Alfred Gatty
Alfred Ollivant
Alice Duer Miller
Alice Turner Curtis
Alice Dunbar
Allen Chapman
Alleyne Ireland
Ambrose Bierce
Amelia E. Barr
Amory H. Bradford
Andrew Lang
Andrew McFarland Davis
Andy Adams
Angela Brazil
Anna Alice Chapin
Anna Sewell
Annie Besant
Annie Hamilton Donnell
Annie Payson Call
Annie Roe Carr
Annonaymous
Anton Chekhov
Archibald Lee Fletcher
Arnold Bennett
Arthur C. Benson
Arthur Conan Doyle
Arthur M. Winfield
Arthur Ransome
Arthur Schnitzler
Arthur Train
Atticus
B.H. Baden-Powell
B. M. Bower
B. C. Chatterjee
Baroness Emmuska Orczy
Baroness Orczy
Basil King
Bayard Taylor
Ben Macomber
Bertha Muzzy Bower
Bjornstjerne Bjornson

Booth Tarkington
Boyd Cable
Bram Stoker
C. Collodi
C. E. Orr
C. M. Ingleby
Carolyn Wells
Catherine Parr Traill
Charles A. Eastman
Charles Amory Beach
Charles Dickens
Charles Dudley Warner
Charles Farrar Browne
Charles Ives
Charles Kingsley
Charles Klein
Charles Hanson Towne
Charles Lathrop Pack
Charles Romyn Dake
Charles Whibley
Charles Willing Beale
Charlotte M. Braeme
Charlotte M. Yonge
Charlotte Perkins Stetson
Clair W. Hayes
Clarence Day Jr.
Clarence E. Mulford
Clemence Housman
Confucius
Coningsby Dawson
Cornelis DeWitt Wilcox
Cyril Burleigh
D. H. Lawrence
Daniel Defoe
David Garnett
Dinah Craik
Don Carlos Janes
Donald Keyhoe
Dorothy Kilner
Dougan Clark
Douglas Fairbanks
E. Nesbit
E. P. Roe
E. Phillips Oppenheim
E. S. Brooks
Earl Barnes
Edgar Rice Burroughs
Edith Van Dyne
Edith Wharton

Edward Everett Hale
Edward J. O'Biren
Edward S. Ellis
Edwin L. Arnold
Eleanor Atkins
Eleanor Hallowell Abbott
Eliot Gregory
Elizabeth Gaskell
Elizabeth McCracken
Elizabeth Von Arnim
Ellem Key
Emerson Hough
Emilie F. Carlen
Emily Bronte
Emily Dickinson
Enid Bagnold
Enilor Macartney Lane
Erasmus W. Jones
Ernie Howard Pie
Ethel May Dell
Ethel Turner
Ethel Watts Mumford
Eugene Sue
Eugenie Foa
Eugene Wood
Eustace Hale Ball
Evelyn Everett-green
Everard Cotes
F. H. Cheley
F. J. Cross
F. Marion Crawford
Fannie E. Newberry
Federick Austin Ogg
Ferdinand Ossendowski
Fergus Hume
Florence A. Kilpatrick
Fremont B. Deering
Francis Bacon
Francis Darwin
Frances Hodgson Burnett
Frances Parkinson Keyes
Frank Gee Patchin
Frank Harris
Frank Jewett Mather
Frank L. Packard
Frank V. Webster
Frederic Stewart Isham
Frederick Trevor Hill
Frederick Winslow Taylor

Friedrich Kerst
Friedrich Nietzsche
Fyodor Dostoyevsky
G.A. Henty
G.K. Chesterton
Gabrielle E. Jackson
Garrett P. Serviss
Gaston Leroux
George A. Warren
George Ade
Geroge Bernard Shaw
George Cary Eggleston
George Durston
George Ebers
George Eliot
George Gissing
George MacDonald
George Meredith
George Orwell
George Sylvester Viereck
George Tucker
George W. Cable
George Wharton James
Gertrude Atherton
Gordon Casserly
Grace E. King
Grace Gallatin
Grace Greenwood
Grant Allen
Guillermo A. Sherwell
Gulielma Zollinger
Gustav Flaubert
H. A. Cody
H. B. Irving
H.C. Bailey
H. G. Wells
H. H. Munro
H. Irving Hancock
H. R. Naylor
H. Rider Haggard
H. W. C. Davis
Haldeman Julius
Hall Caine
Hamilton Wright Mabie
Hans Christian Andersen
Harold Avery
Harold McGrath
Harriet Beecher Stowe
Harry Castlemon
Harry Coghill
Harry Houidini

Hayden Carruth
Helent Hunt Jackson
Helen Nicolay
Hendrik Conscience
Hendy David Thoreau
Henri Barbusse
Henrik Ibsen
Henry Adams
Henry Ford
Henry Frost
Henry James
Henry Jones Ford
Henry Seton Merriman
Henry W Longfellow
Herbert A. Giles
Herbert Carter
Herbert N. Casson
Herman Hesse
Hildegard G. Frey
Homer
Honore De Balzac
Horace B. Day
Horace Walpole
Horatio Alger Jr.
Howard Pyle
Howard R. Garis
Hugh Lofting
Hugh Walpole
Humphry Ward
Ian Maclaren
Inez Haynes Gillmore
Irving Bacheller
Isabel Cecilia Williams
Isabel Hornibrook
Israel Abrahams
Ivan Turgenev
J.G.Austin
J. Henri Fabre
J. M. Barrie
J. M. Walsh
J. Macdonald Oxley
J. R. Miller
J. S. Fletcher
J. S. Knowles
J. Storer Clouston
J. W. Duffield
Jack London
Jacob Abbott
James Allen
James Andrews
James Baldwin

James Branch Cabell
James DeMille
James Joyce
James Lane Allen
James Lane Allen
James Oliver Curwood
James Oppenheim
James Otis
James R. Driscoll
Jane Abbott
Jane Austen
Jane L. Stewart
Janet Aldridge
Jens Peter Jacobsen
Jerome K. Jerome
Jessie Graham Flower
John Buchan
John Burroughs
John Cournos
John F. Kennedy
John Gay
John Glasworthy
John Habberton
John Joy Bell
John Kendrick Bangs
John Milton
John Philip Sousa
John Taintor Foote
Jonas Lauritz Idemil Lie
Jonathan Swift
Joseph A. Altsheler
Joseph Carey
Joseph Conrad
Joseph E. Badger Jr
Joseph Hergesheimer
Joseph Jacobs
Jules Vernes
Julian Hawthrone
Julie A Lippmann
Justin Huntly McCarthy
Kakuzo Okakura
Karle Wilson Baker
Kate Chopin
Kenneth Grahame
Kenneth McGaffey
Kate Langley Bosher
Kate Langley Bosher
Katherine Cecil Thurston
Katherine Stokes
L. A. Abbot
L. T. Meade

L. Frank Baum
Latta Griswold
Laura Dent Crane
Laura Lee Hope
Laurence Housman
Lawrence Beasley
Leo Tolstoy
Leonid Andreyev
Lewis Carroll
Lewis Sperry Chafer
Lilian Bell
Lloyd Osbourne
Louis Hughes
Louis Joseph Vance
Louis Tracy
Louisa May Alcott
Lucy Fitch Perkins
Lucy Maud Montgomery
Luther Benson
Lydia Miller Middleton
Lyndon Orr
M. Corvus
M. H. Adams
Margaret E. Sangster
Margret Howth
Margaret Vandercook
Margaret W. Hungerford
Margret Penrose
Maria Edgeworth
Maria Thompson Daviess
Mariano Azuela
Marion Polk Angellotti
Mark Overton
Mark Twain
Mary Austin
Mary Catherine Crowley
Mary Cole
Mary Hastings Bradley
Mary Roberts Rinehart
Mary Rowlandson
M. Wollstonecraft Shelley
Maud Lindsay
Max Beerbohm
Myra Kelly
Nathaniel Hawthrone
Nicolo Machiavelli
O. F. Walton
Oscar Wilde
Owen Johnson
P.G. Wodehouse
Paul and Mabel Thorne

Paul G. Tomlinson
Paul Severing
Percy Brebner
Percy Keese Fitzhugh
Peter B. Kyne
Plato
Quincy Allen
R. Derby Holmes
R. L. Stevenson
R. S. Ball
Rabindranath Tagore
Rahul Alvares
Ralph Bonehill
Ralph Henry Barbour
Ralph Victor
Ralph Waldo Emmerson
Rene Descartes
Ray Cummings
Rex Beach
Rex E. Beach
Richard Harding Davis
Richard Jefferies
Richard Le Gallienne
Robert Barr
Robert Frost
Robert Gordon Anderson
Robert L. Drake
Robert Lansing
Robert Lynd
Robert Michael Ballantyne
Robert W. Chambers
Rosa Nouchette Carey
Rudyard Kipling
Saint Augustine
Samuel B. Allison
Samuel Hopkins Adams
Sarah Bernhardt
Sarah C. Hallowell
Selma Lagerlof
Sherwood Anderson
Sigmund Freud
Standish O'Grady
Stanley Weyman
Stella Benson
Stella M. Francis
Stephen Crane
Stewart Edward White
Stijn Streuvels
Swami Abhedananda
Swami Parmananda
T. S. Ackland

T. S. Arthur
The Princess Der Ling
Thomas A. Janvier
Thomas A Kempis
Thomas Anderton
Thomas Bailey Aldrich
Thomas Bulfinch
Thomas De Quincey
Thomas Dixon
Thomas H. Huxley
Thomas Hardy
Thomas More
Thornton W. Burgess
U. S. Grant
Upton Sinclair
Valentine Williams
Various Authors
Vaughan Kester
Victor Appleton
Victor G. Durham
Victoria Cross
Virginia Woolf
Wadsworth Camp
Walter Camp
Walter Scott
Washington Irving
Wilbur Lawton
Wilkie Collins
Willa Cather
Willard F. Baker
William Dean Howells
William le Queux
W. Makepeace Thackeray
William W. Walter
William Shakespeare
Winston Churchill
Yei Theodora Ozaki
Yogi Ramacharaka
Young E. Allison
Zane Grey